PRAISE FOR *SATURDAY FRIGHT AT THE MOVIES*

"Amanda's stories are so fucking weird she scares me!"

—#1 *New York Times* bestselling author Christopher Pike

"Slashers and creatures and blood, oh my! Lang's collection is a trick-or-treat bag full of gruesome goodies that every horror fan will delight in savoring."

—Brian McAuley, author of *Curse of the Reaper* and *Candy Cain Kills*

"*Saturday Fright at the Movies* delivers the perfect choose-your-own-adventure of horror nostalgia. In these thirteen tales, Amanda Cecelia Lang births unique monsters, brutal slashers, kick-ass final girls, and creepy urban legends that will leave you screaming for more. Grab some popcorn and get ready for a gory good time!"

—Angela Sylvaine, author of *Frost Bite* and *Chopping Spree*

"*Saturday Fright at the Movies* deals with matters of life, death, and pop culture. While most stories ignore it, Lang's stories often feature pop culture as essential to either salvation or the terror. I can testify from experience that these stories are a great way to spend the time you had originally reserved for sleeping."

—Robert E. Harpold, author of *When the Gods Are Away*

"*Saturday Fright at the Movies* delivers oodles of horror-filled treats and B-movie tricks to its readers."

—Drew Huff, author of *Free Burn* and *The Divine Flesh*

SATURDAY FRIGHT AT THE MOVIES

13 TALES FROM THE MULTIPLEX

A note about reprints can be found on page 281.

Edited by Rob Carroll
Book Design and Layout by Rob Carroll
Cover Art by Dan Fris
Cover Design by Rob Carroll

ISBN 978-1-958598-75-7 (paperback)
ISBN 978-1-958598-80-1 (eBook)

darkmatter-ink.com

SATURDAY FRIGHT AT THE MOVIES

13 TALES FROM THE MULTIPLEX

AMANDA CECELIA LANG

For Kevin,
my favorite author and long-distance friend,
every story goes out to you.
Always.

CONTENTS

Introduction 11

Choose Your Own Destruction 17

Latchkey 31

The Ash Collector 64

Zombie Unicorns from Galaxy 13 75

Apprehension Engine 96

The 31st of October in Locust, Maine 120

Salting the Meat 136

Medusa with the Heads of Men 149

Station 99 180

Attack of Melvin 198

Tricksters 216

Ashes Upon Ashes Upon Ashes 223

The Clover Café 245

INTRODUCTION

THE FIRST HORROR movie I ever watched was *An American Werewolf in London* when I was three years old. An HBO Saturday Night Movie, it's one of my earliest memories. David and Jack backpacking along the misty English moors in those iconic red and green puffer jackets, the you're-gonna-bloody-die vibe at the Slaughtered Lamb Pub, the beware-the-moonlight howls clawing up the night—and there, up ahead, it's probably just a sheepdog…

That opening scene burned itself into my three-year-old blood like the wolf's curse itself. It's the first movie that ever made me scream (and laugh) my freaking lungs out. The chills, the thrills! I spent the rest of the night delightfully afraid to go to bed— and the rest of my life as a werewolf-hugging, slasher-smitten, creepshow-digging horror junkie.

Like most tried-and-true latchkey kids from the '80s, my formative scares came from an experimental tonic of monsters. A shocking close encounter with E.T. in the cornfield. A sneak-peek of a little blonde girl and her possessed television. A trip to the theater with my new friends the xenomorphs and every face-hugging, chest-bursting jump scare. What a blast!

Fast-forward to the VHS boom of the late '80s and my local video store where I was about to shake the bladed hand of Mr. Freddy Kruger. I adored Freddy's MTV vibe, and *Nightmare on Elm Street 3: The Dream Warriors* was my gateway slasher. Alongside those phantasmagoric frights, the dream warriors resonated with me on a personal level. Like the kids in *E.T.*, these teenagers had real-life problems outside their nightmares. Divorce, bullying, these were the kids who were a little weird, a little haunted. Yet they could take their fears and dreams and flip them into fantastical powers. The power to fight back, the power to be unapologetically themselves. Equally inspiring, in this world where adults are quick to dismiss the kids, we get Nancy, the ultimate dream warrior, who does exactly what the dreamers need. She sees them.

Watching that, *I* felt seen, too.

If I dare close my eyes, I can still see that iconic VHS cover, the heavy metal dream warriors walking the blades of Freddy's glove. It waited faithfully for me, lurking in my video store amid so many other eye-grabbing VHS covers. Punk rock zombies with a spray-painted gravestone, a twisted vampire face misting over a suburban home, a slasher girl standing with her back to the camera, showing off a hidden butcher knife and hair braided into a noose…

Like Michal Myers, I had finally come home.

This was my sanctuary, this popcorn-stained aisle. On those hallowed grounds, I met *Halloween 4, Creepshow 2, Return of the Living Dead Part II, The Texas Chainsaw Massacre 2, Hellraiser II, Friday the 13th Part II, III, IV, V, VI, VII, and VIII*—when it came to franchises hacking their way into my heart, I always seemed to unearth the sequels first.

And there were countless others, campy, freaky, bonkers. *The Blob*, that ooey-gooey remake with the riotous theater scene. *Night of the Creeps*, featuring the all-time best cheesy Tom Atkins line (if you don't know, watch the trailer). *The Lost Boys*, I was obsessed, I even named my dog Nanook after Corey Haim's dog. *Critters*, because what's better than shapeshifting, bounty-hunting alien rock gods? *Pet Sematary*, Zelda still haunts my bed.

On and on, my trusty VCR rolled...

Into the '90s, there was even more candy to choose from, with *Freddy's Dead, Are You Afraid of the Dark?, Army of Darkness, Buffy the Vampire Slayer, The People Under the Stairs, From Dusk till Dawn, Interview with a Vampire, The Craft*. As a teenager growing ever-thicker skin, it took a lot to scare me. But despite all that snappy bubblegum horror, the '90s stirred up some ruthless nightmares. The cold, uncanny valley of the bare-fleshed aliens in *Fire in the Sky* was the first time I had to bury my face in my hands. Then there was the relentless misdirection of ghost scares in *The Sixth Sense*; rope-hung, wrist-cut, vomit-chinned, all leading to that final gut-punch twist. And I'll never forget the absolute stunned silence of a packed theater as the final credits rolled for *The Blair Witch Project*.

Of course, we can't go on a '90s-horror spree without bowing to my master. In 1996, a movie came along that was the love letter I'd been writing to my VCR for years.

What's my favorite scary movie?

Damn right it is.

Scream blindsided me. It had everything I loved in a popcorn slasher—a smart, badass female protagonist, a whodunit mystery, crackling tension and riotous laughs, fun, fun, fun. But then it went and did something that, in all my blood-splattered years, I'd never seen.

It dissected itself.

It showed us the rules. Booze, virgins, *I'll be right back...*

In a post-*Scream* meta-savvy world, it's easy to forget that audiences weren't always in on the joke. I saw *Scream* in the theater, and the audience reaction to Randy explaining slashers (not to mention those final killer monologues) was pure, super-charged electricity. I sometimes think the shock to the system I felt might be on par with the thrills early movie-goers experienced with films like *Nosferatu, Frankenstein,* and *Psycho*.

Like a bolt of lightning, *Scream* awakened something new in me, a sort of movie X-ray vision. I left that theater feeling effervescent. Here it was again, that thrill-ride I kept chasing. *Scream* and its sequels lifted me higher and higher…

Only to drop me like a corpse into the torture-porn 2000s.

If you're a fan of Eli Roth, absolutely more power to you. But movies like *Hostel* had me questioning my life choices—and that's coming from someone who'd stomached everything dished up by brutes like Leatherface and Jason *Kill-Kill-Kill* Vorhees. Suddenly, everyone who'd ever wrinkled their nose when I said I loved horror seemed to have a point. What was it that drew me to this stuff? It certainly wasn't the abject gore. Was it?

Armed with the powers granted to me by *Scream*, I started to take a more analytical approach to my moviegoing. The 2000s weren't a total wasteland—witness the brilliant ghostly oasis of *The Ring, Session 9, The Others, The Grudge, Paranormal Activity,* and *Lake Mungo*—but I found myself gravitating back in time.

I dug into pre-1980s classics that had fallen off my radar. The mindless consumerism of *Night of the Living Dead*, the madness and dysfunction of *The Shining*, the unflinching feminism of *Black Christmas*. I fell in love with every episode of *The Twilight Zone*, Rod Serling's twists and clever social commentaries. And I discovered the most terrifying haunted house ever seared onto celluloid. *The Changeling* turned me into a quivering puddle of fear unlike any other movie. That trippy ghost-cam séance, the relentless wheelchair chase, hell, the whole movie is an atmospheric chef's kiss of terror—not to mention a seething rebuke of ableism and classism.

After that, I revisited the '80s slashers and creature features of my youth with a critical eye on the gore and the monsters who splattered it. The practical effects were often campy and delightfully over-the-top, and there were countless more that sung with artistry and creativity. Freddy's boiler burns, the grotesquely deformed boy-child splashing from Crystal Lake, that werewolf transformation in London—these were masterpieces. But while the thrills and gimmicks of the monsters had certainly drawn me in, I realized something else had kept me there beyond that sweet adrenaline rush of terror. Not just blood, not just mayhem.

But survival.

It wasn't the Freddys and Jasons and Michaels who electrified me in the end.

No, it was the final girls. The misfits and wallflowers and illustrious virgins who, despite the gruesome odds, rose up with resourcefulness and intelligence, and sometimes machetes, to drop their respective monsters to their knees. On some level, I had always been aware of this. After all, my favorite characters were final girls. Lori Strode, who escapes the shape of evil, again and again. Nancy Thompson, who conquers one nightmare, then goes on to help other warriors survive her sequel. And I could never forget Stretch from *Texas Chainsaw 2*, little Jamie from *Halloween 4 & 5*, Alice from *Nightmare 4 & 5*… the list spirited on, right up to Sydney, Gail, and Dewy, that beloved final trio from *Scream*. It was fun to be afraid with them, but it was even more fun to watch them kick ass. By the final credits, they all became beautifully savage and screamingly triumphant. They took back the power their monsters stole from them.

And they fucking survived.

They made me want to cheer, they made me want to triumph against real-world monsters. After all, what is it we're all surviving? What hideous social injustice does each new monster represent? Sexism, racism, sensationalism, just name it. That's the shapeshifting beauty of horror.

And as movie reels streamed into the 2010s and beyond, survival would become elevated.

In sleek and stylish movies like *The VVitch*, *Midsommar*, and *Get Out*, our heroic survivors transcend their human demons and reach cathartic new heights. Living deliciously around the bonfire, smiling coyly at the burning bear, and that insane swell of relief amid the flashing red-and-blues when the car door opens and Chris's friend from the TSA steps out. Brilliant. Powerful. These movies shook my bones.

As the years rolled onward, I would find evermore films to fear and celebrate and feed my empowerment-hungry soul. The spine-chills inside the *Conjuring* universe; the mix-and-match genre worship of *American Horror Story*; the latchkey monster-fright nostalgia of *Stranger Things*; the evocative and emotional heartbeats of *The Haunting of Hill House*, *The Haunting of Bly Manor*, *The Midnight Club*, and every other beloved literary IP graced by Mike Flanagan; not to mention the golden renaissance of a silver-screen Stephen King…

On and on the movies play, but there are too many gems to mention here, midnight is fast approaching, and in the end, I think that's the point. Because horror is boundless. The creeps and evils of the real world will always exist. When one falls, others inevitably spawn, reinventing old nightmares. But horror sees them, and decade after decade, it paints them as the monsters they are—just as it sees and honors the legions of warriors, protectors, and final girls who will forever rise up and fight.

Gory special effects, sequels, and all.

This collection is *my* love letter to the Saturday fright movies that terrified and delighted me, to the monsters who lured me in and the heroes who ignited a path through the darkness. It's a celebration of everything horror has to offer. Thrills, chills, monstrous mayhem, ghoulish laughs, and a chance to survive the night.

Now, grab your popcorn and remember, in this theater, everyone can hear you scream.

—Amanda Cecelia Lang
September 2024

CHOOSE YOUR OWN DESTRUCTION

YOU JERK AWAKE in the back row of the ancient Rialto Theater and gag on the fistful of popcorn crammed inside your mouth. Something metallic clicks against your teeth. Choking on disorientation and rancid imitation butter, you spit the crunchy-sharp wad at the floor. What the actual hell?

You don't remember passing out. You remember buying a ticket for the midnight screening of your favorite horror flick, remember peering over your shoulder, nervous your Watcher with the spidery silhouette and that glowing, flickering gaze might've followed you in off the street.

The shadowy creep hadn't.

You didn't buy popcorn, but you remember sitting in a packed theater, a center seat with a clear view of both aisles, both exits. Three endless days of this, of seeing him everywhere. Important to stay alert. Stay around people. You're an expert. You've devoured all the best scary movies and know what happens when morons doze off with lurkers slinking around.

Still, there's no denying it—you passed out. Hard.

Now, spitting out the last invasive bits of popcorn, blinking woozy sleep from your eyes, you realize two things at once:

You're alone in the blackened theater.

And along with that popcorn wad, you're pretty sure something metallic scraped your teeth when you spat just now. Feels undeniable, an echo inside your skull: something clattered down the slanted concrete floor.

You try standing, and your wrist shackles snap taut. Insidious chains, rusty bracelets, they lock you to the arms of your chair.

Your guts sink, your mind starts plummeting.

Did your Watcher do this? Where's he now? You force yourself to go numb. If you panic, whatever fresh hell this is will end badly before survival even begins.

You're wondering if it's futile to scream for an usher when the projector spins to life and a flickering message dominates the silver screen.

I'M CLOSE. CAN YOU ESCAPE ME?
QUICK, CHOOSE ONE:

• SCREAM FOR HELP.

• FIND THE KEY.

Okay, deep freaking breath. You've seen these movies, read these books.

You know this game.

Another thing you know: the odds won't be kind to you, the hapless victim. Still, there's usually a razor-slim path to victory.

It's no fun if you die right away. That's why the first choice is always an easy one.

Clearly, anyone still hanging around the projector booth or the popcorn stand is dead.

Finding their gory, jackknifed corpses will prove quite dramatic if you manage to make it to the lobby. So, no point screaming. That leaves the key—which was definitely that metal object you spat out with the popcorn earlier. It gleams dully in the half-chewed kernels oozing under the seat before you.

You test your shackles. The wrist cuffs are tight, cutting off circulation. But with dim relief, you discover you've been sitting on chains. Your right shackle has an arm's length of extra give.

Enough to reach under the seat.

Your hand feels deadened and oddly stiff—your whole body, actually—but you twist forward and tweeze the key with your fingertips.

Something under the chair bear-traps down on your wrist!

A hand! Your Watcher's bony, spidery, nightmare hand! Clamping you in place, he slices out with razor-fingered brutality, opening grinning gashes across your knuckles.

You scream, shriek, bellow, and finally yank free.

Like you suspected, nobody rushes in from the lobby to rescue you.

Instead, a crooked silhouette unfolds from the dark row ahead, standing silently. Like always, he's wearing your clothing—or tattered replicas. Same pants you wore to the theater, same shirt, even your favorite jacket. All of it shredded at the seams, too small for his distended form. Except that's not the worst of him.

Those shimmery, high-beam eyes have always cast the rest of him in ambiguous bent-bone shadows. But he's tall, so tall his unseen face turns fish-belly pale as he rises into the projector light and—

That's not a face!

No mouth, no nose, just a featureless, egg-smooth terror dotted with two spherical lenses. Movie projectors for eyes? They ignite, and he angles his gaze upon you, dazzling your vision. Your shackles rattle as you shield your eyes.

Silent as the first films, your Watcher waves at you with one gloved hand, waggling long, razor-tipped fingers like the first time you caught him prowling—three nights ago, outside your bedroom window. Like something from the endless horror movies you use-and-abuse to escape your stressful life, fake kills to distract from the troubled pains of daily existence. The sight of him warps your reality. Your hyperventilating mind can't keep up. That razor-blade glove is famous—like, MTV-famous—though you feel anything but starstruck.

You shrink back into your seat and press your hacked-up hand against your chest. Blood slicks your fingers, but despite yourself, you grin. The key digs into your palm.

Your Watcher observes you with a daft tilt of head, flickery gaze blinding and amused. He could easily reach over the seat and end you fast—*slash, slash*—but where's the carnival in that?

He taps one razor-sharp finger against his forehead, then slices a red-rimmed line from brow to chin, splitting his egg-face with a gruesome vertical smile. Twin flaps of flesh curl away, one broken disguise blooming to reveal another.

Studded with shining eyes, the face beneath once gave your great-great-grandparents gaunt-cheeked nightmares. An undead horror with pointed ears and pointier teeth. Victorian victims drained of blood, filmmakers accused of plagiarism, it all flashes before you in a black-and-white blur. Then your Watcher swings his projector stare away from you and begins a leisurely, ghoulish stroll down his row, gliding past seat after seat. Where's he going?

Quickly, trembling, you open your bloody hand.

And hell. Holy face-flaying hell! The key isn't a key.

It's a razor blade—no, it's one of *his* bladed fingernails. That was in your *mouth*? It gleams at you, a sharp rusty wink.

Something else gleams, too…

Between the sliced-to-gills flesh of your index finger, where you should find bone, you catch a glint of steel.

Above, in the Rialto's projector booth, the spinning *flick-flick-flick-flick* of the movie reel pulses like a heartbeat. The message on the screen changes.

EVERYTHING YOU NEED IS ALREADY INSIDE YOU. ARE YOU BRAVE ENOUGH? CHOOSE ONE:

- **FIND THE KEY.**

- **WAIT RIGHT THERE.**

"You're a monster!" you shout and snarl, but your Watcher already knows this. It's the point of this game. He reaches the end of his row and swings into yours, taking his demented time, drawing out the terror, twenty seats away. Nineteen now. Long dagger-teeth, classic movie-ghoul shamble.

His gaze sprays sharp-cut light across your row, and you can't believe what you see. Everywhere the beams shine, the scenery ripples and blurs, revealing a milky, movie-glossed glimpse into an alternate reality. In this black-and-white otherworld, every abandoned seat appears occupied, a jam-packed theater. All around, patrons slump in their seats, heads lolling on the bone—only they're not sleeping. You shudder, swallow hard on raw panic. The ragged bite marks staining every throat promise they're as dead as you're about to be.

"Stay away!" you scream, shackles rattling. Page eight in the invisible script, and you still haven't found the damn key!

Your index finger—besides being sliced to gills—won't bend. An infected incision runs the length of your finger, knotted with thick, black stitches where the twisted bastard sewed you together again—where he inserted a surprise.

You pinch the malformed tip of your finger. The key's teeth poke sideways like a growth beneath the skin. No time to think about this. Grave-shovel footsteps scraping ever closer, your Watcher sweeps rays of throat-massacred illusions across the theater like the flashlights of a gawky usher.

Wielding the razor blade in your good hand, you saw open your stitches, popping them one by one. Now the worst part:

refusing to scream. You peel yourself open, parting pale meat and tendons—but there's no pain. No pain even as you tug and twist and slide the tip of your finger away. No pain. Shock, adrenaline—or maybe he anesthetized you? Ghastly toxins in the air, a quick injection in your neck, something lacing the popcorn? You might never know.

The key head protrudes from your finger, wickedly, triumphantly.

Ten seats away now, your Watcher's gaze transmutes the neighboring seats. Beside you, a moviegoer appears with a silent throat-torn scream, her milky, dead eyes imploring you to hurry! You jam the key into the keyhole. You twist, your cuffs rattle, but the lock doesn't give.

Instead, the end of the key spins slickly inside your finger stump.

Quick, you jerk the key from the cuff. Clamping your teeth around it, you wiggle it loose, hollowing out your finger. The flayed flesh droops, boneless as snakeskin.

Your Watcher looms, five seats away now.

The end of the key is just a tiny bar—nothing to grip—so you clamp it between your teeth and screw it into the nearest keyhole.

This works! The left cuff slings open and falls off your wrist.

Two seats away now.

You stand and pivot just as your Watcher swipes at you. Hideous hooked fingers scrape your shoulder. Scrambling, you grab the unlocked shackle and swing the chain wildly at his pasty, movie-vamp face, hoping to smash those projector eyes.

Instead, that ghoulish, toothy leer shatters like porcelain. You catch a shuddery glimpse of the hockey mask beneath and back away.

The chain cuffing your right hand snaps taut.

Shaking, fumbling, using your teeth, you frantically unlock the second cuff just as your Watcher raises a machete. Where in movie-franchise hell did *that* spawn from?

Your Watcher's new oversized blade splits the air near your spine and lodges in a seat cushion as you escape down the row.

Or almost escape.

Three seats deep, your right leg buckles. You collapse sideways onto someone's cold, spectral lap. In the furious projector spray of your Watcher's glare, you discover a corpse dressed like a camp counselor with an arrow through one eye. The Rialto's sticky popcorn floor turns verdant, outdoorsy. A path of pine needles points you onward between a forest of bloody trees. You recognize these corpse-splashed woods, you've hiked them a dozen-odd times thanks to the power of your old VCR.

Holy slasher! But there's zero time to freak out. You've got a bigger problem. You pull yourself off the camp counselor's skewered corpse and instantly you know: something's hideously wrong with your right leg. What did that monstrous freak do to you?

Your Watcher yanks his machete free and towers over you, blazing-eyed in his hockey mask.

You lurch away on your good leg. The elongated shadow you cast in his furious light cuts a line of sticky-floored reality between the woods. Using the chair backs as crutches, you hobble out into the aisle and stagger toward the tangible reality of the silver screen.

Your Watcher stomps after you, sweeping the theater with his leer, illuminating unexplored trees. Over where you last spotted Rialto's emergency exit, a ghostly archery range appears. Heavy boots clomp into the aisle behind you.

You don't look back. You grit your jaw and shamble in the general direction of the emergency exit. In the illusory blaze of his movie light, the archery range draws closer with every step. You're not certain how the physics of this nightmare operate, but if you can't reach the emergency exit, you figure the archery range is the next best option. Maybe you can arm yourself. Arrows won't do much damage against zombified psycho-slashers in masks, but it's the only plan B you've—*slam*!

You smack face-first into the back of the theater, and the illusion of summer camp crashes to black. Starbursts dash your vision, blood trickles your nose. You barely notice. Nearby, the emergency exit's hallway sits at an angle untouched by your Watcher's light. This is your chance! You start to limp down the dim prefab hallway only to balk. He barred the door at the end with chains. A trap if you go down there without a key—and the only key you know about is still lodged inside the shackles you abandoned in the top row.

You stagger back out into the theater. Nearing the front row now, your Watcher angles his light your way, the maniac woods return, a 35mm mirage superimposed upon the seats. Butchered moviegoers hang pinned to trees, while overhead, the message on the silver screen changes. You can barely read it through the blur of greasy, dizzy tears.

EXITS AREN'T AN OPTION, I'M AFRAID. YOU KNOW WHAT HAPPENS NEXT. CHOOSE ONE:

- **FIND A WEAPON.**

- **RUN ALL NIGHT.**

Never do what your attacker wants—that's *Survival 1-0-freaking-1*. What attackers want helps them, not you. If they tell you not to scream, you scream. If they tell you not to struggle, you struggle. But in this case, your Watcher offers sound advice.

Run, find a weapon.

No point begging for mercy. Sometimes sick bastards are just sick bastards. And this one wants a showdown worthy of a franchise. A chimera of cinema, and you stumbled right into his lair. Fool.

You try to run, despite your right leg's dead weight. Reclaiming the seats as crutches, you lurch along the front row. With every drag of your foot, the bones inside your leg shift and swim apart with a hideous metallic clatter, like meat and silverware.

One row from the front, eyes glowing behind that hockey mask, your Watcher raises his machete.

Ahead, skeletal branches paint the aisle and side with a dense and hopeless forest, the light of fiction rippling like lake water. You pivot up the side aisle of the theater, not daring to look behind you, trying to see beyond the trees.

As you reach the middle rows, your Watcher's machete slices past your head, whirling like a helicopter blade. It lodges into a nearby evergreen—and the Rialto's wall.

You don't waste a heartbeat. You hobble over and yank, but the machete remains buried handle-deep. Your strength feels gooey, transient—still, you put all your weight behind one more tug. The machete doesn't budge.

"No!"

Your skin prickles with desperate futility. Your Watcher shines at you from the foot of the aisle now, a dozen-odd rows below. The machete's a lost cause. You gotta leave it. Tumbling through phantom branches, you land hard on all fours and scramble up the remaining half of the aisle. Behind you, the hockey mask clatters to the sticky floor like a snake molting—revealing a new nightmare? Gut-sick, you glance over your shoulder.

Your Watcher still lurks near the bottom row. All at once, the woods and his projector-glow drop away as he collapses into a fetal ball. He grips his lake-bloated skull, clawing at himself again with that bladed-glove hand. Red raw gashes open up, but instead of blood, they sprout fur. Rabid, wiry fur. Ears turning pointy, teeth and maw elongating, savage claws hooking the air. All of this in a stop-motion flash— still, you know what you're up against.

The exit at the back of the theater isn't an option. More chains cocoon the double-doors leading to the lobby. Desperate, completing an insane loop, you spill back into the top row and hobble, chair by chair, right leg meaty and clanking.

You can't avoid it any longer—your attention shivers downward. Before the evening got going, your Watcher must've split your pant leg to the hip. What you glimpse now between the swinging bell of fabric is *not* your leg. This jagged, bruise-mottled horror-show with the bulging lumps and the festering zipper of black stitches *cannot* be your leg!

"What did you do to me?" you gasp, voice strangling.

With a viscous stretch-and-tear of flesh, and a grisly snap-and-fuse of bone, your Watcher completes his transformation and raises his slathering, blazing attention your way.

Vandalized by movie light, the Rialto intercuts once again with paintbrush streaks of midnight trees. Different this time, though. Black-and-white and full of wolfsbane. Amid the distant seats, you glimpse a quaint thatched-roof village nestled between hills of rolling fog. A bloated full moon hangs in the sky beside the projector booth.

Near the front row, your Watcher throws back his toothy maw, howls silently, then leaps with ferocious agility onto the back of a seat. Everything about his snarling, muscle-ripped silhouette promises he's ready to pounce.

You scuttle deeper down the back row, hunting for the shackle with the key, praying it's your razor-thin chance at survival. But the shackles have vanished, and with every unsteady step, tightly-packed horrors shift and poke inside your jagged, serrated leg. With every step, pointed objects protrude from your stitches.

You think you see the tip of a dagger jutting below what used to be your kneecap.

Bloody leg-splitting hell. You know what you have to do.

You reach the end of the top row, putting as much distance between you and your Watcher as possible. No way you can outpace him. He's relished the chase, cherished toying with you, but if he decides to pounce, you're dead.

Drenched in moonlight and fog, you drop into the Rialto's final seat. Your leg juts sideways. That's definitely a dagger poking between your stitches like a compound fracture.

Gritting your jaw against a vertigo-wave of dizziness, you grip the dagger's tip with your good hand. Every vein in your body turns to ice. You're seriously going to do this!

You tug.

Your fingers slip on the blood-slick blade. You cry out in ragged frustration.

You try again, wiggling the blade like a loose tooth. The only mercy is there's still no pain—only numb, surreal horror.

Your Watcher sniffs the air. His predatory stink mingles with the rancid-butter promise of popcorn. You hold your scream. What's he waiting for? But, naturally, you know.

He wants you to do this. Dig deep for a weapon so he can see what you're made of.

Fine. The dagger slides, blade and hilt, from your ruined knee, slicing putrefied flesh and popping one of your stitches on its way out.

A pathetic match against any snarling, snapping beast.

Even so, you grip the dagger and stand, hell-bent on going down fighting.

Too bad your leg has other ideas. Jarred by your unstable weight, the sharp contents of your fleshbag-calf shift and clatter. Your entire leg cracks like a lightning bolt.

Shrieking, you spill sideways into the aisle, and the light shifts as your Watcher springs across the theater. He lands in the aisle above you with feral grace, claws digging into the red carpet, embedding you both in a foggy, wolfsbane meadow. The legendary flower is lethal to shapeshifters, but something tells you the weapon you need doesn't reside in the world of unreality. Time to dig deep, remember?

Freaking literally.

You grip the dagger and start with the bottom stitch, near where your ankle bones used to live. You pop your stitches. One by one. Desperate, shaking, sanity swimming on the edge of blacking out, *pop-pop-pop* from ankle to mid-thigh, until your flesh splits open like a rifle case.

You gasp. Instead of bone, an arsenal of meat and metal spills out.

From this gut-twisting muck of hamburger and horror spills blades and crucifixes and tiny alchemy bottles.

No going back, your Watcher crouches again, eager to finish you.

His shadow darkens over you: hooked hands, fingers like a skeletal forest preparing to tangle around you.

From the booth, the Rialto's projector light *flick-flick-flickers*, the contents of your oozing leg-sack gleam, and on the haunted screen the message changes.

LOOK AT YOURSELF, RARING TO SURVIVE, OPEN TO ANYTHING. CHOOSE ONE:

- **DISCOVER MY WEAKNESS.**

- **I DISCOVER YOURS.**

He's right. You've come this far. You'll do anything to survive—even reach inside the hollows of your own jacked-up slaughterhouse-leg to fish for salvation.

He's filled you with every cinematic possibility.

Bronze dagger, crucifix, a machete, bundles of white sage, alchemy jars of holy water, a Zippo, a wooden stake, a sawed-off shotgun, and a scattering of silver bullets. Everything needed to slay a silver-screen monster.

Your mind fast-forwards through a montage of creature films—stakes for vampires, machetes for undead psychos, silver for werewolves—but what's guaranteed to stop a film-obsessed chimeric abomination like your Watcher?

You seize the sawed-off shotgun.

You rip it wetly, gruesomely from your calf. Boneless flesh slithers as you scoot against the wall and face your Watcher. Silver bullets won't fit—you aren't fooled. You can only hope the shotgun comes with buckshot and that it still works.

For the briefest two-frame flicker, you consider turning it on yourself. Ending this nightmare, ending the soul-wrenching anxieties of your everyday life. It would be so easy…

You raise the barrel, take aim—but your trigger finger sags, more deboned flesh. With a desperate, sickened scream, you switch hands.

His shadow twitches, and you aim wildly and pull the trigger.

The barrel detonates with a gun-powder flash and kicks you against the wall.

Your Watcher's wolfy shoulder explodes, backscattering tendrils of meat and fuzz into the Rialto's projector light.

But he doesn't stop. He rages at you with beaming eyes. All around, the wolfsbane meadow swirls with Technicolor plumes of crimson-fury fog. You don't need audio to feel the low rumble of his growl. His sharp-toothed maw snaps open, and he pounces!

You scream out and raise the shotgun again. This time your aim doesn't shiver.

The buckshot blasts him square in that projector-lens glare, shattering his light.

All around you, the foggy forest cuts to black.

Your Watcher drops to his knees.

His werewolf pelt splits down the middle, peeling away, layer after layer, falling loose like exorcised masks, revealing a lake-bloated killer, a Victorian vampire, a blade-handed nightmare stalker. Horror after horror until all that remains is a buckshot-charred pile of shadow and bones and the tattered echoes of your clothing. Two ruined projector lenses tumble loosely down the heap.

But you've seen these movies, read these books, know this game.

You cock the shotgun, aim, and squeeze the trigger. There shouldn't be any ammo left, but this is your movie. The gun fires.

High above, where his full moon once shined, the buckshot shatters the projection booth window. The theater falls to darkness. Only thing left is to roll the final credits, but naturally, you've made sure that can't happen.

With the shotgun clamped in your hand, you slump against the wall and welcome the darkness. Relieved this creep show is finally over.

Whatever trippy drugs your Watcher used on you must be wearing off. Your mangled, deboned leg tingles with the first needling, shuddering screams of lifelong misery. Still, you can't help but smile. The pain means you're still alive.

The pain means you won.

Laughing wildly, dazedly, you shove yourself upright.

You're just starting to wonder how you're going to puzzle the chains off the exit when the projector in the booth *fliiiiiiick-fliiiiick-fliiick-flicks* back to life, an immortal heartbeat, refusing to fade.

Every pulsing victory inside you plunges into a dark theatrical pit even as a Hollywood glow beams from the fragmented window above, ever-lighting the silver screen.

Inside the flesh of your mangled leg, something twitches. Something hideous pokes, squirms, a new nightmare being born.

A bladed arachnid hand bursts from your flayed flesh!

You scream and scream as that festering stump-gash births a nightmare arm with shadowy bones. It coils, snakelike, and the bladed hand rears back, ready to strike. Ready to cleave you down the center and open you wide, exposing every real-world tragedy you ritually hide from.

You grope for a weapon while the projector ticks out a grainy movie reel countdown.

4... 3... 2...

A final message appears on your beloved silver screen.

YOU CHOSE WRONG. THE MONSTER I AM IS THE MONSTER IN YOU. READY FOR OUR SEQUEL? CHOOSE ONE:

• FACE YOURSELF.

• GAME OVER.

LATCHKEY

"THE LAST KID who lived in my house disappeared," Jonah tells his fifth-grade teacher after school one Monday afternoon—just spits the Bad Thing right out.

Mr. Fetner makes a funny noise in his throat. "Did you say *disappeared*?"

"Disappeared and was never seen again."

"Well then…" Mr. Fetner closes his grade book and raises an eyebrow at Jonah's ratty Velcro sneakers and too-big eyeglasses. When Jonah asked if he could stay after school, the old man probably never dreamt of this, probably thought Jonah wanted to cry about his "D" in math, or all his missing homework.

But Jonah doesn't know who else to confide in. It's either tell Mr. Fetner, or tell the police officers who show up sometimes at the 7-Eleven at the end of his street—the one with the MISSING posters and all the graffiti. His mom said never to stop there, *always* go straight home, no matter how bad he wants a cherry Slurpee or to play Pac-Man. Bad Things happen to kids who talk to strangers and don't go straight home after school.

Only, that's not always true…

"His name was Billy," Jonah tells Mr. Fetner. "The other kids say a man in a clown mask crawled in his window when he was home alone. Billy was just sitting there in his chair watching his afternoon cartoons and eating a bowl of Trix when he got snatched. They say the bad guy took him to a basement somewhere and chopped him up into soup and—"

"I wouldn't put much stock into anything your classmates tell you," Mr. Fetner cuts him off, stern but still sorta nice. It's this same teacher-y niceness that made Jonah hope he might help. "I assume you're talking about William Walker? Hadn't realized you were living in his old house."

Jonah nods. "His bedroom, too."

"I had William in my class last year. Good kid, quiet kid, kind of like you, Jonah. He even had trouble turning in his homework on occasion. I'm sure the stories your classmates tell about him are quite spooky. But can you keep a secret?"

Jonah shrugs. He's kinda breaking a promise right now just by talking to Mr. Fetner.

"William's parents were in the middle of a nasty divorce and fighting over custody," Mr. Fetner says. "That means: which one of them he would live with."

"Oh, I know what it means."

"Well, the police think his father took matters into his own hands. Kidnapped him, moved him to Canada. Awful, yes, but even William's mother believes he's still alive."

Jonah shakes his head. His stomach knots, his heartbeat races and tingles. The fluorescent lights glint jagged stars off his glasses as if the Bad Thing is happening right now. "But you're wrong. Everyone's wrong. I know what really happened."

"Now, Jonah…"

"I know because Billy told me!"

Mr. Fetner sits forward, kind eyes suddenly sharp and alert. His mustache twitches. "You've spoken to William Walker?"

A staticky, white-cold warning buzzes inside Jonah's ears and crackles downs his spine, freezing him solid for a short eternity. Billy said nobody would believe him. Billy said not to tell.

But he has to try.

"I talk to him every day."

Praying his friend is wrong about adults, Jonah tells Mr. Fetner all that's been going on at home after dark. He spits out every secret Bad Thing.

"SO THAT'S ALL I wanted to tell you," Jonah says with a mouth that's gone dry, as if the truth sucked the Kool-Aid right out of him. "If I disappear now, too, my mom will know I wasn't kidnapped—not in the regular way. You'll tell her, right? My mom and ex-dad don't get along very nice either, but my dad won't disappear me. He doesn't even want me."

"You haven't told your mother any of this?" Mr. Fetner says.

Jonah shakes his head. He doesn't wanna make her even more sad. Not with her two jobs and two mean bosses. He promised to act like a big boy now, like the man of the house. He just never figured on the Bad Things.

Mr. Fetner sighs, and a goober of melting hope sinks through Jonah's guts.

"You know, Jonah, sometimes when something scary happens that we can't quite explain, we invent big fantastical stories to help us feel better about the mystery." Mr. Fetner raises an eyebrow at him. "Do you understand what I mean?"

Jonah understands. Billy was right.

"Living in a new house might feel strange—heck, even scary—but a house is just a…"

Jonah's ears start ringing, drowning out his teacher's voice. Through the classroom window, a glint of low sunshine hits his glasses. Oh jeez, when did it get so late? He scoops up his backpack and glances at the hands on the clock above the chalkboard.

"Sorry, Mr. Fetner, I gotta go." He scurries from the classroom, fast as he can. Hot tears sting his eyes, and already he knows this is the last time he'll mention Billy Walker and the Bad Things to an adult.

Mr. Fetner calls after him—maybe something about doing his homework—but Jonah's head is too busy spinning, working out a math problem all his own.

Little hand on the five. Big hand just past the three.

A twenty-minute walk home.

The *1986 Farmer's Almanac* in the school library said today's sunset is at 5:47 p.m., and so far, it hasn't been wrong.

All that equals only ten minutes to prepare!

If he runs, maybe he can add a few lucky minutes to his time. Too bad he's never lucky.

Right away, the slippery November snow-slush sucks at his sneakers, filling his socks with soggy, wet ice. His puffing breath fogs his glasses and the sidewalks ahead. The traitor sun sinks faster from the sky, and the brick-track houses around him glow orange and cold and alien.

As he passes the 7-Eleven, he biffs it, slipping on ice and skidding on his knees.

A police officer on a coffee break laughs gruffly. "Slow down, kid!" Probably laughing like how Billy will laugh when he finds out Jonah tried to ask for help.

Jonah runs faster. No help for him anywhere, not even from his neighbors. After dark, everyone seems to go blind and deaf.

The sun is a half-ball on the horizon by the time Jonah reaches the cracked cement stoop of his front porch. This house isn't nearly as big or nice as the one they lived in with his ex-dad. They don't *have* nice things since the big jerk married a younger lady. Usually, Jonah feels pretty sad about that for his mom's sake, but today there's no time.

He fishes inside his shirt for the key he wears on a shoelace around his neck. His fingers feel like grape Popsicles, and only now does he realize he forgot his coat and mittens somewhere at school. His mom will be upset if he loses anything else to the lost-and-found, but there's no going back now.

He rattles his key in the deadbolt, then dashes inside, pausing only long enough to peel a bright orange envelope from the door. *Final Notice.* A fresh knot of worry ties itself in his gut as he locks the door behind him.

In the dim twilight of the living room, lumpy shadows crouch all around him.

Jonah gets straight to work.

He scrambles for the wall switch. The overhead lamp pops on and the living room brightens, revealing saggy brown furniture and as-yet empty corners.

Jonah throws off his backpack. Then, giant deep breath, he races on squishy shoes through the remaining gloom, flipping switches in the kitchen, the hallway, his mom's bedroom, the bathroom, the bedroom that used to be Billy's but now is his. He doesn't exhale until the whole house is bright and shadowless.

Next, he yanks open all the window blinds. His mom doesn't like it when strangers can see inside, especially at night, but Jonah keeps hoping maybe someone *will* see.

He forgot to check the clock on the VCR when he got home. Now that he does, he yelps.

Seven minutes until sundown!

He drags a kitchen chair into the living room and sets it up two feet from the 19" Sony TV his mom got in the divorce. The piece of junk has tin foil wrapped around its bunny ears, but Jonah wouldn't still be here without it.

Six minutes until sundown.

He dives for the shoe boxes he keeps near the TV. Each is clearly marked:

GOOD GUYS. BAD GUYS.

Normally the two forces would never team up, but as Billy once told him: extraordinary circumstances call for extraordinary measures.

Jonah dumps his action figures onto the rug and arranges them around the chair. One by one, even though his stupid hands won't stop shaking.

He-Man next to Skeletor.

Optimus Prime wheel-to-wheel with Megatron.

Luke Skywalker, Han Solo, and Chewbacca in a lineup with Darth Vader.

The G.I. Joe attack team mixed up with the goons from Cobra.

And last but definitely not least, Johnny Galaxy with Vamptor and Wolf-Dude, leading the whole squad.

Each tiny protector brandishes a plastic weapon, bravely facing the surrounding room.

Three minutes until sundown.

"Stand by, soldiers!" Jonah hops over his perimeter and beelines for his and Billy's bedroom. He lands on his knees in the corner and pries the metal air vent from the floor. As always, his stomach gives a sick twist, and he's certain his secret weapon will be missing.

But as always, it's right where he found it after his first few nights in this bedroom—after weird cartoony dreams about a boy named Billy prying up this very same vent and hiding something amazing. Jonah reaches his hand in and feels that same electric tingle of awe.

He pulls out the VHS tape.

A Maxell T-120 with two hours of tape and a label with Billy's crooked handwriting:

IT KEEPS THE *BAD THINGS* AWAY

Jonah books it back to the living room and slams the videotape inside the VCR.

Two minutes to sunset.

He takes a seat in his action-figure-guarded chair and switches on the TV.

His pulse buzzes with the static on the screen. With a tingly prickle of dread, Jonah hits PLAY on the VCR. The tape rolls.

One minute to spare.

"Oh, blast it!" He bolts upright and runs for the kitchen, kicking Chewie and Han down the hallway as he goes. No time to rescue them! Jonah flings open the cupboard. Never much to choose from. A dusty box of Rice-O-Roni. The last can of Chef Boyardee.

He grabs at a tattered box of Pop-Tarts. It's light enough to be empty, but there's a lone cherry tart rattling inside. Have to eat it untoasted. He snags the pitcher of red Kool-Aid from the fridge, then slams back into his chair. His glasses slip down his nose. He pushes them into place just as the digital numbers on the VCR flicker to 5:47.

Outside his gaping windows, the sun disappears into Elsewhere.

Just like Billy Walker.

And just like they did for Billy Walker, the Bad Things come.

IT ALWAYS STARTS the same way.

The wheels whir inside the VCR. The snowy TV static flickers to a commercial for New Coke starring Max Headroom, the blond AI with the digital stutter.

Jonah leans closer to the screen and clutches the Pop-Tart and Kool-Aid in jittery hands.

Somewhere deep in the house, hangers rattle and a closet door whooshes slowly open. A floorboard moans with horrible footsteps. If Jonah glances sideways, he might catch a tall, wiry, white shadow slipping from his bedroom at the end of the hall.

But he doesn't look; he keeps his eyes glued straight ahead.

Max Headroom thanks him for being a Cokeologist, then the commercial break snap-cuts to black. A squealing guitar solo rips from the TV. Cartoon thunderbolts and music notes flash across the screen, spelling out a jagged, heavy-metal logo:

JOHNNY GALAXY AND THE SLASHERS OF THE NIGHT BEASTS!

In the kitchen, condiment bottles rattle as the refrigerator door pops open on its own. Cupboard doors groan and whine, and fleshy bare footsteps trudge across the linoleum.

Jonah's lungs scream, but he doesn't dare breathe.

Doesn't dare blink.

On the screen, Johnny Galaxy's logo explodes, and a cartoon teenager with orange leather jeans and an acid-green mohawk leaps from the blast, brandishing an electric guitar. "Greetings, headbangers! I'm Johnny Galaxy, defender of Darktopolis and leader of The Slashers, the wildest garage band ever to headline this monster-infested city!"

Jonah mouths along on auto-pilot, like reciting prayers with his mother before bedtime—only now, he's heard by all the wrong ears. Without moving a muscle, he tries to shrink smaller and smaller. If he doesn't move, if he becomes the size of Johnny Galaxy on the TV screen, nothing Bad can get him.

Except he knows that's a lie.

The toilet lid clatters open. Unearthly wet footsteps. Slow movement in the hallway.

A long white shadow gleams along the edges of Jonah's glasses. Neck and limbs as thin and rubbery as linguine. Large pale head. Turning his way.

On TV, Johnny Galaxy thrashes out a power chord on his guitar. Lightning zaps outward, and between the *zip-zam-zolts*, the rocker's ragtag bandmates appear.

"Meet my friends!" Johnny Galaxy cheers. "Veronica Van Hell-Sing—The Slashers' fabulous, fearless drummer! Midnight Jones—born to chew bubblegum and tear up the bass! And every screaming girl's favorite heartthrob—Davey Oscillator on synth!"

Streaks of fluorescent color dance across Jonah's glasses, all mixed-up with the reflection of that approaching shadow. Sickly pale limbs slow-glide down the hallway, getting closer. Nothing Chewie and Han can do to slow the Bad Thing down. Maybe nothing his other soldiers can do either, not with a broken perimeter. He wishes he would've saved his fallen *Star Wars* heroes. He wishes Mr. Fetner was here to see he wasn't lying.

Another Bad Thing creeps at the edge of the kitchen. It grips the doorframe with too-long, spidery fingers. Jonah's glasses slip down his nose, but he doesn't dare push them back into place. On the screen, his cartoon heroes become brightly-colored blurs.

"By day," Johnny Galaxy says, "we're high school seniors rehearsing for our next big show. But by night…" The rocker's sunny, instrument-filled garage turns foggy and spooky with moon-clouds. *Zip-zam-zolt!* Thunderbolts strike Johnny Galaxy's guitar and Midnight Jones's bass, transforming them into spiky battleaxes. Veronica Van Hell-Sing's drumsticks sharpen into stakes. Davey Oscillator's keyboard guitar glows with wavery, toxic-yellow music notes. "By night, we become The Slashers! Sworn to defend our unsuspecting classmates from Vamptor and the other horrid night beasts of Darktopolis!" A purple silhouette materializes behind the bandmates—fanged, clawed, caped, and reaching.

Behind Jonah, the springs inside the couch cushions let out a slow metallic screech as something huge rises and stands. On the tip of his nose, the lenses of Jonah's glasses reflect the nightmare and swim with white-washed shadows. Unlike Vamptor and the other horrid night beasts, the Bad Things don't reach out with their reedy arms. They don't need to. As they close in from all sides, Jonah's brain screams: *don't look!* But even with his eyes glued to Johnny Galaxy's world, Jonah can't help but see the stretchy-huge grins filling the Bad Things' empty white faces.

Billy said those grins are hungry.

Billy said those grins can swallow a kid deep down into Elsewhere, the very bad place where they're from.

"Join us on our latest slamming-jamming adventure!" Johnny Galaxy raises his battle axe and lightning shoots from the blade, right toward the audience! Jagged slashes of cartoon thunderbolts stab the glass of the TV screen and explode outward.

Zip-zam-zolt!

They strike Jonah squarely in the chest, but they don't hurt because they never do.

The Bad Things reach his action-figure perimeter.

In a neon flash, Jonah goes from sitting in his living room to standing in the side yard outside Johnny Galaxy's All-American garage. Just like every day after school since moving into his new house, Jonah hears The Slashers in there, tuning instruments, warming up for their latest episode.

And just like always, a grubby cartoon kid springs up from behind a nearby shrub and rushes over to greet him.

"Jeez, dude, what took you so long?" Billy Walker says.

"YOU STAYED AFTER school to ask for help?" Billy snickers, pacing the shadows behind Johnny Galaxy's garage. Fluorescent purple music notes pour from a nearby window. "Wowza, dude, you really are a doofus!"

Jonah hunches over in the cartoon grass, real elbows on real knees, still dizzy-sick from his mega-close call back in the real world. He straightens his glasses, side-eying the reflections of the Bad Things as they glide along the edges of his lenses, testing the perimeter with their linguine limbs. He forces himself to concentrate on Billy in front of him.

The cartoon kid wears the same Bermuda shorts and *Karate Kid* T-shirt he had on the last time his mother ever saw him. In fact, he looks pretty much like the picture on the MISSING poster at the 7-Eleven. Hooked nose, milk-chocolate eyes, dirty mop of hair—only now, the missing kid is a genuine cartoon hero, same as Johnny Galaxy and The Slashers. Sharp black outlines, bright video-arcade colors.

Billy takes an enormous crumbly bite of the Pop-Tart Jonah brought him. "What'd you think? Old Man Fetner was gonna go all Mr. Miyagi and save the day? Adults aren't dialed in to the right frequency. The Bad Things will walk right through them and swallow you up anyway. Face it, there's only one escape, Jonah-san, and you've already found it."

In Jonah's glasses, the Bad Things start circling, searching for an opening into this world. He hopes Luke and Vader will summon the Force and hold the line where Chewie and Han fell.

"They keep getting closer," he whispers, all quivery even though he tries to act brave around Billy. "I think they're gonna get me soon."

"That's what Bad Things do, doofus." Billy taps his paper finger between Jonah's eyebrows. "Keep returning to the real world and they'll eat you whole. One gulp! Gone! But it's like I told you an infinity-zillion times, they can't step foot in Darktopolis."

"You're *sure*?"

"*I'm* still kicking, ain't I?" Billy swallows the last of his Pop-Tart then takes a long swig of Kool-Aid. "Take it from me, Jonah-san, you should stay awhile."

Jonah watches him eat, ignoring the low growl in his stomach. Billy's way nicer when Jonah brings him snacks, so Jonah always does. According to Billy, the food here in Darktopolis tastes like ink and cardboard. Secretly, Jonah keeps hoping real food might turn Billy into a real kid again. But so far, it's just the opposite. It's always kinda strange and uneasy watching his friend eat. The shimmery ruby Kool-Aid changes to flat cartoon droplets the instant it touches Billy's mouth. Even his cherry mustache turns animated.

According to Billy, to stay here forever, all Jonah has to do is call out Johnny Galaxy's Power Words. Then lightning will transform him into a cartoon, like Billy. Sounds easy enough, but boy does Jonah's stomach like to twist around at the thought.

"I can't stay here," he tells Billy for like the infinity-billionth time. "My mom needs me to be the man of the house."

Billy snorts. "That's just what moms tell their sons when they're sick of taking care of them."

"Not true. My mom wishes she could be home with me."

"Think about it," Billy says. "How many minutes a day does she actually spend with you? Bet you could set an egg timer by it. She'll never miss you. Heck, she'll be relieved not to have to feed you and dress you and bother with you. Without you, she could quit her jobs, find a *new* man of the house, someone to take care of *her* for a change."

"Don't say that."

"Why not? She'll be happier without you, just like your ex-dad is happier without you."

"You're wrong," Jonah says, but the words taste like cardboard. For a kid that got himself trapped inside a videotape, sometimes Billy is wise in the meanest ways.

He sucker-punches Jonah's arm. "C'mon, don't be such a downer, Jonah-san. Look! There's a bad moon rising!"

Right on cue, the sun drops like a tennis ball from the sky, and when it bounces back up, it's a full silver moon. The sunny sky deepens to a spooky purple nightscape streaked with long arms of wispy midnight clouds.

Somewhere at the end of Johnny Galaxy's street, a lone wolf howls. *"Ah-woooo!"*

The two boys hurry up and peek through the window. Inside the garage, the drums cut short, and the guitars screech to silence.

"Hear that?" Midnight Jones cries.

"I'm catching wolfy vibes," Davey Oscillator says.

"Sounds like a bad moon rising," Veronica Van Hell-Sing agrees, just like she has infinity-billion times before. Billy winks at Jonah.

Inside the garage, The Slashers form a circle and wail the Power Words with rock-n-roll voices: "For the heroes of Darktopolis, power chords to power us all!"

The moon over the garage crackles with purple veins of electricity.

Zip-zam-zolt!

A neon thunderbolt blasts from the sky and electrifies the bandmates. Their street clothes morph into spiky heavy metal body armor. Their instruments sharpen into mighty weapons. Lightning splinters outward, electrifying the whole garage like those static-filled plasma globes they sell at Spencer's Gifts. Billy and Jonah press their hands against the window glass and their hair bristles like mad scientists.

Usually during this part, Jonah likes to puff up his chest and feel a rush of courageous power! Heck, sometimes, he even feels like he might be ready to recite the Power Words himself and go all Looney Tune.

But tonight, all he feels are vampire-bats fluttering crazily inside his gut.

A second howl shakes the night.

The Slashers high-five with their weapons, then pile into their rusted-busted tour van. The muffler coughs a cloud of orange smoke, the radio slam-jams to life, then the van squeals tires down the driveway.

Billy and Jonah race out and leap onto the back bumper, just like infinity times before. Usually by now, Jonah stops seeing the Bad Things in his glasses and enjoys the ride. After all, this is the special extra-long episode where Johnny Galaxy first meets Wolf-Dude. It's one of the all-time best.

But tonight, those shifty white-washed reflections don't go away.

Tonight, lumpy bulbous heads tilt closer, breaching the perimeter, widening their mouths. If Jonah squints sideways, he'll be peering down the barrel of a bottomless black grin. There's no telling what Elsewhere will be like, but he bets there won't be cartoons or action figures or anything that makes life not-so-scary. Billy once said Elsewhere is just mountains of chewed-up, unwanted dead kids. And the still-alive kids who get sent there run around dirty, barefoot, and starving—*so* starving, they gobble the legs off the dead.

And now it's Jonah's turn.

The Bad Things lurk closer and closer until—

Jonah's sweaty fingers slip from the back of The Slashers' van.

"Hey," Billy cries over the rock-n-roll and the wind. "Get a grip, Jonah-san!"

Too late.

Jonah topples back and hits the street in a dizzy-making somersault. Up becomes down, and the cartoon pavement tumbles around him, scraping grit into his knees. His eyeglasses pinwheel off, and he jolts to a stop on his butt. The speeding-off-without-him-van and the bad-moon-rising fuzz into unrecognizable paint smudges. Anything could be coming at him now—Bad Things, Vamptor, Wolf-Dude…

Jonah paws the ground for his glasses.

Blurry hands reach out of the blurry darkness.

With a scream like a wet burp, Jonah skitters backward on his butt.

"Jeez, doofus, it's just me," Billy laughs. "I've never seen anyone backflip off a speeding van before! That was actually kinda awesome."

"I told you," Jonah gasps, trying to get his wind back. "Something's different. The Bad Things are hungrier tonight. They're watching me right now."

"Of course they are. You're *inside* your TV."

Jonah shakes his head. It's not that. "Why aren't you afraid of them anymore?"

"Because, doofus. I've got better things to be doing. Here." Billy pops Jonah's glasses back onto his nose. The right lens is cracked into a spiderweb. In each of the hundred slivers, a Bad Thing widens its mouth.

Jonah's insides lurch, and he yanks the glasses off his face, squelching his eyes tight against a sting of embarrassing tears. He shoves his glasses up at Billy. "I think they're breaking my perimeter. If you're not afraid, then just look."

"No flipping way!" Billy skitters backward. It's the first time Jonah's heard his voice crack. "Get away from me with those things! Those are *your* Bad Things, got it? I've already escaped mine."

"But I can't face them alone. If I do, I'm toast. I don't know how to stop them."

"Jeez, doofus, how many zillion-billion times do I have to tell you? Just say the Power Words, stay with me in Darktopolis."

"I can't." Jonah buries his face in the tattered knees of his jeans.

"Then you really *are* toast. And one day, the Bad Things are gonna swallow you whole." Billy faces the direction the tour van zoomed off in. "Now look what you did. The Slashers are getting away. We're gonna miss the first wolf battle!"

Down the street, howls and fireworks and power chords explode against the Darktopolis cityscape. Neon sparks dance across Jonah's squished-up eyelids. He already knows how Johnny Galaxy's fight ends. Heroes like The Slashers make bravery seem ultra-easy. He's watched them blast the fur off Wolf-Dude a zillion times and won't ever get sick-to-death of it.

Only, tonight feels different—like an egg-timer ticking down inside the buzzing goo of his stupid kid-brain. *I want my mommy!* But he doesn't dare say it out loud, not in front of Billy. Instead, he just slumps there in the street, arms blanketing his knees, trying to hold still as ice, even as he can't stop shivering.

"Sometimes, you're a major bummer," Billy groans, nudging Jonah's leg with his paper sneaker. But Jonah can't help himself. If he moves so much as a pinky toe, something Bad will happen. He knows it.

Eventually, the fireworks in the distance flare out and Billy gives up on dragging Jonah to The Slashers' next battle. Instead, he helps him to his feet—"Come on, Jonah-san, it'll all be okay"—and guides him, squelched eyes and all, back to Johnny Galaxy's garage.

Jonah sits on Veronica Van Hell-Sing's drum stool and buries his face in his knees. "If I stay, do you think my mom might be able to visit me here?"

Billy snorts. "Wowza, you've got a lot to learn, doofus."

Only, for the rest of the episode, the cartoon kid doesn't say much—just paces restlessly, tapping his fingers across the drums and tunelessly plucking the strings on Johnny Galaxy's backup guitars.

At last, far-away lightning crackles outward from the moon—*zip-zam-zolt!*—and defeated howls vibrate the paper-thin air.

A power chord later, Johnny Galaxy's electric garage door hums victoriously to life and starts to rise. Headlights streak across Jonah's eyelids as an old beater rumbles into the driveway and coughs to a stop.

His heart gives a little skip, and before he knows it, a pale icy hand reaches out from the real world and squeezes his trembling shoulder.

"Hey there, Little Man, I'm home."

JONAH LIFTS HIS head from his lap and blinks at his mom's blurry silhouette. He scrambles for his glasses, eager to see her, but by the time he fumbles them onto his face, she's already turning away.

"Sweet goodness, Little Man, haven't I told you not to sit so close to the TV? It's bad for your eyes." In his splintered right lens, a hundred kaleidoscope Moms glide dreamily across the living room. She peels off her yellow second-hand puffy coat, revealing her brown cashier's uniform like a bruised banana.

"I love you," he says, but his voice chokes on a lump.

"And just look at this place!" she clucks. "All the lights in creation blazing, toys scattered everywhere. You promised to pick up after yourself."

Jonah blinks. His *sorry* sticks in his chest. His action figures lie battle-blasted all over the living room, sprawled on their backs with plastic limbs twisted at spooky, jagged angles.

"I see you've had dinner; that's good." His mom plucks the empty Pop-Tart box off the rug then heads for the backpack he heaped by the front door. "Did you finish your homework?"

"Yes," he lies, barely hearing himself. It's worse than he feared. The Bad Things actually destroyed his perimeter! The torn-off heads of He-Man and Optimus Prime stare blankly back at him.

"Oh God," his mom says, holding up the bright orange envelope he pulled off the door earlier. *Final Notice.* She presses a hand to her mouth as she reads the letter, growing paler and paler, like maybe it's more unfair papers from Jonah's ex-dad. Since the divorce, shadow-clouds always hover around her eyes, but now they darken to storm clouds.

No lightning, though. This one's a rainstorm.

"What is it?" Jonah asks, suddenly afraid. A new kind of afraid.

"Nothing," she lies. Her gloomy blue gaze drifts up from the paper and meets Jonah squarely in the eye—straight through his broken glasses. He braces himself for trouble— he promised to take better care of his stuff—but she doesn't seem to notice the shattered lens. In fact, she doesn't seem to notice Jonah at all. For a long second, she goes very far away, transported to an Elsewhere reserved just for adults. Then:

"Clean this mess up and get ready for bed." Her voice sounds suddenly all shook-up like a can of Coke about to burst. "And turn off all these damn lights when you go!"

"But you just got home—"

But she's stopped hearing him. She disappears into the kitchen and starts banging the cabinets closed and cursing Jonah under her breath for leaving the refrigerator wide open.

If only she knew what *really* happened in there.

Jonah crawls around, collecting his busted-up action figures. His stomach gurgles, upset and empty. His knees burn from tumbling off Johnny Galaxy's van. Worse, the carnage in the living room shows how mean the Bad Things can get. Heads twisted backward. Limbs hanging loose on bony plastic knobs. Skeletor, nothing left but a muscular torso. Luke Skywalker, snapped in half and missing his light saber. Darth Vader, helmet crushed flat as the Empire. Jonah fills his shoe boxes like coffins. When he finishes the head count, his heart sinks.

Han Solo and Chewie are MIA.

Vanished from the hallway. Vanished from sight.

The Bad Things got them. Took them Elsewhere.

Only Johnny Galaxy seems to have survived unharmed.

On the TV, the cartoon's end credits cut to commercials. The Trix rabbit appears behind a tree, spying on a group of kids with rainbow bowls of cereal. Billy sits with them. He turns and winks at Jonah, then the scene fuzzes with static and the videotape runs out.

Jonah hits REWIND, resetting the video for tomorrow.

While the VCR whirs, he hovers silently near the kitchen doorway. His poor mom sniffles, then the phone rattles off the cradle. The dial tone buzzes through the lonely house, as if she's trying to figure out who to call.

With heavy feet, Jonah slinks back to the VCR and grabs his videotape. As he retreats for his and Billy's bedroom, his mom says, "Hey, Vick, it's me…"

Icicles stab Jonah's back at his ex-dad's name. Even though eavesdropping isn't polite, he leaves his door cracked while he re-hides the videotape and shrugs into his too-small PJs.

Like always when talking to his ex-dad, his mom starts shouting almost right away.

"Because he's your son, too, damn it! You want him sitting here all alone in the cold and the dark? Please, Vick! How am I supposed to come up with a spare two hundred bucks by Thursday? I'm already working fifty hours a week! I don't give a shit that you just bought a second honeymoon to Mexico! They're gonna turn off our electricity, you asshole!"

Every word is awful, but as Jonah crawls into bed, the part about the electricity squeezes him to a jittery pulp. He buries his head under the pillow, trying not to cry while he does the math. His ex-dad being a jerk plus zero money by Thursday equals three days until the power goes away and Jonah is toast.

At last, his mom slams the phone down so hard the bell jingles.

Footsteps in the hallway.

His door creaks open and a sliver of golden light shines in.

"Little Man? You still awake?"

Without mentioning his ex-dad, she pulls Jonah up into a hug and nuzzles his hair with her chin. "Who needs electricity, right?"

"I need electricity to watch Johnny Galaxy," Jonah whispers. He can't help himself.

His mom lets out a surprised bark of laughter. "Oh, Little Man, c'mon now. Cartoons? You can survive without Mister Galaxy for a little while, right?"

She won't believe the truth, so Jonah nods and hugs her back, hiding his sad-scared tears like a big man—even as he shrinks inside her arms, so, so small.

"Chin up. It'll be an adventure, right?" But she sounds like she's hiding tears, too. "We'll pretend we're camping. Flashlights, our warm coats, and mittens."

And just like that, piled high atop a heap of worries as tall as a mountain of chewed-up dead kids, Jonah remembers the puffy coat he lost at school.

TUESDAY AFTER SCHOOL, Jonah searches the lost-and-found for his coat. He digs down so deep, his feet come off the ground. But it's bad luck as usual. His coat has disappeared into Elsewhere along with his mittens and Chewie and Han. He holds up an ugly orange ski jacket that isn't his and considers taking it.

So far, he's in the clear. His mom didn't notice his missing coat this morning before leaving for her shift at the café. She didn't even spot the hole in his glasses where he'd popped out the broken lens. Though, Mr. Fetner noticed—just like he noticed Jonah's ripped-up knees and missing homework. "I think it's about time I speak to your mother, Jonah," he warned him after math class.

And now this. Jonah holds the orange ski jacket against his chest like his mom does at the thrift store. He frowns. The color reminds him of *Final Notices*. Plus, he doesn't want his mom thinking he's a burden *and* a thief. Besides, who needs a coat anyway?

Truth is, he won't get chilly on Thursday when the power goes out because he doesn't plan to be around that long.

Come Wednesday night, he's gonna say the Power Words and stay in Darktopolis. It's his only chance of escaping the Bad Things before the electricity goes Elsewhere. His mom might miss him for a little bit, but after a while, she'll be happier—like how his ex-dad is happier.

Jonah tosses the ski jacket back into the lost-and-found.

A spot of green flutters from the pocket.

Jonah blinks. A ten-dollar bill?

Ten bucks isn't much. Still, he imagines handing it to his mom and the sun-beam smile she'll wear, like he saved the day. Of course, he's not so dumb he thinks ten bucks could save anything, but it'll be nice to see her smile at him. He peeks down the hallway to make sure there are no teachers, then shoves the cash in his pocket.

And now he spots something else in the heap of lost goodies.

A tiny, hot-pink mohawk. Jonah glances down the hallway again, then reaches into the bin. Can this be real? A brand-new Midnight Jones action figure! He pulls her loose, followed by a shirtless Davey Oscillator and a winking Veronica Van Hell-Sing.

With his Johnny Galaxy back home, they complete the band. With their power weapons, they can take the places of his disappeared *Star Wars* heroes.

He shoves The Slashers into his backpack, then races home through the shivery snow. He ducks his head low, hoping the gray clouds won't flatten him with a thunderbolt for being a thief.

At home, he turns on all the lights. Pulls up all the blinds. Builds a new perimeter around the TV and VCR. He poses The Slashers first. Standing together, friends-'til-the-end, their plastic battle-punk armor gleams.

Next, Jonah performs emergency surgery on the daring heroes who fell trying to protect him. He pops arms and legs into sockets, screws heads onto necks, and explains the importance of this next battle.

"Tomorrow, I vanish from this world forever," he tells them. His brain buzzes with a blurry-eye headache, and his chest cramps at the thought of his mom hanging MISSING posters at the 7-Eleven. But if he wants to survive Thursday's blackout, Darktopolis is his only choice. "Guard the perimeter one last time, so I can say goodbye to my mom tonight."

Johnny Galaxy and The Slashers stare back at him with painted eyes.

Outside his windows, the sun drops from the world.

Jonah drops into his chair and hits PLAY.

THE BAD THINGS have him surrounded. More than ever—at least ten, but maybe two hundred. Long-necked, hideous and towering, their reflections crowd the entire left lens of his glasses. Their deformed roly-poly heads dangle over Jonah's action-hero perimeter, peering down at him, grinning.

But tonight, he doesn't fall off the back of The Slashers' van.

"Woo-hoo!" Billy howls beside him, his cartoony mop of hair whipping wildly in the wind. "This is your life now, Jonah-san!"

Well, it's not his life *yet*—he's still gotta say goodbye to his mom. But ever since Jonah told Billy about his decision to move to Darktopolis, Billy's been celebrating as if Jonah already called out the Power Words.

Johnny Galaxy cranks up the power anthem on the radio and swerves into the parking lot of an abandoned fireworks factory.

Evil howls shake the moon.

"Looks like we found the dog pound," Veronica Van Hell-Sing snickers.

"Let's muzzle those hounds!" Midnight Jones cries.

Billy and Jonah trade high-fives and leap off the bumper just as The Slashers burst from the tour van with their instruments blazing. Even before the fur and fireworks fly, thunderbolts and star-filled music notes explode above their heads.

Sparks of DayGlo-color paint everything, including Jonah. The skyscraper city of Darktopolis shines, more neon than ever. Sharp, clear lines, dazzling colors. Jonah rubs his right eye through the hole in his glasses frame—and it hits him!

Even with his missing lens, his vision feels 20/20. He pulls off his glasses and nothing changes. "Whoa."

"What are you doing now?" Billy whines, tugging him toward the action.

"My glasses," Jonah says. "I don't think I'll need them in Darktopolis."

"No duh, doofus. The food might stink but everything else here is grade-A awesome."

Just to be sure, Jonah holds his glasses back up. Stupid. All he sees are Bad Things hovering in a frenzy around his perimeter, their starving grins the size of black holes—like they know their chance at a big meal is running short.

"Get away, you jerks!" Jonah shouts. "Just stay back!"

At the sound of his voice, the Bad Things recoil and skitter around the living room as if he lit fireworks in their faces. It surprises Jonah, too. He's never dared speak to them before.

Quick as they scatter, they swarm him again like flies to dead kids. *But still…*

"Billy, check this out," Jonah whispers, holding his glasses out. "I think I spooked them!"

Billy slaps his hand away and his eyebrows darken to angry cartoon slashes. "I told you to keep those things away from me, doofus!"

"Don't be a bummer," Jonah says. "Say something to them. They can't get you. They're stuck behind my new perimeter. I got some new toys." Jonah tells him about his discovery in the lost-and-found.

"You found ten bucks?" Billy's eyes glitter with tiny cartoon dollar signs.

"Well yeah, but that's not the point. The action figures practically appeared like magic!"

"Forget that." Paper drool trickles from the corner of Billy's mouth. "Here's what you do, Jonah-san. Tomorrow, during your last day in the real world, you're gonna hustle that ten bucks up to 7-Eleven and buy us a celebration feast. Nerds, Bonkers, Big League Chew—the works!"

Jonah's stomach grumbles, but he shakes his head. "It's for the electric bill."

"Don't be a doofus, doofus. Two hundred minus ten still equals lights out. Anyway, don't you think good-old Mom will ask where you got it? Want her to think you're a thief?"

Shoot. Jonah can't argue with that.

He sighs. "Fine. I'll buy snacks. *If* you try on my glasses."

Billy's eyes flatten to angry tough-kid slits. "Jeez, what's your weird obsession with me and your nerd-glasses anyway?"

Jonah's mouth goes dry of answers—at least, dry of answers that might impress Billy. With a shrug, he says, "I don't wanna be the only one who sees the Bad Things."

Billy rolls his eyes. "You know, doofus, we're missing the best action again for this bologna." In the background, lightning sizzles and—*zip-zam-zolt!*—ignites the fireworks factory. Wolf-Dude yowls as fur and cherry bombs explode from the windows.

"I'll throw in some Pop Rocks," Jonah says.

"Fine, doofus, hand them over." With a sideways smirk, Billy snatches Jonah's glasses and shoves the frames onto his face.

Almost instantly, the missing kid's mouth scoops open with an enormous gasping scream. Before Jonah can ask what he sees, Billy flings the glasses across the parking lot. The remaining lens shatters.

Only, before it does, the wildest thing happens.

For a flash-instant, Billy Walker's cartoon face flickers with the fleshy nose, mouth, and eyes of a real boy.

"YOUR TEACHER CALLED, today." Jonah's mom flips the TV off so zippy-fast he doesn't even get to tell Billy and The Slashers: *see you tomorrow.*

Jonah blinks up at her. His fingers fly to his glasses. Both lenses broken and lost to Elsewhere. In this world, his vision is still all blurry.

Only that's not exactly true. His mom's disappointment is crystal clear. He's let her down again. Electricity-gobbling lights blaze all through the house. And in the living room, the bloodbath is brutal. Every last member of The Slashers has been chewed apart.

Jonah grits his teeth, bracing for his mom to shout at him like she does his ex-dad.

Still wearing her coat, she slumps into a puffy yellow heap on the couch and hides her face in her hands. She weeps real tears and shrinks smaller and smaller.

"Mom?" He puts his hand on her shoulder, warm and soft, not paper-thin.

"I'm so tired, Jonah." She lifts her stringy head. "How did I miss all this? Mr. Fetner said you haven't done your homework in weeks, and your glasses… God, just look at you." She flutters her hands at him.

"You're doing your best, but I make it impossible." She shakes her head. "And you've been telling wild stories? Missing boys and a magic videotape?"

"And the Bad Things," he adds in a whisper.

"Oh, Jonah, just stop! You're too old for boogeyman and imaginary friends. Don't you see I have enough to worry about?"

"But Billy Walker *is* my friend. And I might know a way to turn him real again before the power goes out—"

"Enough, Jonah, enough!" she snaps. "Just go to bed."

But he lingers, wanting to hug her and tell her about what happened when Billy tried on his glasses. "Shouldn't I pick up my toys?"

"Don't bother. It'll be a while before you get to play with them again."

"I'm sorry, Mom," he whispers. "I love you." But she's too far disappeared in her own Elsewhere to hear him. He slinks down the hallway and closes the door softly behind him.

This isn't how he wanted their last goodbye to end.

But as Billy would say: there are no happy endings in the real world.

"HEY, KID, IT'S freezing out!" a police officer shouts outside the 7-Eleven on Wednesday afternoon. "Does your momma know you're out here without a coat?"

But Jonah's already learned his lesson about confiding in adults. He ducks his head, hurrying past the window of MISSING posters, and runs home hauling $9.75 worth of Bonkers, Big League Chew, Nerds, Pop Rocks—the works.

Tonight, he and Billy are gonna become friends-'til-the-end and share the best-ever celebration feast.

Because tonight, Jonah is gonna say the Power Words.

If only his stomach didn't feel so sour.

If only he could stop picturing that flash-second when Billy's face turned real.

If only his mom hadn't stayed awake most of the night, digging through the junk drawers and closets, searching for his ancient pair of eyeglasses from third grade. They were waiting on his nightstand this morning along with a note:

LITTLE MAN, I HOPE THESE GET YOU THROUGH THE DAY. I LOVE YOU.

After reading it, Jonah tucked the note into his pocket. Except for Billy's candy, it's the only thing he plans to take with him to Darktopolis.

Arriving home, shivering, Jonah performs his pre-sundown ritual one last time.

Lights, shades, chair, TV. No action-figure perimeter, though. His mom hid his Good Guy, Bad Guy shoe boxes as punishment for not doing his homework and being a lousy son.

Today's sunset is at 5:46.

At 5:36, with ten minutes to spare, Jonah writes his mom a note:

I'LL LOVE YOU FOREVER.

At 5:38, he pulls up the metal air grate in his and Billy's bedroom. It's empty.

Jonah's heart drops out and hits the floor. His secret weapon—gone!

He races back to the living room. Praying, hoping. His mom sent him to bed before he could re-hide the videotape.

But the VCR is empty, too.

5:40—six minutes until sunset.

His mom must've hidden the videotape with his action figures!

Heart racing his feet, he rushes from room to room.

5:41

He bangs open cabinets.

5:42

He yanks open junk drawers.

5:43

He even flings the cushions off the couch.

5:44

But his mom must've hid the VHS tape Elsewhere.

5:45

He slams open her bedroom closet.

And drops to his knees in dizzy relief.

His shoe boxes peek out from beneath the hems of his mom's summer dresses. The VHS tape sits on top.

IT KEEPS THE *BAD THINGS* AWAY

The lamp flickers. Jonah's glasses slip down his nose as he reaches through the gloom.

A floorboard creaks. Hangers rattle.

Two twiggy white legs materialize in the back of the closet.

Jonah's hand freezes on the videotape.

Pale, spidery fingers part the curtain of his mom's dresses, reach down and curl around the videotape.

He's never looked directly at a Bad Thing before.

At first, Jonah can only wheeze with a silent scream. The Bad Thing's neck is long and scrawny, like a rope tied to a lumpy balloon. It stretches its hideous black mouth—only not black, not really. Its mouth cavity is lined with the rotting corpses of dead kids.

"Get away from me!" Jonah cries.

At his voice, the Bad Thing recoils on its spindly legs, topples backward.

The videotape clatters free. Jonah snatches it and bolts toward the living room. As he passes the kitchen, several spidery white bodies tumble like newborn nightmares from the open cabinets.

Jonah slams the video into the VCR and pushes PLAY. Again, again, like punching the call button for an elevator.

At last, the wheels in the VCR whir. The static on the TV snaps to video. The Trix rabbit appears behind a tree, spying on children.

The end of the video! He never rewound it!

All around, the Bad Things skulk from doorways, corners, all the hidden edges of reality.

Jonah hits REWIND, then jerks a glance over his shoulder.

A hideous long-necked creature with slimy fish-belly skin spider-crawls up from the couch cushions. It reeks like the blood of action figures, and when it opens its grin, the dead kids lodged inside that hellish twisty-slide throat scream out for Jonah to run.

But there's only one place to go.

"Stay back!" Jonah screams. "Stay back! *Stay back!*"

All around him, linguine bodies flail, clamping hands to bulbous skulls and toppling backward.

The videotape hasn't finished rewinding all the way, but Jonah smirks at the fallen Bad Things and hits PLAY.

IT'S THE FINAL battle between Wolf-Dude and The Slashers.

The moon hangs high and bright over the abandoned Lucky Dog pet food factory—a.k.a. Wolf-Dude's secret lair. High above, on the rooftop, The Slashers hang in chains over a giant steamy can of molten puppy chow. A caped figure with furry ears, a tail, and a spiked leather dog collar stalks back and forth, howling with villainous laughter.

"No more battle of the bands for you tuneless punks!" Wolf-Dude grips the lever that will release The Slashers to their bubbly, meaty-dog doom. But Johnny Galaxy and his bandmates smirk and exchange secret glances. They always have a lightning-packed trick up their sleeves.

Meanwhile, Jonah climbs the fire escape to the roof, up and up, fast as he can. His time is running out! His glasses fill with spindly white static as the Bad Things stand and swarm closer.

But he doesn't lose his grip.

"Get back!" he cries, and the Bad Things stagger again.

Hopping onto the roof, he whips off his glasses and scans the chaotic standoff of fur and rock-n-roll. Wolf-Dude's four-legged minions circle the Lucky Dog can with slimy dripping tongues, eager to feast. Crackles of electric-blue lightning gather around the moon.

In the murky shadows behind Wolf-Dude, a lost boy stands with tear-stained cheeks, watching his favorite cartoon heroes for the infinity-zillionth time.

"Billy!" Jonah cries.

Billy whip-flips his head around and lights up at the sight of Jonah.

"I thought you ditched me forever." He runs over, scraping embarrassed tears from his cheeks with the back of his hand. "Not that I would've missed you or anything, doofus. Did you bring my candy?"

"Forgot the candy! The videotape is gonna run out soon! You have to put these on!" He shakes his glasses at Billy. "You have to make yourself look at the Bad Things! You have to face them. If you do, you'll turn real again." Fingers crossed.

"Are you mental? I don't *want* to be real again!" Billy shoves Jonah backward toward the edge. "I don't *want* to face the Bad Things!"

"Even if it means you get to see your mom again? Go to school? Be a normal kid?"

"My mom was never home! School was hard! The other kids tell spooky stories about me! Why would I ever wanna go back there?"

"Because *I'll* be with you." Jonah glances at The Slashers. Together, dangling over certain doom, the bandmates link hands. Jonah says, "And I have a plan—at least, *I think* I have a plan."

"The *plan* was to celebrate with candy!" Billy cries. "The plan was for you to shout the Power Words and hide out with me forever!"

"Just listen! In the real world, we might be able to fight the Bad Things. *Together,* friends-'til-the-end. We'll shout at them until they go away!"

Billy snorts. "Haven't you been paying attention, doofus? The Bad Things will never go away! Even if one *does* die, there's always another one to take its place."

Across the roof, the furry villain growls a final warning. Maybe Billy's right. Heck, even here in Darktopolis, Wolf-Dude and his pack arrived as replacements for Vamptor after The Slashers slayed him in a previous episode.

But that doesn't mean The Slashers stop fighting.

Together, the bandmates raise their hands and wail their Power Words:

"For the heroes of Darktopolis, power chords to power us all!"

The entire sky crackles with a neon plasma ball of moon-lightning and power chords and courage. A heavy metal thunderbolt strikes the puppy-food can. *Zip-zam-zolt!* A starburst of Lucky Dog's finest explodes outward, splatting Wolf-Dude in goopy brown slop. At once, his growling, starving wolf pack pounces, knocking him on his tail and slurping the muck off his dazed, spiral-eyed face.

Meanwhile, The Slashers flex their super-charged muscles and explode from their chains in a burst of high-fives. Johnny Galaxy, Veronica Van Hell-Sing, Midnight Jones, Davey Oscillator! Each shines neon with blazing inner strength. Together, they tap drumsticks, strum guitars strings, jam on synth, until a pulsing spooky tune fills the air around them.

Jonah does the math. One last song plus a final fur-flying showdown equals:

"The show's almost over!" He rattles his glasses. "Please, Billy, take them. Don't make me leave you behind. If it's between you or my mom, I choose my mom."

The cartoon color in Billy's cheeks heats to a boiling-cauldron-red, and he shoves Jonah again, inches from the edge. "You swore you'd stay here! You swore you'd bring me candy!"

"There's candy in the real world," Jonah promises, refusing to lower his glasses. "Have a look. The Bad Things are there, sure. But so are the Good Things. Maybe even secret powers we didn't believe we had."

"There's no such thing as secret powers in the real world, Jonah-san! There is no magic, no Good Things! Only liars like you!" Cartoon flames flare inside Billy's eyes and curls of steam rise from his ears. "I'll never go back to the real world! You can't make me!" He yanks the glasses from Jonah and hurtles them over the edge.

Maybe there are no such things as secret powers.

But that doesn't mean there aren't treasures in the real world that make you strong.

Jonah pats the letter in his pocket. "I'll miss you, Billy Walker," he says. Then he stage-dives like a rock star over the side of the Lucky Dog pet food factory. After all, he isn't about to let the glasses his mom stayed up late to find get broken.

The factory zooms by, windows blurring into painted action-lines. Jonah snatches his glasses from the air and shoves them onto his face a billion-zillionth of a second before smash-landing onto the rug of his living room.

"*Oof!*" He rolls onto his back, gasping.

The Bad Things peer down at him.

Misshapen skulls atop necks as long as arms. Each stands taller than the sky, yet lurks close enough to cast an endless shadow. They breathe in deep with those cavernous hellscape grins, taste-smelling the scent of Jonah's terror.

"Go away!" he shouts. "Go away, go away, go away!"

With a chorus of furious wheezing screeches, the Bad Things recoil back.

Then they slingshot forward again and swallow Jonah alive.

SPIRALING DOWN THE Bad Thing's twisty-curvy throat, shrinking smaller and smaller, Jonah prays to be back in his living room, back in Darktopolis, anywhere but Elsewhere.

He squelches his eyelids shut. But he can't stop seeing the nightmare circus of trash and body parts twisting past. Empty food wrappers, broken eyeglasses, mangled action figures, forgotten homework, bright orange *Final Notices*, puffy winter coats, VHS cassettes with black tape spilling out like intestines, all tangled up with the soupy remains of unwanted dead kids. Chopped-off heads, torn-away limbs.

At first, they're only strangers, faces from MISSING posters at the 7-Eleven. But as he slides deeper, they become people he knows.

Mr. Fetner and the snickering police officers at the 7-Eleven.

The kids at school who tease him about the house he lives in.

His selfish ex-dad and his greedy new wife.

And at the bottom, crouching in a pale, hungry-empty pit of loneliness and sadness and desperation, Jonah sees his mom.

"I'm so tired, Jonah," she weeps, with a voice that echoes around him and through him.

At the sound, deep in the stomach cavity of Elsewhere, more shadows stir, hangers rattle, a door groans, and more Bad Things drift like phantoms from the gloom—colorless and spidery and long-throated as ever. Only, inside their gaping grins, the soupy carnage is slightly different: mean bosses, ex-husbands, icy houses, empty wallets, a troubled son.

His mom's Bad Things. They surround her.

It's just like Billy said. They're everywhere. They never go away.

But that doesn't mean Jonah will stop fighting.

"Hey, jerks, over here!" He rises on wobbly knees and puffs out his chest.

Because, sometimes, even moms need heroes.

Giant deep breath, Jonah whispers *his* Power Words:

"I won't run away, Mom. I'll be strong for you. I'll make you proud!"

Thunderbolts don't strike.

Jonah doesn't transform into a heavy metal cartoon warrior with electric superpowers.

But something hidden and Good begins to shine.

He stands ready for the fight. But he doesn't rush toward the crouching figure. That hunched and bony shadow isn't really his mom—just his deep-down scary idea of her.

He knows where his real mom is.

He starts to climb.

Up and up, through the nightmare throat of the Bad Thing. Past all the worries that twist his stomach. Past all the hardships that make him hide. He won't cower in cartoons any longer. And he won't let the Bad Things swallow his life. His ex-dad, *Final Notices*, MISSING kids. Awful, scary, yes—but hapless villains compared to the blazing power of the Good Things.

Like the note in his pocket:

LITTLE MAN, I HOPE THESE GET YOU THROUGH THE DAY. I LOVE YOU.

Jonah nudges his glasses up and cranes his neck. Far above the tangled dark mess, the Bad Thing's half-moon grin glows with the hopeful light of his living room.

Jonah climbs and climbs and grows bigger and bigger.

Until he spills, un-eaten, from the Bad Thing's mouth. Until he hits the rug, gasping. Until the golden light of his mom's headlights glints across his glasses.

LATE THURSDAY MORNING, while Jonah sits in math class, the power in his house goes off. Murky shadows and a misty white chill creep from the corners, filling the silent rooms. Deep in the house, hangers rattle, a closet door opens, and a spidery hand grips the doorframe. More follow, as they always do. They wander, linger, gather in the growing twilight and wait for Jonah to come home.

Later that day, a key rattles inside the deadbolt. The front door moans, and a dark silhouette with large reflective eyes steps inside. He almost reaches for the light switch, then remembers the flashlight and fluffy warm blanket his mom left for him by the door.

Click. A beam of light cuts across the living room, briefly illuminating a white-washed forest of legs, arms, and necks.

Jonah whispers his Power Words.

Then, with a wobbly but brave little smirk, he heads to the kitchen table and unzips his backpack. And with his mom's blanket warming his shoulders, he settles in with his flashlight and finishes his math homework.

Just like the Little Man he's become.

THE ASH COLLECTOR

THE SAGEBRUSH COUNTY coroner always looked forward to disposal night. That was when the unclaimed cadavers stored in his deep freeze were transferred to his crematorium. Though the territory he served consisted of barren desert and one tiny town, the number of unclaimed dead had been satisfyingly high for over three years now. The nearby interstate was a favorite hunting ground for the Chrome-Face Butcher. The killer—besides preternaturally eluding the bullets of the local authorities on two separate occasions—also had a talent for picking victims with no next of kin. The castaways, the lonely hearts. Every few months, their corpses would wash up on the side of the interstate with the fast food wrappers and cigarette butts. Pretty girls with artistic wounds and nobody anywhere to claim them. To the coroner, who was lonely himself, they felt like offerings.

He wasn't a murderer. Working with the dead was as close as he'd come to feeding the slithering urges inside. But on those glorious mornings when the sheriff called him to a fresh crime scene, the coroner always felt like a VIP. Heck, crossing into the spectacle of police tape and flashing red-and-blues was like finally gaining entrance to an elite after-party. And though the guest of honor had already departed, Chrome-Face never failed to leave behind plenty of favors. Weapons still lodged inside bodies, clothing shredded to streamers.

Cause and manner of death were obvious in these cases. *Sharp Force Trauma, Homicide.* But wow did the instruments of destruction vary spectacularly! Pig splitters, pitchforks, bolt cutters, even a bear trap once. Such genius!

It was an honor to probe and catalog each victim's wounds, to fingerprint them and ID them and officiate their impressive demise. On those mornings, as the coroner wheeled their dripping gurneys into his autopsy suite—and on disposal nights, of course—he liked to believe he was in league with old Chrome-Face, a partner operating on the back end. Chrome-Face created the masterpieces, and the coroner curated them.

Currently, he kept Chrome-Face's victims on display at the back of his crematorium. A stark violation of county policy, which mandated all unclaimed cremains be buried en masse. Despite that—or maybe because of it—his private collection kept him gleaming with pride. Thirteen silver urns at last count. One day soon, he fantasized, the killer would arrive to claim his trophies and they would become great friends. Maybe not the type who went trout fishing or puffed cigars at the local girlie bar or anything—unless Chrome-Face was into that—but theirs would be the kind of rosy secret bond that lasted a lifetime.

Chrome-Face and the Ash Collector. Oh yes, he liked the sound of that.

Tonight, he would add three more masterworks to his collection.

Billhook, Tent Spike, and Javelin.

Those weren't their legal names. Naturally, the coroner had forgotten those almost as soon as he'd released them to the press.

As expected in these cases, there were no weeping parents, no heart-shattered fiancés. Any distant relatives he'd attempted to contact never returned his calls—not that he went out of his way to follow up. The revolving door of state detectives and their gooney forensic pathologists had exhausted their need for the remains. And now the mandatory twelve-month sleepover inside his deep freeze had expired.

Barely containing a cheese-moon grin, the coroner slicked the eager sweat from his receding hairline, then slipped on his favorite long, rubber apron. No wet-work tonight—the getup was merely ceremonial. After all, every aspiring sidekick needed a snazzy trademark costume. Sucking in the gentle bulge of his stomach, he tied the apron strings securely and checked his dull reflection in the side of the freezer like a schoolkid primping for a date. Nobody was ever going to call him a heartthrob, but he hoped he looked appropriately macabre.

As he pulled open the individual lockers and rolled the naked freezer-burned beauties onto gurneys, the coroner indulged a shiver of nostalgia. He would miss visiting them, running his ungloved fingers inside the intimate contours of their injuries, whispering to them in the abandoned hours of the night. Maybe it was silly, but sometimes when he pressed his mouth against their cold ears, he'd pretend that Chrome-Face—wherever he was when he wasn't hunting—could hear him.

It was always a relief to talk about the shadows hanging between himself and the rest of humanity. Like the lucky jars of spider legs he'd kept as a teenager, or the pocket-tin of cadaver teeth he used to shake like a nervous rattlesnake all through med school. Somehow, he felt certain Chrome-Face would understand:

It was never his intention to chase people away. They'd simply ran.

All his fidgety, weak-stomached first dates. His holier-than-thou tattletale peers. Those narrow-eyed professors who'd suggested he aim low and never work with living patients. Lucky for all of them, he'd long ago resolved himself to being alone with his dark intrigues.

That is, until Chrome-Face's victims rolled into his life, and he realized he had a kindred spirit somewhere out there.

And, oh, how he envied Chrome-Face's ability to assert himself with such bravado! Each new canvas came decorated in a frenzied flourish of stabs, slashes, gashes, and chops—the coagulated red autographs of a legend.

Such stories they told!

The coroner found the defensive wounds especially expressive. Nearly all of Chrome-Face's victims had them, exquisite documentation of their desperate final moments. The coroner could envision it all. The scraped knees as they ran and stumbled. The abrasions on their elbows as they scurried backward across the pavement. The split palms and severed fingers as they tried to fend off the nightmare.

Whistling to himself, the coroner wheeled the gurneys, one by one by one, through the morgue's back door and across a moonlit walkway to the deceptively charming brick building beyond. Nothing else around for miles except desert grit and Joshua trees and the hard-baked ribbon of the interstate. Once the gurneys were lined up inside his crematorium—first Javelin, then Tent Spike, then Billhook—the coroner propped the heavy steel security door open with a brick to let in a breeze. It violated policy, but if someone wanted to come all the way out here for a peep, who was he to deny them?

His own instrument of destruction waited at the back of the large sterile room: a hungry black metal box with a smoke stack and a corpse-sized loading hatch. On both sides of the cremation chamber, his silver urns lined the walls. The polished surfaces reflected the new arrivals, bending the outlines of their cadavers into devious smiles. The coroner smiled, too.

Three empty urns waited on the nearby counter.

With flamboyant flips of switches and twists of knobs, the coroner ignited his furnace, preheating it to a toasty 1100 degrees Fahrenheit. Then he stood back and appraised the exposed flesh of the three victims, with bright incendiary eyes.

To preserve the dignity of decedents, ethics and health standards mandated that cadavers be placed inside a flimsy pine box that would burn around them. But that involved sifting coffin nails from the cremains afterward and was far less cozy. The coroner preferred having an intimate view of those pretty gaping wounds as he slid them into his pyre.

The first tonight was Javelin.

Female, brunette, 5'4", 143 lbs. with her organs intact. Lovely purple contusions and tiny crescent-shaped incised wounds decorated her neck. Those, as well as the angle of the entry and exit wounds through her upper torso, suggested Chrome-Face had hoisted her by the throat before inserting his weapon. The resulting wound tract pierced her sternum, heart, then spine. The strength needed to accomplish such a feat was a savage miracle. Oh, to have been a fly on a corpse during that murder spree! In fact, those rare cunning girls who saw the legend and *lived*, told investigators he was relentlessly tall and muscular, with a face of smooth featureless chrome. They said he was uncanny and inhuman. They said he appeared like a phantom between the dust and the shadows and the streaking white lines on the highway.

They said many things.

Heck, some even believed Chrome-Face had died years earlier out on the interstate, the victim of a hit-and-run. They said he'd crawled into the surrounding desert with the motorist's shiny bumper still twisted around his skull. There, beneath the cold-bladed moonlight, he'd vowed to slaughter every unsuspecting soul who ventured alone along his road at night. Yes, the coroner liked the sound of that: an immortal loner hellbent on making the world hurt as bad as it had hurt him. Certainly, no cadavers fitting Chrome-Face's description had ever come through the coroner's autopsy suite. Not even after those spitfire deputies unloaded their guns into Chrome-Face's retreating shadow. They *swore* the bullets had struck him, but of course, they never located any blood trails.

And although his victims' struggles usually ended with split and mangled fingernails, the coroner never found any trace evidence of Chrome-Face in his scrapings and swabs for the lab. No hair, blood, saliva, not even clothing fibers.

That wasn't to say discovering interesting debris on the victims was uncommon. Javelin, for instance, had arrived with loads of goodies embedded beneath her nails—tiny crescent-shaped divots she'd gouged from her own neck while trying to pry Chrome-Face's hand away. The coroner had detailed each stunning bit of flesh in his report. He always took great care with his findings, describing the finest scratches and abrasions with the pen of a poet. The state detectives were endlessly impressed with his thoroughness. And whenever their over-cocky pathologists nosed in, they failed to find even a single pinprick the coroner himself hadn't already logged. Naturally, handing over his findings never felt like a betrayal, because Chrome-Face had proven himself a god beyond capture.

While the cremation chamber finished preheating, the coroner transferred Javelin onto the conveyor and let his fingers say goodbye to her wounds. It was a shame that such stimulating pieces as this were destined for the fire, like master paintings lost to history, but the coroner, being a romantic, preferred to see their transformation into ash as symbolic of something everlasting. These objects of fleeting carnal beauty connected him to Chrome-Face in a way that gave the night dimension.

After the ashes settled, what remained was a brotherhood.

Or perhaps he was being overly purple. A habit in his profession: smoke-and-mirror phrasing to obscure the sharp force blows of death. Heck, even the concept of "ashes" was a gentle lie: they weren't *ashes* at all. Take Javelin here, for example. During her imminent cremation, the ruthless heat would incinerate every bit of her flesh, organs, and blood before ushering her skyward through the smokestack. What would remain after the coroner's fire receded were naked vulnerable bones, brittle as relics. He'd chop them up and sweep them into another hungry little device: his cremulator. There, the crushing force of ball bearings would pulverize the bone slivers to dusty sand.

Not ashes at all, but something so much more…gritty, everlasting.

In a way, Chrome-Face was like those ashes.

The coroner slid his fingers from Javelin with a sweet shudder. How lucky she was to have met the legend in the flesh. He envied her, even as he checked the temperature on his oven and rolled her into the hatch. Even as he watched through the viewing window as her eyelids crisped away. Had those same melting-egg eyes widened in existential awe when Chrome-Face approached with his javelin? Oh, how her cries must've gone from desperate pleas to thrashing mortal screams!

"He's killing me!" Javelin wailed—a banshee's voice that ricocheted around the walls of the crematorium. Startled, the coroner recoiled and looked back over his shoulder.

"Please! He's right behind me!"

It was a female. A live one. Blue hair, tattoos, approximately 5'8", 125 lbs. with organs intact—though she appeared to be missing a respectable slice of her right shoulder. She staggered into the open entryway. For an elated instant, the coroner wondered if she had come to view his collection. Then she spun and fumbled wildly with the security door, tugging on it with the full panic of her body weight, a freak show of shaking hands and dripping mascara. The door scraped inward, but his brick doorstop held the gap like a foot. The coroner watched, fascinated, wondering if she would solve the dilemma in time. He thought he glimpsed a flash of chrome out in the desert.

With a wildcat scream, the girl kicked the brick into the night. Her autopsy would surely reveal an array of fractured toes.

"Does it lock?" she cried, pawing at the doorknob.

"Automatically." The coroner tilted his head, his heartbeat turning giddy. "The question is: *will it hold?*"

"What?" She didn't seem to be hearing straight. "You gotta listen, man, he's a monster, he's after me! You gotta call the cops." She staggered away from the entrance, then went rigid as her eyes caught the gurneys with Tent Spike and Billhook.

Tent Spike, with thirty-three distinct stab wounds, was especially well-decorated. The coroner studied the Live One, anticipating an extravagant hysterical break, but her actual reaction was rather disappointing.

"Holy hell, you've got to be kidding me." Her terror stalled momentarily on a scathing laugh of dark-carnival irony. "Of all the places along the highway— This is a fucking morgue?"

This was his *calling*. But before he could offer to show her the viewing window, a force like a Mack Truck struck the security door, bowing the metal. The bricks lining the doorframe trembled again and again.

The Live One shrieked and bolted for the coroner's wall of urns. Her shoulder laceration dribbled a pleasing bright red abstract across the tile floor. "Tell me there's a back door!"

The coroner shook his head. "No phone, either."

"Oh hell, oh God…" She doubled over as if she might vomit, clawing at her hair. A split-second later she shot up, eyes like lunatic moons. "Man, don't just stand there like a freak!"

Baring her teeth, she shoved the gurneys recklessly toward the door, toppling them, creating a barrier of splayed legs and arms and desperation. It wouldn't be enough. She grabbed the steel poker the coroner used to crumble their well-cooked skeletons, then she, herself, crumbled.

She dropped into a fetal crouch against the side of his blazing cremation chamber and readied the poker with her good arm. It shook feebly.

One by one, the hinges on the door popped like knuckles.

"This can't be happening… I wanna wake up…" Her voice was devolving into feral, nasal moans, the kind of riveting firsthand detail autopsies never uncovered. "…just lemme waaake uuuuup…" Ironic words, ha-ha, since the coroner was the one living the dream.

"I'll take fine care of you," he promised as the door clanged inward.

The Chrome-Face Butcher had to duck to fit through the doorframe. A brute of midnight leather and gleaming heavy-metal flourishes, he radiated fury and artistry, just like the coroner always knew he would. Magnificent. Though the mask-plate covering his face had no eyeholes, the chrome was polished to mirror-like perfection and reflected the crematorium with surgical sharpness.

Hastily, the coroner finger-combed his sweat-greased hair and straightened the edge of his apron. Jeez, he sure hoped he looked menacing enough. Standing in the presence of such unbridled greatness, he felt suddenly underdressed.

The moment was a whirlwind.

Chrome-Face crashed past the gurneys, sending Tent Spike and Billhook pinwheeling to the side, too focused on his latest creation to admire old masterpieces.

Behind the coroner, the Live One's moans had choked to silence. As Chrome-Face angled for her, the coroner reached back and pried the poker from her petrified fingers.

He held it out before him, and with an awkward croaking frog in his throat said, "I heard through the grapevine you love sharp force objects." Delicately, he flipped the poker and extended the handle. "I'd be honored if you used one of mine. I'm your biggest fan."

Chrome-Face paused mid-stride. Possibly nothing like this had ever happened before. The coroner saw himself reflected in the chrome: a blushing and balding boy-wonder framed by a porthole of fire. His collection of silver urns floated on the periphery like spider eyes.

With a hand gloved in leather and glistening blood, Chrome-Face accepted the poker.

The coroner stepped sideways and extended his hand to offer up the Live One.

But Chrome-Face seized his upper arm with a superhuman grip.

A crunch, a hideous pop, then the coroner's humerus tore from the socket. Rapturous, white-hot agony erupted through his arm and shoulder.

Chrome-Face leaned in close with his shiny face-plate and raised the poker to throat level. The coroner saw the glinting tip reflected in his own widening eyes, and his veins went cold with a nameless awe.

Behind him, reflected in chrome, the Live One stood, taking the opportunity to dash for the exit. With apex reflexes, Chrome-Face hurtled the coroner against the wall of urns, then caught her blue hair with his fist. Everything a whirlwind. Urns crashed down in explosions of ash. The crematorium filled with a dusty haze and earsplitting shrieks.

It was exquisite.

Chrome-Face yanked the Live One close. Her bulging eyes hung inches from his mask-plate as he drove the poker home.

The coroner barely noticed the point of entry.

The surreal gaping terror as the girl watched herself die— *that* was the spectacle to behold!

She stared into the portal of her own eyes, a gallery of tragedy, of pains and regrets and ambitions. Every cruel, ugly thing the world ever did to her. Every hopeful, courageous thing she would never become. All of it skewered, devastated, obliterated. Gurgling, tears wetting her face, she watched it all fade.

A final pulse beat later, her body hit the floor.

Now Chrome-Face turned his bulbous, genius head to regard the coroner. Every lung in the crematorium held silent.

Then Chrome-Face stormed toward him through the ashes.

Scrambling, the coroner reached for the closest urn and held it in front of his face.

"I kept them for you," he rasped, so starstruck he wasn't certain he was making sound. He read the engraving on the urn. "You did this one with a bone saw."

Chrome-Face paused. He leaned in close with a gleam and a tilt of curiosity.

The urn reflected his face-plate, and the face-plate reflected the urn, and somewhere in that endless hall of mirrors, their grisly souls sparked.

Chrome-Face and the Ash Collector.

"United at last," the coroner whispered.

Chrome-Face knocked the urn aside.

Then he gripped the coroner's disjointed arm and manhandled him up onto his feet. Resplendent pain stabbed through the coroner's shoulder, a cherished memento of this night, which he would carry with him for his remaining days.

With a single rough-yet-gentle stroke of his hand, Chrome-Face dusted the ashes from the coroner's shoulder. For several raging heartbeats, they simply stood there admiring one another. Two lovely, lonely monsters born to walk behind the shadows, born to celebrate the messy surrealism of death.

Chrome-Face nodded once.

The coroner offered up a bursting, gleeful salute.

Then the legend turned and tromped back into the night, an immortal vision of passion and rampage, off to add more pieces to their collection.

ZOMBIE UNICORNS FROM GALAXY 13

LISTEN, MISTER ARMY or Marine Dude or whatever the heck you are, you wanna hear how I saved the world? Then stop barking questions about hostile horses and take a chill pill. They weren't horses, for one thing. And there's a whole galaxy more to *me* than bubblegum and high-tops. Seriously, not every hero needs helicopters and creepy top-secret interrogation bunkers. So, you gonna wipe that big crusty scowl off your face, or should we kick back and wait for the second invasion?

Fantabulous.

For the record, it all started with my big sister Teagan, make-out queen of Sagebrush County. She lost her dang brain. She set me up on a blind double date with one of her new boyfriend Chad's gooney wrestling buddies. Inane locker room talk, slurping spaghetti by candlelight, all of it out in public where people could see us. Just try to imagine a more soul-sucking waste of a Saturday night, I dare you.

So, I countered with a demand: *if* I agreed, we had to attend the drive-in screening of *Monsterbeast 7: The Final Splattering*. Some critics say the franchise jumped the shark with the whole Robo-Beast gimmick in part five, but I'm a die-hard fan. And bonus: creature features wreak havoc on Teagan's stomach. Just the idea of her barfing up her popcorn in front of our dates had me glowing. Gotta make the best of a bad situation, right?

See, a week ago, our parents ordered us to spend our Saturday nights together. Like, forever, until the end of summer. That's when Teagan was supposed to head off to college. If we didn't buddy-up soon, Mom was afraid we'd turn into strangers and ruin Thanksgiving like my dad and uncle do every year. As if a few measly Saturdays were gonna fix fifteen years of mutual sisterly neglect. I mean—

I *am* getting to the point, Colonel Jerk-face! Jeez. Keep interrupting and watch this take all night. Like seriously, dude, some of us have curfews.

Anyway, we got to Chad's house, right. And guess what?

My date wasn't there.

"Sorry, babe," Chad told Teagan, all slobbery and fake. "Guess he flaked when he figured out who his date was."

Teagan actually sad-smiled like she felt sorry for me, which was beyond lame. I might not be super-ultra popular, but it's not like I show up to life smelling of beef onion soup. I bet Prince Charming never even *asked* his friend. Not that I cared about swapping spit with some jock in the backseat. It was just rude.

"We'll still have fun," Teagan promised me.

We took Chad's '66 Mustang convertible to the movie. Candy-apple red. Wind in our hair. That car was his one redeeming quality. The whole way there, he squeezed Teagan's knee and joked about ditching me on the road. You know, the kind of jokes people tell when they're not joking. Teagan just giggled and hugged up next to him, which was bogus since she's an A-student and completely beyond that kind of pandering.

Anyway, the Dead-End Drive-In was packed. Had to be three-hundred cars there, easy. All the prime spots near the concession stand were already taken.

While we drove around searching for a spot, I put on my 3D glasses. Tried to imagine all the queasy shades of green Teagan was about to turn, the traitor.

So then Chad was all, "Hey, dorkus, you know this movie isn't in 3D, right?"

And I was all, "These are special glasses. Guaranteed to turn any movie into an extra-dimensional experience."

"Oh yeah?" he snorted. "What, you order those from the back of a comic book?"

So, here's the thing: I did. *Creepy Tales International*, $3.99 plus shipping and handling. Took six weeks by mail. I was absolutely itching to try them on the Dead-End's super-massive screen. Didn't do much to our TV at home— just made the colors all twisty and funky—but I figured they'd work at the drive-in.

I tossed my backup glasses to Teagan. They were supposed to be for my date, but whatever.

"Um, thanks, Spence," she said, tweezing them between her Lee Press-On nails. "But these relics aren't actually my style."

They did sorta resemble the glasses our parents wore in the olden days: the cardboard kind, with red-and-blue lenses. But whatever, they looked rad to me. Retro. Besides, that wasn't the point.

"Who cares what you look like?" I said. "The movie's gonna be so much bet—"

That's when Chad hurled Teagan's glasses out the roof and swerved to crunch them. "*I* care what she looks like."

"Wow," I said, like so not shocked. "You're a creepoid *and* you owe me $3.99. Plus shipping and handling."

"I owe you squat, loser. You got scammed."

"I'm not a loser."

"Then how come Teagan says all you do is hole up in your basement watching movies alone? Like a *looo-serrr*."

Well, I didn't exactly have a comeback for that whole basement thing. It's not like there's an instruction video for making friends or whatever.

Teagan turned in her seat. "No offense, but it *is* weird, all those movies you watch. I mean, gag me with a spoon: *Monsterbeast*?"

"They're classics!" I protested. "Cutting-edge special effects, gross-out monster transformations. Plus, Stretch Lee always does her own stunts."

"So do I," Chad snickered, pawing Teagan's thigh.

"Wait until you see it…" But my mouth was going dry.

Movies like *Monsterbeast* added color to my grayscale existence. The heroic endings got into my veins. Honestly, sometimes Stretch Lee was there for me when nobody else was. But no way was I saying that in front of dumb old Chad.

"Get real, Spence, these movies are a waste of time," Teagan said. "You spent your whole freshmen year just…hiding. Didn't you wanna go to a party or hang out with friends?"

"I don't know," I said, kinda salty. "Maybe if someone had *asked*. Now tell your jockstrap of the week to pull over! I'm getting out."

I did, too. Didn't even let the Mustang come to a complete stop. In my head, I was a leather-clad rebel like Stretch Lee in *Monsterbeast 3*, leaping from her Pontiac Firebird. In reality, I biffed it and gave the nearby cars a good chuckle. Chad, too.

I sprang up, 3D glasses askew.

"Wait," Teagan said. "Where're you going?"

"Concession stand."

"Here." She leaned over the side. "Twenty bucks. Get whatever you want. And hey, Spence?" She tightened her grip on the cash, all sheepish.

"Yeah?" I said, stupidly hopeful, like she had something meaningful to say.

"Don't tell Mom about this, okay?"

I rolled my eyes. "Just whatever. Go park. Maybe I'll find you guys."

"Or maybe you'll watch *Monsterbeast* from the concession stand," Chad called after me, because super-mega jerkwads always pipe in.

I stormed off, not bothering to search for Teagan's 3D glasses. And I wasn't about to take mine off—I was making a statement.

I should mention, dude, by then it was getting dark and there were already stars in the sky. Like ultra-colorful neon stars. Kinda eerie, but I figured it was just my glasses.

Inside, the popcorn line was a mile of shiny, laughing people, goofing around, swapping one-liners. I stood at the back, instantly fidgety. Being alone can feel so conspicuous, you know? Chad and Teagan's voices floated all echoey inside my head. They'd called me a loser. And weird. Weird! For some reason, that one stung. Was it my taste in movies?

Or just me?

I mean, *Monsterbeast* fans were all over that drive-in. Some even had piercings and spiky punk hairdos. Weirdos, right? Except nobody seemed as awkward as I felt.

Anyway, I loaded up at the counter: large popcorn, Coke Classic, and a butt-ton of Pixy Stix. You know, the little wands of flavored sugar? Only these were the size of swords. I grabbed every last stick on the counter: six Sour Grapes, four Blue Razz-Berries, three Very Cherries. Why skimp, right? It was Teagan's cash, and she hated the things.

I holstered the Pixy Stix onto my belt and went to pay the cashier. Except she didn't take the money. In less time than it took to fetch my popcorn, something outside had snagged her attention. Her eyes gaped, wide as moons.

I spun around—afraid *Monsterbeast* was starting without me—and yelped.

Rainbows were shooting from the sky!

They hurtled toward the drive-in like giant, sparkly party streamers.

"Whoa, you see that?" I cried. A boneheaded question—or it would've been if anyone answered me.

The other moviegoers just stood at the window frozen, like someone hit their pause buttons, staring outside all moon-eyed, same as the cashier. Even stranger: they weren't gawking at those psychedelic rainbows.

A freaky chill sunk through me.

They were gawking at *Monsterbeast 7*.

I mean, okay, yes. I was as die-hard as any fan there, and what I glimpsed of that opening scene *did* look rad. An adorable prickly Monsterbeast hatching from a stony, mercury-filled egg—it absolutely shrieked origin story, which any other night would've kept me riveted. But, *hello*. Rainbows! Shooting from the sky!

What was everyone's damage?

That's when the obvious hit me like a 3D fist. My glasses! Maybe they were giving me some spooky extra-dimensional sight. Maybe I was witnessing something nobody else could see.

Testing the theory, I pushed my glasses up onto my forehead.

The scene in the sky didn't change.

But, dude, the one on the movie screen sure did!

Okay, so, this next part's kinda hard to describe. The screen turned, like, completely white. Looking at it felt like being mind-sucked into some bizzaro eggshell vortex. White nothingness floated *everywhere*. I couldn't look away! Worse, I didn't care. My thoughts started stretching like spaghetti and turning bright white. Crazy, right?

Until suddenly, *Monsterbeast* reappeared on the screen!

Snap. Poof. Quick as that.

Get this, dude. My 3D glasses had dropped back onto my nose, blocking that brain-vacuuming whiteness and jolting me from my haze.

"Holy mail order," I whispered.

That's when the first rainbow smash-landed near the ticket booth. *Ka-pow!*

Two more struck near the screen.

Suddenly they were everywhere—blazing balls of color hurtling between the cars! One hit the bumper of a Cadillac and flipped it like a coin. Another annihilated the picnic tables in front of the concession stand. The whole building rumbled. Popcorn buckets jittered. Bells ring-a-dinged inside payphones and pinball machines.

I ducked and covered, but the other moviegoers didn't even blink!

Not even when a spectacular horned creature emerged from the crater dust.

"No. *Way*." I staggered to my feet as a colossal sparkling shadow lurched past the window. Then, in an absolute wonder-daze, I chased after it out the door.

After all, it's not every day a weirdo like me encounters a real-life unicorn.

NICE POKER FACE, dude, but I know what you're thinking. Heck, *I* was thinking it, too. Only, the proof was right there, shambling through the sidewalk debris.

This thing was twice the size of your standard Earth horse. Exquisite white coat, shimmering mane, long golden horn.

At least, that's what it was *supposed* to look like.

The creature in front of me was a hot mess.

Like a total *goonicorn*.

Mane all frizzled, flesh mangled from the crash. Rainbow meat dropped away from its diamond ribs and crystal skull like soggy birthday cake. Its horn had busted in half, and the pointy end dangled by a fiber.

But, dude, the craziest part: instead of eyeballs, tentacles of pink-and-blue goo squirmed inside its eye sockets.

Then, get this: a glob of that goo twitched free, splatted to the ground with its tentacles splayed, and started crawling.

Crawling!

A sticky goo-booger the size of a tarantula, it made a beeline for the concession stand and the zonked-out moviegoers inside.

"Oh no you don't!" I kicked the door shut. "Ha!"

That's when the goo-booger sprang at me like evil bubble-gum! Its tentacles suctioned to my 3D glasses, started pulling them off my nose. Gah!

Frantic, I peeled the goo-booger loose and flicked it to the sidewalk. It hit with a *splat* and immediately started glowing. Bright as neon.

Nearby, Sir Broken-Horn's goopy eye sockets lit up with the same neon light.

The beast pivoted my direction and—before I could mutter something witty—it charged. I scrambled sideways and it head-butted the door. Glass shattered.

Then, dude, I swear to you, the goo-booger on the sidewalk let out this sinister squishy snicker and snot-rocketed inside the concession stand.

Like, whoa! Right? I think that slimy thing actually *mind-controlled* the goonicorn.

More snickering goo-boogers bounced from Sir Broken-Horn's crystal skull and skittered through the shattered door. Definitely *not* how I'd imagined my first encounter with mystical alien creatures.

No fool, I ducked behind a nearby Volvo.

That's when I noticed the spooky iridescent space-laser beaming down from the stars, like straight into the projection booth above the concession stand. The cause of this whole mess—I'd bet my entire basement of VHS on it!

Goonicorns wreaked chaos all over the drive-in, galloping between cars with hooves like wrecking balls, dripping rancid bubblegum monsters from their glowing crystal skulls. Those tentacled goo-boogers pounced toward the concession stand.

And, dude, I'm telling you, not a single moviegoer screamed or fled in panic. Nobody even sneezed. They just sat in their dented-up cars, moon-eyes glued to the movie screen, getting mind-sucked.

I could've made a break for the desert—but oh heck. That's when I remembered.

"Teagan!"

Real fear zipped through me. I bolted halfway down the first aisle before realizing I had no clue where dumb old Chad had parked.

How hard could it be to find a candy-apple red Mustang convertible?

Turns out, dang near impossible. In total pandemonium, I dashed between convertibles, ditched past red paint jobs, and tripped over my own feet, like, *a lot*.

Meanwhile, on the big screen, Monsterbeast spiral-crawled toward a pair of clueless coeds sucking face on a park bench.

"Teagan, dang it!" I tried to envision the lamest parking spot at the drive-in: behind a lamppost, or maybe next to a Porta Potty.

That's when the scorchingest rainbow of the night blasted from the sky.

With a mega-disco-ball flash of color, it landed in front of the movie screen, and the most magnificent creature I'd ever laid eyes on burst into my world!

Smooth rippling muscles. Flowing golden hair. Blazing multicolored aura.

Now *that* was a unicorn.

My turn to go all moon-eyed. As I gawped, the unicorn stepped forth to survey the scene. He stood resplendent like a god and wore 3D glasses. Blue-and-red and retro, same as mine.

"Heck yeah," I whispered.

He lowered his mighty horn and charged the nearest goonicorn.

"Go for the goo-head!" I hollered. But the *Monsterbeast* soundtrack had kicked into feast mode. Violins, bass drops. The unicorn didn't hear me.

He impaled his foe's chest and ripped sideways until its magical heart splatted the dirt like a scoop of rainbow sherbet.

But the goonicorn didn't die. Its goopy skull blazed brighter, and it attacked! As the two clashed horns, the neon eye sockets of the surrounding goonicorns flared up. They pivoted toward the action.

The unicorn was about to be outnumbered! I had to create a distraction! But how?

I looked around. Smashed bumpers, flattened speaker poles. I'd lost my popcorn at the concession stand. Though I did have one thing…

I reached for my belt-load of Piy Stix. Then, summoning a battle-cry like Stretch Lee storming the discotheque in *Monsterbeast 2*, I unleashed a sparkly cloud of Blue Razz-Berry into the nearest goonicorn's tentacle-filled eye sockets! Like tossing salt onto a slug, only the payoff was way sweeter.

An ululating squeal erupted from inside its skull, matching pitch with Monsterbeast on-screen. The goonicorn crumpled and skidded across the dirt. Goo-boogers sprang from its eye sockets, tiny tentacles sizzling, dissolving. I yelped and fell onto my butt, kicking them off my high-tops.

Meanwhile, the unicorn bucked his opponent through the Dead-End's fence, then galloped over, peering down at me in those 3D glasses.

"Come with me," he said.

"If I wanna live?"

"Precisely."

No way was I gonna say no.

The unicorn knelt down, and I did what any rational movie-nerd would do.

I climbed aboard.

WHOA, LIEUTENANT FREAK-OUT, stop acting all bristly and paranoid! You know you'd do the same thing. Seriously, dude, I'm telling you, the unicorn was a friendly. We blasted skyward, and I held on tight, buried my face in his strawberry-scented mane.

"Who are you?" I called over the rush of wind.

"Greetings, I am Ambassador Adonis Valiant Demetrius Wynstar the Third."

"Spencer Tiffany Kapowski the First here. Cool if I call you Wyn? Because wowza, that's a mouthful."

Then, I swear to you, he was all, "If it so pleases you, enchantress."

Enchantress!

So, naturally I had to go and make it awkward. "Um, you talking to *me*?"

At once, he performed this phenomenal cosmic nosedive. The wind swirled with stars, my stomach flew into my toes. We touched down in the desert behind the drive-in.

I dismounted onto legs quivering like protoplasm. Had to steady myself against him else I would've toppled sideways from too much exhilaration.

"Forgive me," he said. "Are you not an enchantress? Then you must be a sorceress? Or perchance an Andromedan warrior fairy?"

So, okay, I admit it. I was blushing pretty hard. There I stood before this stunning mystical creature, and he thought *I* was magical? I was super tempted to play along, call myself the grand mistress of the sprites or something, but it's never cool to start a friendship on a lie.

I fessed up. "Sorry, nothing enchanting here. I'm just a weirdo."

He inspected me through his 3D glasses. "Saw it myself: you abolished the Trollvekians with a wave of your wand. Expelled them from the skull of my fellow ambassador."

I rubbed my temples. My giddy was catching up with me. "Whoa, back up. The Troll-what-kians? Those goo-boogers have an actual *name*?"

"Yes, noble weirdo. They are the Trollvekians, and you are the first in the galaxy to defeat one."

"Holy Pixy Stix," I muttered.

But he wasn't done: "As an ambassador for Galaxy 13 of the Intergalactic *Silver Screen* Federation, I humbly beg your assistance."

"Did you just say 'the Intergalactic Silver Screen Federation'?"

"Indeed. It is the Federation's duty to monitor star systems with intelligent life. We watch and wait, hoping others will discover the most powerful element in existence."

"The A-bomb!" I guessed, because living out in this desert, who *hasn't* read the UFO and A-Bomb conspiracy literature—right, Mister Area 51?

Except, I was so wonderfully wrong.

"It wasn't weapons that alerted us to you, noble weirdo," Wyn said. "Your species discovered cinema."

"*Cinema?*"

"Cinema. As in filmmaking, moving picture shows?"

I gawped at him, all super-ultra mind-blown, like my brain was confetti. *Pow.*

"Oh, balderdash," he said. "Is my universal translator glitching again? They're stellar for eliminating subtitles but—"

"No, no," I said, un-choking my voice and probably dripping with the planet's nerdiest grin. "You're totally speaking my language."

I'd known it all along, of course—that movies were mankind's all-time grooviest achievement. But to be validated on an inter-galactic level? It was so bitchin'!

Plus, it made total sense. Movies mesmerize us, transport us, empower us. Bigger-than-life characters, action, danger! Heck, get lost in your favorite movie and *you* become the hero. Most powerful element in existence?

I mean, *yeah*, duh.

See, dude, turns out that when a civilization starts making seriously rad movies like *Monsterbeast*, the Intergalactic Silver Screen Federation deploys a fleet of ambassadors to their planet. They make first contact—"we come in peace" and all that—then invite them to enter the Intergalactic Film Festival. The filmmakers who win Best Picture become ambassadors for their respective galaxy. It's mondo-super prestigious. Wyn represents Galaxy 13—a.k.a. *our* Milky Way.

Awesome, right? Our galaxy has more movie-lovers than stars in the sky. Unfortunately, there's always some jerkwad who wants to wreak havoc on the fun.

"They are the Trollvekians," Wyn told me. "A globule species of vile critics. They entered our festival with their film *Q'seivometahew.*"

"*Q'seivometahew*?" Just saying it was like hocking up a loogie. Loosely translated, it means *Wall of Eggshell*. We're talking 720 hours of paint drying. In slow-motion. A film so mind-numbing, the Federation declared it a health hazard and banned the Trollvekians from the festival.

That's when the little creepoids vowed to destroy every filmmaking civilization in Galaxy 13. Wyn and his fellow ambassadors had just reached our moon when the invasion began.

"No ships," he told me. "They beamed *Q'seivometahew* across the galaxy. It contains a subliminal signal that mutates brains and eyeballs into Trollvekian larvae. It infected our fleet's in-flight movie marathon and overtook my fellow ambassadors. Now, the Trollvekians will use them as puppets of chaos until their entire brains melt into larvae."

"All because they loved movies? That's despicable."

"I was spared, thanks to my 3D glasses. I ordered them from the back of *Creepy Tales Intergalactic*. But I only had one pair…"

"Wyn, I'm so sorry, I…" I didn't have the words. What would it be like to find a whole movie crew of friends, only to lose them?

"Now, noble weirdo, I fear *Q'seivometahew* has premiered at your drive-in."

"Oh jeez, Teagan!" I glared at that revolting space-laser. Just imagine our Thanksgivings if my sister came home with aliens oozing from her skull. My poor mom. "We gotta stop those scum-suckers! My sister's out there!"

Wyn bowed. "It would be an honor to fight beside you."

"Sweet. Because I might have a plan."

I GAVE WYN the skinny as we flew back over the Dead-End. It was Armageddon down there, but from our height, Teagan was easy to spot. We landed between Chad's Mustang and a fallen dumpster. Gah! Figured.

"Make haste, noble weirdo!" Wyn shouted. Around the drive-in, neon-skulled goonicorns lit up and pivoted our way.

Chad's engine had a massive horseshoe-shaped dent, but the passenger door still opened. The make-out queen and Prince Charming sat in the backseat, drooling on each other and staring all googly-eyed at the screen.

I tugged Teagan's arms, but she wouldn't budge. I tried blocking her view of the screen and *Q'seivometahew*, but she went on gawping.

A goo-booger appeared in the corner of her eye and pounced my 3D glasses. Gah! The thing wiggled and snickered and might've once been a teaspoon of my sister's brain. Hopefully it was the part that liked idiots. I flicked it away, resisting the urge to aim at Chad's drippy jockstrap face. This was all his fault! The scum-wad had destroyed my back-up glasses!

"Oh jeez, Wyn, look at them," I cried. Another goo-booger squirmed outta Chad's nose. "Are we too late?"

"Their hourglass runs low. We must get to the projection boo—"

"Look out!" I jumped onto the seat, launched myself over Wyn's back, and dusted an incoming goonicorn with a cloud of Very Cherry. Goo-boogers leapfrogged from its sockets, fizzling, squealing. The empty-skulled goonicorn went down for the count.

"Stellar reflexes, noble weirdo!" Wyn cried as I landed on my high-tops. "I'm reminded of Stretch Lee in *Monsterbeast 3*."

I couldn't believe it. "You've seen *Monsterbeast 3*?"

"Seen all your classics. Lee's stunt-work is exquisite. Another enchantress. Fierce, with inner power."

"Her courage totally inspires me."

"Me, too, noble weirdo."

I peered into his 3D glasses, gobsmacked. He was checking all my boxes. Forget space dramas and alien invasions—getting to know Wyn was a most excellent adventure. For the first time, like, *ever*, I actually got why Teagan was so bedazzled by her friends.

Oh heck, speaking of Teagan!

Before I could overthink it, I reached for the glasses on my nose.

"Noble weirdo, no!" Wyn cried. "What are you doing?"

"Giving her my glasses. Her brain's crawling out. I gotta do something."

"You must fulfill your plan!"

"Saving her *is* the plan. I can't leave her like this. You go!" I held up my arsenal of Pixy Stix. "Pure sugar. My secret weapon."

But Wyn wouldn't take them. "You are the only weirdo in Galaxy 13 ever to destroy Trollvekian larvae."

"I'm telling you it was just the sugar."

"And I am telling you I know an enchantress when I see one. Take my glasses, save your sister, save your world!"

"Wyn, I can't let you—"

With a shake of his golden mane, he loosened his glasses. "Godspeed, noble weirdo. We shall celebrate your victory with an intergalactic film marathon—if the enchantress so wishes."

Before I could say "heck yes," Wyn tossed me his glasses.

Q'seivometahew zonked him instantly.

I wasted three giant seconds standing there with his glasses dangling in my hands. Was I really gonna let the unicorn of my dreams go all goo-brained? I mean, we made a rad team, and I couldn't save the world alone. Goonicorns rampaged all around, closing in. Plus, I was pretty sure the Trollvekian larvae had a hive mind. Their slimy exodus into the projection booth had grown eerily synchronized, like tentacled, DayGlo ants.

But Teagan had college in the fall, and if we were ever gonna buddy-up, she'd probably need her brain.

I leaned into the back seat and popped the 3D glasses into place.

Full disclosure: I put them on Teagan *and Chad.*

I know, barf, right? But Wyn's glasses were oversized enough for both their sappy heads.

The awesome power of 3D was instantaneous.

Chad woke up, cussing at the sight of me.

Teagan's expression turned all soupy and awestruck. Not at me—at something on the silver screen. "Oh, neat!"

I turned just as Monsterbeast bloomed to full spiky-winged glory and chomped a scientist in half with its spiral-toothed mouth. Stellar special effects! The guy's intestines spaghetti-ed out.

So did Teagan's dinner.

Mom's Linguine Surprise hurled straight into Prince Charming's lap. *Ker-splat!*

"Nasty wench!" Chad bellowed.

Before I could stop him, he shoved Teagan and the 3D glasses away, scrambled outta the Mustang, went mooned-eyed—then got dropkicked by a charging goonicorn!

Don't worry—the dumpster broke his fall, the loser.

"Chad!" Teagan cried.

"Plenty of jockstraps in the sea," I reminded her.

That's when she took a wide-eyed look around. We were practically surrounded. "Spence, what the flip? Are those uni—"

"No time to explain." I yanked her from the back seat. "Keep those glasses on and follow my lead!"

I'M TELLING YOU, dude, it sucked leaving Wyn behind like that—already his moon-eyes looked oozy—but if I was gonna save him, I had to act fast.

With Teagan freaking out, but sticking by my side, I zig-zagged through the aisles. Channeling the rebel-fisted grit of my inner Stretch Lee, I dusted every brain-sliming Trollvekian I passed with Sour Grape revenge.

Ten cars from the concession stand, a blazing trio of tentacle-skulled goonicorns barreled out to block us. My old pal Sir Broken-Horn galloped on point.

"Get ready!" I cried, ripping open the last of my ammunition.

"Ready for what? Spence, this is bonkers!"

But Teagan wasn't an A-student for nothing.

And I'd studied Stretch Lee all my life.

As the goonicorns hurtled our way, Teagan grabbed a fallen speaker pole and chucked everything she'd learned in AP Physics at Broken-Horn's front hooves, toppling him into a somersault. The goonicorns in the rear crashed into him, sending the three-corn pile-up skidding our way.

Like Stretch Lee playing sneaker-chicken with a grenade-charred Monsterbeast, I charged into the dust and dosed the goonicorns' rolling eye sockets with a rainbow cloud of sugar. Split-second before they bowled me over, Teagan yanked me sideways. Horned skulls crashed into a nearby Buick and goo-boogers whiplashed out. Sizzling and screeching and doomed!

Teagan and I locked eyes in disbelief.

Who knew? My sister was a badass.

We raced inside the concession stand. Trollvekian goo-boogers twitched across every wall, ripping down movie posters on their way to the stairwell.

"What are those creepoids doing?" Teagan whispered.

"Ruining my movie. Trying to take over the world. You name it."

"Ew."

"Don't worry, we're gonna stop them." I bolted to the pop-corn stand—only to grab an empty Pixy Stix carton. Dang! I'd cleaned them out earlier.

No time to panic, Wyn was counting on me. I asked myself: what would Stretch Lee do?

Heck, she'd improvise! Like in *Monsterbeast 5* when she sprayed Silly String into Robo-Beast's gears. I grabbed a popcorn bucket and dumped everything sugary inside: Bonkers, Nerds, Pop Rocks. Then I primed Teagan about what came next. Ducking behind the candy stand, we jammed our heads together beneath Wyn's glasses, swapping out so I had the giant pair.

I gave Teagan the candy bucket and a fierce hug. "You were right."

"I was?" She looked dubious.

"I *was* hiding. From school, from friendships. From you."

That sad smile again. "I saw you struggling, stuck in your shell. I'm such a bogus big sister. I should've been there for you."

"Be there for me now?"

"Totally."

"Rad."

Together, we snuck upstairs to the projection booth. And, dude, talk about a creep show! In the flickering doorway, we clung to each other and tried not to gag.

Hundreds of squirmy DayGlo goo-boogers dangled like spit-wads from the ceiling above the projector. Lumpy, tentacled, and *uuuug*-ly. That evil space-laser shone straight through the ceiling, incubating them, transforming them into even bigger jerkwads!

Not to mention the nasty things that neon light was doing to the projector. The *Monsterbeast 7* reel spun and vibrated, possessed by 720 insidious hours of paint drying.

"Cover me!" I cried, dashing forward.

Teagan didn't let me down. As I raced for the projector, she tossed the candy at the goo-boogers above my head. Only, instead of fizzling to death, they absorbed the sweets like fruit-salad inside Jell-O and snickered heinously.

Oh heck! Were Trollvekians only allergic to Pixy Stix?

Or was Wyn right? Was the magic really mine?

No time to wonder.

At the projector, I reached for Wyn's 3D glasses, ready to block that eggshell light. But too late!

The Trollvekian hive mind flared a blinding pink-and-blue neon, and the goo-boogers pounced. A thousand sticky tentacles rained down on me like a giant sneeze.

GAAAH!

I mean, you have no idea! Inside that squirming, rancid-bubblegum nightmare, every negative review ever spewed by a critic squished over me. Zero stars, a billion thumbs down. I was covered head to high-tops in protoplasmic rotten tomatoes! Didn't these freaks have anything *nice* to say?

Teagan screamed my name, a girl-shaped blur on the other side of the slime. Just imagine the Thanksgivings she must've been picturing! But what could she do?

I'll tell you: she reached out with her Lee Press-On manicure and clutched my goo-infested hands. "All these creepoids can suck it! I believe in you, Spence!"

Pretty sure she meant it, too.

No way was I letting my big sister down.

There was only one way to destroy a gang of vile soul-sucking movie critics.

Enchantress or not, I summoned the magic already inside me.

All the punk-rock, devil-may-care heroism of Stretch Lee, every badass, backflipping stunt, every eye-popping B-movie spectacle, every gore-splashed monster-slaying victory. Loud and proud, I invoked the transcendent power of my fandom and all my favorite flicks.

"*Monsterbeast! Monsterbeast 2: Splatter Boogaloo! Monsterbeast 3: Beast Warriors! Monsterbeast 4: Splat Galore! Monsterbeast 5: Robo-Beast! Monsterbeast 6: Splatter Chicks!*"

The goo-boogers screeched and jiggled, started to fizzle. It was working!

Harnessing every die-hard, shining-star, cult-classic review in my guts, I cried out:

"*Monsterbeast 7: THE FINAL SPLATTERING!*"

Cosmic-levels of movie love surged my veins and blasted outward, going supernova, slamming through the goo-boogers and the projector.

With a death-wail like a thousand writhing Monsterbeasts, the Trollvekians exploded off me! Fizzling guts painted the walls, the reels—and Teagan, too.

Ker-splat!

"Go *Monsterbeast!*" she cheered. Then she ralphed into her candy bucket.

"Most powerful element in existence," I said, knees rubbery with amazement.

Above the spinning movie reels, the glowing space-laser guttered and vanished like a one-hit-wonder. Just to be safe, I wrapped Wyn's glasses around the projector, officially banning *Q'seivometahew* from Earth.

Monsterbeast 7 appeared on the big screen for everyone to enjoy—just as Stretch Lee, glossy with creature gore, strutted into the sunrise and the closing credits.

Sticky and victorious, Teagan and I linked elbows and rushed down to the parking lot. The last Trollvekian goo-boogers sizzled outta skulls, and without their snotty influence, the final goonicorns slumped like string-cut puppets.

All around us, moviegoers started waking up, wigging out and gagging at the steamy Trollvekian aftermath.

Wyn galloped over, magnificent as ever.

"Noble weirdo, brave enchantress." He bowed before me. "That was most triumphant."

And wowza, dude. You should've seen my sister's face.

I introduced them, feeling like the winningest weirdo in Galaxy 13.

"I must report back to the Federation," Wyn told me. "After all is settled, might the enchantress still be interested in that intergalactic movie marathon?"

"Always," I said. "Cool if my sister tags along?"

We made our plans—and no, you're not getting those details, Sergeant Black-Ops, so wipe that evil gleam from your eyes.

We bowed our heads as the lovely, mystical forms of Wyn's friends and fallen ambassadors glittered and evanesced and beamed into the sky. Godspeed.

"I wish I could've known them," I told Wyn.

"They would have adored you, noble weirdo."

So, yeah, dude, I guess that's about everything. Your helicopters were just cresting the sky—late to the show, I might add.

"Go!" I told Wyn. "You can't be here when they arrive. They'll dissect you."

"You're pulling my hoof."

"I'm not. Haven't you watched our sci-fi?"

"Fair enough, noble weirdo." With that, he streaked skyward in a spectacular rainbow flash. As he faded into the night, Teagan and I stood shoulder to shoulder in awe. She nudged me. "Looks like the beginning of a beautiful friendship..."

So, yep, that's my story. I'm sure you'll wanna concoct your own about swamp gas or whatever to explain to our parents why we broke curfew. Also, you'd be smart to stockpile some 3D glasses in case the Trollvekians try for a sequel.

And if you ever need an enchantress, you've got my number.

Now, dude, if you'd kindly take me to whichever creeptastic underground interrogation cell you've got my sister in, we're gonna blow this top-secret Popsicle stand. It's messy work saving the world, and I'm ready to kick back with some Pixy Stix and my new crew, and bask in the projector-glow of victory.

Heck, who knows, I might even catch a sneak peek of a whole lotta weird.

After all, once *Monsterbeast* ends, there's a galaxy full of movies on my horizon.

APPREHENSION ENGINE

THIRTEEN NIGHTS AFTER Chuck Legion macheted off his own ears, then dive-bombed from his attic window, I lurk outside the gates of his not-so-secret hideaway, trying to grow a pair. Police tape drapes the bars like a demented smile, and in the silent distance, the house's silhouette practically dares me. Dude's dead, what's the harm? Climb a fence, break a window, take a sneak-peek around. Maybe discover some lost Hollywood relics. I give the bars a futile shake and watch the dead-end road, pretty sure the chick from the bar is standing me up.

This is batshit anyway. Bunch of big-talk to impress some random bartender because my fake ID actually fooled her and I was feeling unstoppable. I should bail. I'm no criminal, not some hardcore creeping fanboy. A horror-score legend rolled into my pathetic nowhere town, holed up a few miles from my college dorm, and not once in two years did I go kicking through his privacy bushes, begging for an autograph.

"Fuck am I doing?"

Who cares if the bleached-blonde bombshell behind the bar whispered her name in my ear and ate up my music trivia—like everything I know about Legion and his monster scores. Like how when news of the composer's death hit the airways, die-hard fans could practically hear the swelling violins and earth-shattering base drop. Hell, she even shot me a coy little grin when I dared her to meet me here after her shift. Now it's past three o'clock, my moment of boneheaded truth, and I can't stop pacing a crooked whiskey line. No way Nikki's gonna show, not a chick with eyes like that.

Probably a good thing.

Best to peddle my underage ass back to the dorm, crank up Headbangers Ball on MTV, maybe pop one of Legion's creature features into the VCR. I drag my ten-speed out onto the sidewalk just as headlights flash around the distant corner.

No time to kick my bike back into the shadows, a cherry Pontiac Firebird rumbles up beside me. The driver's window glides down and the primal pulse-beat of Billy Idol spills out.

"We doing this, monster boy?" Nikki purrs.

I'd let out a rebel yell, but I can hardly breathe. She sizes me up with those aquamarine eyes, chewing red-alarm lips like some lace-and-leather glam-rock vixen. No way am I telling her no. I unchoke myself, try not to squeak like the sophomoric rodent I am.

"Oh, we're doing this." I nod toward the thicket of dead-end shadows. "Park down there. I found a spot for us to climb over."

"No need." Engine revving, she rolls past me to the gate's keypad and stabs a random zigzag of numbers. No way that's gonna—

The gate swings open.

A shiver of *what-the-fuck* ices through me.

Nikki winks. "Hop in, monster boy. Fast times ahead."

Before I can overthink it, I ditch my bike and slam into her shotgun seat, grabbing the oh-shit handle as she squeals tires up Legion's winding gravel driveway.

"You have Legion's gate code?"

That coy grin again. "Crazy thing being a bartender, never know who's gonna pop in."

"You actually met him?"

"I've met lots of people." Nikki slams the Firebird to a fish-tailing stop, aiming the headlights toward the front door. The house dwarfs us, three-stories high, taller than it is wide, with attic spires and murky windows. "Didn't I mention that?"

"Pretty sure I'd remember."

She kills the engine, kills the headlights. "Few weeks ago, guy staggers in, looking like something Ozzy hocked up. Buggy-eyed, twitchy, beard all ragged, one gold tooth, and he's wearing these massive headphones. Doesn't take them off for nothing, talks overloud like his music's blasting. Thing is, he's plugged into thin air, cord just dangling, and he's spewing on about some new movie with this obsessed shine in his eye. Nutjob, right? But guy pays in large bills and says he lives in the big tall house on the edge of town. Fast-forward through a bottle of mezcal, and I offer to taxi him home. We get here, he spits out the gate code, and voila!"

Nikki blows me a kiss then slips outside, smooth as a lynx.

"Wait." I scramble out after her. "Legion was working on a new movie?"

"Try to keep up, monster boy." She pops the Firebird's trunk and grabs a crowbar and a flashlight. "Had no clue guy was such a big deal, not until weeks later when I flip to *MTV News* and see that gold tooth. Disgraced Hollywood whatchamacallit, stone-cold dead at sixty-three."

"He did it all," I remind her. "Writer, director, but he's most famous for his horror scores. We're talking the wraith song in *Night Shivers*, and in *Skelentacle* how he—"

"But it's not like guy was a rock star, right?" Nikki cuts in.

"If you've got the right ears he was. His music put this primal tension into his movies, like it gave his monsters life. He only ever used one instrument, called it his apprehension engine. It created these insane otherworldly soundscapes, and leitmotifs that needle your spine."

"Leitmotif?"

"The signature sounds of his monsters. You hear that metallic *thrum-thrum-thrumming* and you know Skelentacle is sneaking up behind you."

Nikki snorts. "Whatever you say, monster boy. At least guy died a rock star's death."

She ignites the flashlight and traces the house's eaves and the attic window with its shattered glass eye and fluttering police tape.

"Now where…?" She aims the flashlight at the driveway, turning a slow circle, boots crunching broken glass and muddy gravel. "You'd think a fall like that would—"

"Fuck me, we're standing in it!" I trip sideways. One, two, three staggering steps before I reach clean gravel. "Man, I think that's Legion's blood."

The stain splatters outward like the world's grisliest Rorschach test. Look, kids, a tentacled Skelentacle!

"Wow," Nikki says. "Never been inside the head of a genius before."

Feels wrong to laugh, but I do. "Rumor is they never found his ears."

"Ooo, treasure hunt!" She hip-checks me and capers over to Legion's unwelcome mat. More police tape zigzags the door. I should man-up, jiggle the handle or something. But Nikki shoves the flashlight into my sweaty hand and jams her crowbar into the doorframe.

"Ever heard of a doorbell?" I tease, when what I really mean is: *you done this before?*

She slam-dances the crowbar back and forth, splitting the wood with a *crack*. The door moans inward, trailing ribbons of police tape. She grins. "You were saying?"

"Anybody home?"

"Doubt guy drove himself back from the morgue." No hesitation, Nikki steps into the black-hole entryway. And this, folks, is that movie moment when a single discordant piano key rings out and something hideous springs from the rafters.

"Shit, Nikki, slow down." I chase her into the void.

"SEE A LIGHT anywhere?" Nikki's voice sounds oddly hollow, far away.

I trip across plush carpet, and my flashlight brightens an inky staircase and a bizarro wall covered with massive black spikes. What the—

Nikki screams, her cries flat and disorienting.

"Nikki!" My flashlight streaks the shadow-studded entryway. I find her right beside me, facing off with a tentacled humanoid skeleton, ready to bash it with her crowbar.

She laughs. "Not a lamp. Hell of a welcome though."

"No way, is that…?" I stagger closer, going all sorts of starry-eyed. Flesh and gunmetal exoskeleton, bony chrome-colored tentacles spiraling from the toothy maw of its headless throat. Skelentacle! That ravenous menace from another dimension. I can practically hear those iconic metallic chords *thrum-thrum-thrumming*.

Nikki thumps a chrome tentacle, rings it like a dull dinner bell. "Boo, just a dummy."

"Not just a dummy." I shine my light along the electronic puppeteer wires jutting from its spine, the chipped chrome paint, the fake bloodstains, the LED lights nesting inside its throat. "I think this is the actual animatronic from Legion's first film. Holy shit, I should've brought my Polaroid."

"Or a U-Haul. Bet this thing's worth a fortune."

"Yeah, right," I say, and my voice sounds funny, we both do.

Nikki fumbles more shadows for a switch, and a chandelier dazzles on overhead. The strange internal texture of the house sharpens into focus.

"Holy batshit," Nikki gasps, and she's not wrong.

It's like we've stepped inside some cavernous alien dimension. Long spikes of high-density acoustic foam jut from the walls and ceiling like craggy sound-swallowing stalactites. My ears echo inward, *thrum-thrum-thrumming*, numbed by the lack of ambient noise. Holy batshit, indeed.

Chuck Legion's house is soundproof.

"The hell? Why would he do this?"

Nikki's eyes glitter. "So no one can hear us *screeeeeam*."

"Are we planning on screaming?" I chuckle, and there's an uncanny sort of vertigo in the way my words resonate only inside my skull. Dizzy echo chambers of meat and teeth and bone amplifying how lame I sound.

"Depends on you, monster boy." Nikki strokes Skelentacle's bony chest plate, wets her lips with a smile. Before I can scrape my quivering brain for a comeback, she pivots, appraises the staircase and an adjacent hallway. "You're the expert. Where do we start? Missing ears, priceless nerd treasures? Maybe find out if Legion had a secret love nest…"

My pulse thumps, hard. "Uh? His private studio? His apprehension engine is supposed to be the holy of holies. He never let anyone watch him record, not even Hollywood bigwigs."

"Holy of holies?" Nikki arches a vixen eyebrow. "Guy really revs *your* engine, huh?"

"Maybe music does." I try not to blush. "I mean, imagine Jason Vorhees without his mother whispering *kill-kill-kill* on the Echoplex. Or the shower scene in *Psycho* minus those screeching violins. Or in *Jaws* when—"

"Okay, okay, I get it. Guy was a rock star among rock stars. C'mon, monster boy, let's find his secret goodies."

We follow a downstairs hallway wallpapered with egg-crate foam, and the *thrum-thrum-thrumming* of my organs spins a disorienting ambiance. The sound is so acute, I actually glance behind us to make sure Skelentacle isn't following. I hear my own bones creaking as the hall opens to a parlor and a kitchen, adjacent rooms infested with spiky hives of soundproofing.

"God, it's like earworms are chewing up all the noise." Nikki enters the parlor, raising her voice to no avail. "No wonder guy lost his shit!"

"His movies took him to trippy places," I say, unnerved by how unnerved I feel. They say don't meet your heroes. Same goes for breaking into their homes. The hell was Legion trying so hard not to hear? After years immersed in psychedelic soundscapes, had the master craved silence? The thrumming inside his own skull?

Amid the parlor's foam stalactites, we find ashtrays full of burnt sage and bloody earplugs, empty liquor bottles and handheld crucifixes. Random furniture sits at skewed angles, draped in slippery satin dust covers like the bed-sheet ghosts of the rich and famous. Nikki yanks the covers away with a flourish, unveiling art deco furniture, an overturned oval couch, a console TV with a shattered screen and speakers ripped out like innards. A static-buzz of electric feedback vibrates through me, sinews creaking and grinding like *Skelentacle*'s opening score.

"Hey, Earth to monster boy." Red fingernails snap me back to reality.

I blink, realize Nikki's looking at me funny. "Shit, sorry. Got soundscapes stuck in my head tonight."

"Yeah? You remind me of him, you know, of guy." She wanders away toward the foam-studded kitchen, leaving me to chew on that. "God, this place is a freak show. What kind of creep lives like this?"

Wait, what?

"Not a creep." I shadow after her, ringing a finger in my ear. "I mean, yeah, there were tabloid rumors. Uptight pricks claiming Legion's music drove his fans to the dark side, but that doesn't mean—"

"The dark side?" Nikki stops dead, looks genuinely interested. "How?"

"Satanic-panic horseshit. Some college eagle scouts or whatever threw this Legion movie marathon then cut off their ears afterward. One even jumped off a bridge, so suddenly Legion's the target of this heinous wrongful death lawsuit. Bunch of poser fans slithered forward to testify. Claimed cranking the volume on his movies made their ears bleed or some dumb shit."

"Whoa, rewind. They cut off their ears? And one jumped to his death—same as guy?"

I pause. "More like Legion died like the fan. But yeah, the tabloids claimed the dude was hallucinating."

"Ooo, what'd he see?"

"Nobody knows. But those zealots at FAIM—you know, the Families Against Illicit Media?—they twisted it into this major moral panic, ruined Legion's career. All because some lightweights couldn't handle spooky music. It's horror, it's supposed to be unnerving. And guess what, I crank Legion's movies every night and have yet to chop myself to bits."

"Yeah, but maybe it tracks." Nikki bounces a hand along a kitchen counter buried in more soundproofing. "Guy I met didn't look like music was doing him any favors. And his *new* movie had him straight-up obsessed."

I try to act cool, try not to reek of some loser with horror scores *thrum-thrum-thrumming* my brain. "Did he tell you about it? His new movie?"

"Guy was rambling at warp speed. How should I remember?"

"You remembered his gate code."

"That I did." Nikki shoots me a sly smile and walks her fingers up my arm. "Okay, say I do recall what guy told me about his movie. What's it worth to you?"

"What do you want from me?" I try to sound suave instead of genuinely dumbfounded.

"Oh, I don't know…" She shoulders past, strolls back down the hallway. "How about you tell me who you *really* are, Mr. Jason Meyers of 666 Elm Street?"

I blank, struck genuinely stupid, then it hits me. Shit. The name my roommate slapped on my fake ID. I scramble after her, face heating up. "Nikki, listen, I—"

"Had you pegged the instant you tiptoed into the bar. Most people don't show up with their IDs in their hands." She circles past the Skelentacle animatronic in the foyer, and I half-expect it to open its tentacled maw, a macabre string-section roar screeching from its throat.

Nikki traipses up the staircase, twitching Jazzercise hips.

"Listen, it was my roommate's idea," I trip after her, head *thrum-thrum-thrumming*. "You know, to crack me out of my shell. I'm not one of those creeps who—"

She turns on me, three steps from the top, and presses a finger over my mouth. "Maybe shut up and tell me your real name before I shove you down these stairs?"

"Travis. Sorry."

"Well, Travis *Sorry*, let me guess…" She draws her finger down my chest. "Music major and a freshman?"

I grip the banister. "Sophomore. But yeah, music composition, minor in film theory. Actually, I was hoping my career might follow in Legion's footsteps, minus the whole freak-house, leaping-to-my-death thing. My parents think I'm insane."

"To be fair, your hero *was* certifiable. But maybe there's a spark in you, I can't tell yet." She tilts her head. "What instrument do you play?"

"Bit of everything, percussion, synth, guitar. I've always been able to pick things up and just play. Like classical to heavy metal. My professors say I have a natural ear, the intuitions of a savant."

"Bet they say that to all the girls." Nikki continues up the stairs. "So, a sophomore. That makes you what? Nineteen?"

"Just turned twenty." I clamber after her. "Didn't mean to lie, it's just the way you smiled at me back at the bar. I mean God, Nikki, you're unreal."

"No, I'm real." She pivots down the second-floor hallway and turns the first doorknob she finds amid the jagged foam landscape. "And if you're half the metalhead you claim to be, you would've recognized me by now."

She disappears inside the room beyond.

"Wait, what's that mean?" A lamp brightens a master bedroom clotted with evermore soundproofing. A headful of whispers flurry through me, and a willowy mannequin greets us from the foot of Legion's round, satin bed. Flowing otherworldly limbs, long steel-wool hair. And damn if that lovely mouthless face doesn't gel with the house's silent chaos.

"Hello," Nikki purrs. "Who's this maneater?"

"The Whisperwraith from *Night Shivers*," I hear myself say, dreamy cosmic bell-tones tinkling between my ears. Inhuman, primeval, devolving into more carnal whispers. I trace a hand along the Whisperwraith's gauzy curves. That's the mark of a master—how even submerged in silence, these echoes of Legion's monsters stir inside me. Polyrhythmic reverbs ingrained in my neural fibers.

Hissing-and-ringing, thrum-thrum-thrumming, looping my veins.

"Kinky," Nikki says. "Does this one like to watch?"

I chuckle, pretty sure she's fucking with me. "Hey, Nikki, why should I recognize you?"

Ignoring me, she rises up on tiptoes and makes a show of kissing the smooth void of the Whisperwraith's mouth, smearing it with red lipstick. Then she thrusts her arms outward like a crucifixion, tosses her head in blissful bleached-blonde agony. My mind flashes, déjà vu visions of this girl dancing inside a spray-painted alleyway.

"Holy shit," I say. "You're the chick from that Twisted Sister video! The one that got banned. 'Sin After Sin,' right?"

Nikki drops her pose. "I'm impressed."

"I caught the world premiere on *Headbanger's Ball*. That was you shackled to a chain link fence. Dee Snyder sacrificed you to the gods of rock-n-roll." I drag an unbelieving hand through my hair. "That video was savage, only ran for like a week."

"Thirteen days," she says. "FAIM got it banned, bunch of pearl-clutching assholes. Their complaints to the FCC called it pornographic and gruesome. It was supposed be my big break."

"You're a model?"

"An actress."

"The hell are you doing bartending in a shithole town like this? No offense."

Nikki glares like she's gonna chew me down to my lying rodent size. Instead, she slumps onto Legion's bed. "Not every dream pans out. Especially not in Hollywood. Your parents are right, showbiz is insane. Sometimes you learn that, then you do what you gotta to survive."

I dare to sit beside her. "For what it's worth, the way you thrashed when that guitar solo electrocuted you was metal as fuck."

"Metal as fuck?" She bites those red-alarm lips, prowling me up and down with that aquamarine gaze. "Tell me how you really feel."

"Ready to make some music…?"

"Is that a question?" She laughs. Any second now, she'll wise up and walk away.

Instead, she attacks me.

Feral, luscious, everything about her kiss tastes likes cherries and fast times and sets my blood spiraling. She clamps my wrists and rakes my hands along her hips, over the swell of her breasts. My entire soul stiffens. And holy fuck, holy fucking fuck, am I about to get lucky on Chuck Legion's bed?

I must be hallucinating.

With the Whisperwraith watching and whispering, Nikki— the chick from the Twisted Sister video!—straddles me and drags her silk and fire tongue along my jawline, sucking my earlobe, breathing waves into me, filling my echo chambers with insatiable gasps and moans. A wet slippery tickle, her tongue enters my ear, and it's all I can do not to pop.

Do not, do not, do not—

At once, she jerks away, sitting up with an arch of her back, hand sliding from my belt buckle. She stabs a finger over my mouth. "*Shhh…* You hear that?"

All I hear is the blood pumping through me.

Except, wait, is that…? Radio static crackles the dead-dull air, or hidden speakers snap on—it's hard to tell. Somewhere distant or very close by, the drone of new music spins to life. Nikki and I lock eyes.

We're not alone.

"SHIT, IS SOMEONE here?" A caretaker, maybe the cops, maybe something else…

I sit up, fumbling my pants. The sound is nowhere and everywhere all at once, tortured and phantasmic, like music box gears meat-grinding a chorus of human windpipes. I glance at the Whisperwraith, but the dirge swells beyond the bedroom door, or maybe inside my skull.

"You do hear it!" Wild light glints in Nikki's eyes.

She glides off the bed and clasps my arm, steers me toward the hallway. I swear the music transcends the air. Traveling to us on radio waves or the fillings in my teeth. Inhuman vocals vibrate my ear canals, bell tones stretching and elongating, cooling into an industrial *thrum-thrum-thrumming*, shivering my meat and my bones.

I resist the urge to glance behind us.

"Nikki, maybe we should bail."

"What, and peddle back to your dorm?" She cuts me down with smoldering eyes, lipstick smeared from our kisses. "The night's just getting good."

Fuck, I'm a sucker. Who cares about cops or caretakers or eerie vibes. I can still hear this girl gasping in my ear. This is the encounter MTV and movie scores were made for.

I follow Nikki and the music down the hallway. That surreal cinematic siren call twists my inner volume dial, reverberating, haunting, alive. Nikki pulls me toward a pair of side-by-side doors, clings to me, nibbles my ear.

"Pick door number one."

I twist the doorknob—and the music scratches to silence. Hollow resonating nothingness. If this was a movie, Legion's corpse would spring from the door, top of his earless skull smashed in, gold tooth and driveway gravel jutting from his forehead.

"What are you waiting for?" Nikki hisses.

"The music stopped," I whisper.

"No, it didn't. It never stops." She shoves past me, pushes through door number one. Sallow flickering light spills out.

"Nikki, wait—"

"This is why we came here." She tugs me inside, and the protest dies in my throat.

"Holy shit."

Triple rows of leathers seats, reels spinning on a projector, a wall-sized silver screen.

"Chuck Legion's home theater." Nikki takes a seat in the back row, tries to tug me down beside her.

I stay standing. I should yank my hand free, but I never know what I've got with this girl. Especially with her red-alarm smile and aquamarine eyes playing larger-than-life on the silent movie screen. "What the fuck, Nikki?"

"Surprise." She tugs again, and I sit. "Remember that movie guy was working on?"

"You're in it?" I say, though the answer is obvious. What I'm seeing is clearly a rough cut. But on-screen, a blood-soaked Nikki throws open the door of this very house and runs out onto the driveway in primal terror, glancing back at some unseen threat.

"I was gonna be the star. More than just MTV eye-candy, a scream queen." She watches herself collapse onto half-naked knees. "It was just another cursed production. Tiny crew, smaller cast. We film, we wrap—then midway through post-production, Chuck announces he won't finish the film. The composite shots of the new creature aren't coming together, neither is the score."

"New creature?" I say.

"He called it the Earworm. It was supposed to unite his cinematic universes—Skelentacle, the Whisperwraith, both made cameos. But his Earworm was incomplete. Chuck needed the music to envision it, except the music was gnawing a hole inside his head. Said he was torturing himself with doubt, like maybe all those satanic-panic FAIM bitches were right about his movies. Didn't care this was the second time fake moral outrage crushed my big break."

On-screen, the blurry silhouette of the Earworm manifests behind Nikki's character like crackling neon mist. A smudge of humanoid static, then empty reels where the monster should be standing. And silence.

"See, it's not complete. Not without the music. You're right, Travis. It breathes life into Chuck's creatures. That was his secret. His final masterpiece is so close to completion, it just needs those special magic touches. It needs *you*."

"I can't finish Legion's monster."

"But you can play his music. You hear it."

I balk, laugh. Feel a tickle in my guts, unease flirting with something electric and dangerous. "I can't do that. I'm just some wannabe with an unrealistic dream."

"You don't have to be." Nikki leans close. "You have a natural ear. You know every heartbeat of Chuck's movies. Have you heard yourself? All you do is wax poetic about music and monsters. It's who you are."

"Nobody's ever been able to duplicate Legion's soundscapes."

"That's because they never saw what instrument he was playing. You said it yourself."

"Right, but it takes more than—"

"But nothing." She stands and hoists me up by my belt buckle. "What if I can show you? I know where it is. His apprehension engine."

My heart skips. "You're kidding?"

"Door number two, monster boy."

On-screen, Nikki's character rises like a minx and presents her half-naked form to the off-screen entity Legion called Earworm. I squint, wondering how he envisioned it, how would he fill in those staticky gaps? What would be its creeping leitmotif?

Nikki kisses me, tongue and talent stirring discordant magic inside me.

"Door number two?" I say, coming up for air.

"The holy of holies," Nikki purrs, "just waiting for you to make some music."

DOOR NUMBER TWO opens to an attic staircase and a naked light bulb. Splintery walls, lofty steps, vibes of something unseen waiting above.

"No acoustic foam," I whisper.

"Yeah, I tore that batshit down. It was even worse up here." Nikki squeezes my sweaty hand. "Ready?"

I don't hesitate, though I know I should. What else hasn't this girl told me? Hand in hand, we climb into Chuck Legion's high-beamed attic, floorboards creaking underfoot, police tape fluttering in the broken window. I always imagined Legion's studio would be packed with high-end microphones, mixing consoles, patch-bays, never mind a mess of exotic instruments.

A lone instrument waits for us in the center.

"There it is," Nikki coos. "Legion's apprehension engine."

The gorgeous black-lacquered monstrosity commands the attic. The size of a pipe organ, it's a Frankenstein's mutant of jutting antennas and ivory knobs, gut strings and steel cranks, malformed piano keys and curious moving parts.

I drift closer, and is the room spinning? Composers everywhere would forfeit their souls to stand where I am.

"Can you play it?" Nikki asks.

Fuck no. My nuts shrink at the very idea.

But I nod. "Got an ear for these things, remember?"

"Make me some music, Travis." She releases me with a shove. This is insane, sacrilege. Where do I even start? My hands tremble across barbed-wire violin strings and a crooked-toothed xylophone.

Nikki clears her throat. "Chuck always started on the other side."

"You saw him play?"

"A few times, during production and post. He was always slipping away like a junkie needing a fix. Maybe I spied a little."

Nerves buzzing, I circle the apprehension engine, stopping before what looks like a dented hurdy-gurdy and a rusty radio antenna. "What was he really like?"

Nikki glances at the busted window. "Intense."

No shit, he was intense. The man sliced off his own ears. Rusty stains drizzle a gruesome circle around the apprehension engine, then break off toward the window. That's a lot of my hero's blood to see in one night. I know his movies from glory to guts, every sinister twist. How stupid do I have to be to experiment with the instrument he was clearly playing right before he died?

Nikki blows me a kiss.

I stroke a slow hand across the apprehension engine's chaotic surface, strum a serrated radio antenna. Needling sparks of electricity prickle through my fingertips as I release it.

It rattles up and down. Discordant, unparalleled, the inverse of bones shaking, that timeless creeping release, that surreal *thrum-thrum-thrumming…*

"Holy shit, that's the leitmotif from *Skelenta*—"

Dumb awe chokes me off.

Behind Nikki, the air shimmers like heat rippling off pavement, and a hazy shape appears. Swirling chrome tentacles, a sharp-toothed glint of throat and maw.

Skelentacle eddies before us like a mirage, eerily 3D and blocking the staircase. Bioluminescent bones and sinews, organic meat and chrome. Adrenaline spikes through me, because holy shit! Glowing teeth gnash inside its throat, and it lunges!

I yank Nikki toward me. Tentacles pass through us with a ghostly electric shock, and Nikki's thrill-ride laughter shakes to the rafters.

Skelentacle ripples and vanishes. Here then gone as the wobbling antenna slows and the *thrum-thrum-thrumming* fades to an echo inside my skull.

"Did you see that?" I cry. The empty air reeks of ozone and fog machine, hums like the energy after a rock concert. "He's got some kind of projector hooked up to this thing. God damn, that looked real."

"Oh, it was real!" Nikki slides up against me, gives a little bounce. "I knew you could do it. Go on, monster boy, play something else."

I glide my hand over a coiled metal theremin, moaning vibrations rising in electric pitch beneath my fingers. The Whisperwraith's keening, hissing siren song ripples the air, that phantasmic bell-tone dirge calling lovers into the void—

"Look," Nikki whispers. Melting silver shadows split the far wall, and two willowy inhuman arms appear, bending at uncanny double-jointed angles, reaching for us...

"Keep playing."

I stroke the coil, and the magnetic pulse of something new thrills my fingertips, a clammy hand twining around mine, taking hold.

I jerk away, stagger backward.

The Whisperwraith's pale grasping arms tremble then vanish, poof, nothing more than murmurs eddying between my ears.

Nikki punches my arm. "Why'd you stop?"

"This is too trippy. I thought I felt—"

"Because you did! You felt the magic. The *music*. This is why you exist, Travis. I wasn't sure at first, but it's you. The music sings in you, like it sang through Chuck. When he died, the entity he'd been summoning spoke to me, said I'd find you and bring you here."

"You were here when Legion died?"

"Chuck was weak, he refused to fulfill his commitments. He got scared, so it took back what was given. But it told me you'd be drawn to me, to *it*."

I shake my head, brain spasming to keep up. "What said that? What the fuck, Nikki?"

"Chuck's Earworm. It's *still* saying it…"

"Do you know what you sound like?"

"Like the truth." Nikki grips my chin, and I can't tell if she wants to rip my skull off or stick her tongue down my throat again. "*Listen*. You're tapping into that wild interdimensional melody that makes all great musicians great. You still hear it. Even after the music stops, you hear it. I know you do…"

She laces her hands atop mine and caresses my open palms along the apprehension engine. My bones tremble, but I crank the mutant hurdy-gurdy, a slow-motion wail like an air raid siren. Something inside my sternum tingles and vibrates and—

Halfway through the spin, the wheel jams, the music lurches to ear-ringing stillness.

"What now?" Nikki says.

"Something's lodged inside." I give the crank a hard jerk, and the hurdy-gurdy wheels around with a tortured human whimper, spitting out twin relics of crescent-moon mystery meat. Are those…?

I recoil. "Oh fuck, Legion's ears!"

"I told you!" Nikki traces a fingertip along one beef-jerkied earlobe. "The Earworm took back what was given…"

I step away from the girl and the instrument, feel the predawn breeze from the broken window on my sweaty spine.

"The fuck, Nikki? This is too messed up"

"No, this is destiny." She flicks the ears aside and laces herself up against me, purring in my ear—and until the day I die, I'll hear this girl breathing inside me. "We're so close, Travis, let yourself feel it. The music's vast inside you. I need to feel it in me, too. Don't you want to feel your own power? Keep playing, finish Chuck's vision, make us legends beyond the stars…"

I side-eye Legion's ears, waiting for them to sprout legs and skitter away.

That would be insane, but something insane *is* happening, something infinitely more intoxicating than any booze I scammed at the bar. And like every other primal instinct, Nikki awakens a shivering truth. Deep-veined, carved into the fine-boned echo chambers of my skull. I can't run from this. The god of Legion's music rumbles, calls. I've heard it all my life, in the primal hours of the night, hidden between the rhythms of MTV and the gritty pulse beat of movie scores, waiting to be unleashed, waiting for the perfect instrument to speak to me in its hidden language.

Something beyond the apprehension engine wants to feel it breathe.

Nikki's rough-cut movie replays inside my head. Her damsel ritual of chase and capture, the static-blur of the half-summoned Earworm. The leitmotif to breathe it to life exhales through me.

So simple, so hideous, so beautifully disturbing.

The apprehension engine contains the song inside its twisted tubular bones, and so do I. Don't know if Legion built it himself or discovered it in some accursed Hollywood tomb. I only know it belongs to me now. The music grows restless. Everything Nikki and I can become with this instrument at my fingertips—fame, fortune, fucking—I'm here to take it.

Right?

I crack my knuckles, flex my fingers, and try not to shudder when an instinct beyond the stars possesses my hands.

IN THE HIGH-BEAMED acoustics of the attic, I unleash myself on the apprehension engine. Caressing knobs, stroking keys, tapping into hidden echo chambers. The smoky inverse of music swells, industrial twists and tubular howls, hidden noise spectrums emerging from the marrow, the aching bone groan of the primordial abyss.

Legion was holding back all these years. This instrument is capable of vastly more than the music he produced. My hands pulse in intoxicated rhythms I scarcely understand, but I give myself over to it, let raw inhuman noises sing out from beneath my hands. Abrasive polyrhythmic heartbeats and gut-twisting bass drops, a low-frequency chaos and the screeching metallic crescendo of worlds tearing open.

The house shudders sideways, floorboards tremble, shards loosen from the window. All around us, the air shimmers, vibrating with broad-spectrum intensity, rising soundscapes folding reality inside out like the pleats of a kaleidoscope.

With a neon flash, the air melts and splits and dual silhouettes darken the ether.

Skelentacle and the Whisperwraith.

They tower forward, live and in person, backlit by starlight and ambient void-song. No puppeteer wires, no LED lights, these are the heavy-metal realities of the cheap replicas Legion slapped on-screen. Skelentacle stands ten feet tall, bioluminescence pulsing inside a tangled-bone ribcage, liquid chrome tentacles coiling and uncoiling with rhythmic grace. Beside it, the willowy, mouthless Whisperwraith shimmers inside a mist of ethereal hair and a ballgown of translucent flesh and lacework arteries, a thousand gnarled heart-organs twitching within.

The apprehension engine mimics the soundscapes of their worlds as my fingertips strum a haunted dance, ragged and bleeding, palms throbbing.

Nikki stands behind me, gripping my shoulders like a shield.

"It's ride or die now," she coos. "If you stop playing, they'll slaughter us both."

As if in agreement, Skelentacle unhinges its tentacled maw and roars, screeching and grinding like it swallowed an entire string section. The Whisperwraith's mouthless alien cranium shivers and rattles, a thousand inner-skull fragments resonating with a keening high-frequency wail that etches new fissures into my bones.

Movie logic dictates that I should be crapping myself, or dead. But the sounds filter through me, vibrating my fingers, sternum, skull, expanding from abstract fury into something that almost resembles tangible words.

I think they're announcing the main act.

Nikki's eyes shine in anticipation. "Strap in."

The apprehension engine shudders, and between neon zigzags of electricity, a staticky shape slashes from the void. Still half-formed, floorboards shaking beneath its ethereal weight, a humanoid shadow of black holes and crackling feedback. Legion's titular Earworm?

"Keep playing!" Nikki cries, stepping out from behind me.

The music ripples my marrow, dissonant trills and atonal fugues, soundscapes upon soundscapes overlapping. Nikki drifts toward the trifecta of monsters and extends her hands. The Earworm bends to greet her, somehow vast despite its human size, just like that uncut scene from Legion's movie.

At the razor peak of a tortured trilling wail, their hands connect with a lightning bolt of static shock. The Earworm explodes into full-focus reality. I can't look away, can't unsee this. A nude humanoid creature embraces Nikki with muscular limbs and fish-belly flesh. No eyes, no nose, no ears, just thousands of cavernous mouths covering it from bulbous head to gnarled feet. Boundless as the stars, every mouth hideous and strange. Lips with scales or scabs or slime, teeth of metal and flames, barbed tongues, forked tongues, tongues with obscene alien cravings.

And every gaping throat echoes with the phantasmic songs of other realms.

Transcendent pain stabs my eardrums, a trickle of warm blood.

Nikki loops her arms around the Earworm's shoulders. "Keep playing!"

And I do. Couldn't stop now even if I wanted. Don't know where I stop and the music begins—or where the music stops and the monsters begin.

The Earworm's vast mouths speak to Nikki in siren-tongue. Promises shimmer on the air, all Nikki's starry aspirations coming true, fame and fortune and ethereal light blowing through her hair. She rises up on her tiptoes and flicks her tongue across that red-alarm smile. Countless alien mouths pucker open, slavering for a kiss, eager to taste the sounds this girl makes.

She chooses a human mouth embedded on the side of the Earworm's cranium, and I recognize the tabloid smirk, that gold tooth.

Chuck Legion.

The legend's mouth wails from inside some meaty inter-dimensional damnation.

Nikki shuts it up with a kiss.

A heavy-metal tongue-lashing unlike anything witnessed by the gods of rock-n-roll. Something passes between those mouths, wiggling from the Earworm into Nikki. A grotesque aching jealousy spikes through me even as I control the freaky cross-rhythms of it all. I strum and drum, and all around, musical monstrous hellscapes rise to a climax.

The Earworm's galaxy of mouths ignites like a disco ball of sonic light, each scream blazing outward, projecting auditory glimpses of the myriad worlds inside.

Nikki moans in horrific ecstasy.

When the Earworm finally breaks the kiss, she clutches its muscular shoulder with one arm, breathing hard through a euphoric half-crazed smile. And there's something fresh and luminous and meteoric about her, like her very presence demands a spotlight and a red carpet.

Like she could command the world.

"It's okay, monster boy. You can stop playing now. We've broken through."

My ragged, obedient fingers strike a final death knell, and I pull back. My hands tremble, sweat and blood *drip-drip-dripping*, every sound magnified, every splash supersonic.

I step away from the apprehension engine, and the music continues. Nikki's right, it never stops. Dynamic, polyrhythmic, acoustic textures I can taste and see and feel. The monsters bask in it, dominate it, standing savage and thunderous. Skelentacle, the Whisperwraith, the Earworm.

And Nikki.

Talk about metal-as-fuck.

My effervescent bleached-blonde goddess clings to the Earworm and curls a sleek finger, beckoning me over. "Come play?"

Jelly for knees, something sharper for a spine, I go to her, electric tension strumming my bones, my nerves, my heart-strings. Have I ever felt more alive? Like a long-sustained high note, like something about to shatter.

Up close, the Earworm dwarfs me, radiates a spectrum of soundscapes so vast my senses tangle. Nikki extends an arm, and she and the Earworm loop me into an embrace. The entity's warped sonic mouths twitch against me, grisly inharmonious hellscapes throbbing beyond every tongue. Licking, nibbling, singing, the Earworm moans with siren promises all my own.

Nikki winks at me, wets her almost-famous smile, and my blood thunders. My own dynamic leitmotif.

"Don't worry, it doesn't want your soul." Nikki nibbles my bottom lip. "It wants to give you everyone else's..."

We devolve into a kiss.

Nikki's tongue tastes of candy and monsters.

The Earworm joins our passion, and the lipstick-smeared nightmare on the side of its bulbous skull unhinges. Chuck Legion's mouth moistens my ear, lips suckling like leeches even as the legend's harried voice escapes inside me.

Bleeding-eared nonsense, fucking satanic panic. "Run, jump, don't listen, there's still time to stop it—"

Legion's mouth spasms to silence, then gargles up something wet, spiraling, drilling closer...

And now I understand why Legion called it his Earworm.

Its tongue pierces my ear canal, wiggling and barbed, a parasite of supersonic meat. Didn't think it could get any louder inside my head until the other realms explode through me.

The full-decibel roar of the stars.

The demonic ambiance of hidden dimensions.

The collective bass drop of billions upon billions of inhuman voices and instruments.

The Earworm's tongue snakes my brain, igniting untold electrons and soundscapes, unfolding my mind through vast alien realities. Groaning ghost-torn worlds and screeching monster nebulas. Wailing wastelands and echoing expanses. Living, pulsing soundstages I fear I'll forget if the music ever stops.

The tongue twitches, resonates, makes me understand.

The Earworm—this rising sonic maestro who uses monster legends like backup dancers, who collects the wild concert screams of other realms—it craves an audience. It loves to be heard and seen. It wants its creeping creature scores to sneak up on Hollywood and our whole unsuspecting world like it's done in countless realms beyond. My fine-tuned soul quivers with the inharmonious possibilities of it all.

This dark musician of the universe, this creature who wears the mouth of my hero like a trophy, this god who took my dream girl as its groupie. It's here to rock out with its cock out.

And it wants me to join the band.

Or whatever the movie monster equivalent of that is.

Its tongue-kiss deepens, and its silver screen vision ignites inside me, scene after nerve-shredding scene reeling through me like a midnight masterpiece. Nikki as my diva, my scream queen, my goddess—and the Earworm as her insidious heavy-metal co-star. Sensational monster sacrifices, hardcore carnal dance rituals—all of it performed against the whimsical polyrhythmic hellscapes of my apprehension engine.

The music swells and my inner movie pans out, and there we stand, Nikki and I, on the red carpet at our first movie premiere.

Flashbulbs, squealing fans, hell-studded MTV glamour.

And inside the theater, the Whisperwraith and Skelentacle rampage across the silver screen, grislier-than-life, flanking the Earworm while it seduces coeds and reaps their chorus of screams. Vast audiences haunt the seats, gaping in mesmerized horror, light and sound reflecting off their awestruck faces, blood oozing from their ears.

And who cares about the sneering pricks with the FAIM T-shirts, who double over in their seats, spilling their popcorn and clutching their heads in brain-thrashing agony? Who cares if they machete off their virgin ears and jump out windows? Who cares if their satanic-panic death-wails constellate in real-time on the Earworm's pock-mouthed flesh?

We play for the true fans.

The metalheads and dread-decibel connoisseurs, the head-bangers holding up devil horns and begging for a sequel. The die-hards who invite us to live in an endless midnight loop inside their skulls. I can practically hear them chanting my name.

The vision pops, my ears finally pop.

The Earworm withdraws its discordant tongue from me, and Nikki slows her red-alarm kiss, tracing a naughty fingertip along my earlobe.

"So, monster boy..." She nibbles my lip, winks at the Earworm and its effervescent backup monsters. "You ready to finish this movie with us?"

I grin at the apprehension engine, bloody fingers twitching, dread-tones pulsing and swelling. And holy fuck, yeah!

"Cue the music."

THE 31ˢᵗ OF OCTOBER IN LOCUST, MAINE

I DON'T REMEMBER my birth-town. But as this road unwinds its final miles through an autumn-spiced forest of crimson oaks and golden locusts, a sense of returning home rises in me like shivery warmth and candy-corn bile.

A signpost waits in the overgrowth ahead.

WELCOME TO LOCUST, MAINE,
POPULATION 1,313

The splintered sign slumps sideways in the weeds, spray painted with layers of unimaginative graffiti: skull-faced jack-o-lanterns and a population reduced to a red-dripping *1*.

I roll the rental car to a stop, several yards before the town limits. Not quite superstition, but something unseen keeps me from daring any farther. A particularly grotesque shadow in the center of the sun-dappled road draws my attention.

"Is that where they found you?" Julie asks from the passenger seat—and I jump so hard I nearly lose my stomach. Almost forgot she's here.

She's been unnaturally silent this whole drive, observing me with her phone. It's more surreal than I imagined. Coming here, spending Halloween with Mistress Julie, influencer and host of *True Tales from After Midnight*. Over the years, I've been approached by countless producers, Hollywood sleaze slobbering to buy my story. My aunt always shooed them away, said I needed to forget this wicked place. But Aunt Bethany died last year, and I'm eighteen now, on my own. Never would've agreed to document the worst day of my life if I didn't need the tuition cash Julie offered.

And, if I'm being honest, her friendship these last couple months.

"I think this is it…" I crack my door and soft-step outside, oddly afraid of dropping off into another dimension. The surrounding trees tremble, restless leaves, and the buzz of late-season katydids swarms inside my head.

Julie follows me onto the road. "First time you've been here since the days following that infamous Halloween. After thirteen years, anything sparking?"

Glimmers, echoes. "I was just a kid, so I don't really remem—"

"Into the camera," Julie reminds me. Just like we rehearsed.

I make uncomfortable eye contact with the phone's black-hole gaze. She promised to keep this tasteful, promised me final approval before she posts. Even so, I already feel Julie's followers dissecting my every tangled word in the comments below. There are people who still don't believe me.

"It's the 31st of October in Locust, Maine…" I start again. "I don't remember that night. My aunt said they found me wandering the road outside town. Five years old, surviving on candy corn, still wearing my Snoopy costume." I can still hear the state patrol skidding to a stop around me, blue-and-reds flashing across my blurred vision.

"How'd they know to look for you?" Julie asks, though she already knows every answer. She's spent months researching, interviewing, preparing for today, our 31st of October.

"For a week after Halloween, my mother didn't answer her sister's phone calls. When my aunt reached out to our neighbors, then the constable, she discovered the same thing. Abandoned phones that just rang and rang. Aunt Bethany was the first out-of-towner to report it. Something had happened to the people here in Locust." Feeling far away, I stare into the camera. "They vanished. Everyone but me."

"And you had no memory of the event?"

"Didn't remember anything—not my parents, my house, not even my own name."

Reagan Morris, Reagan Morris, it pulses through me. Same mantra I used to repeat into the mirror during the months after Aunt Bethany took me in, desperate to feel like the person she told me I was. *Reagan Morris,* over and over, until it blurred and so did I.

"But you did remember one thing," Julie says. "You remembered your big sister."

"Yes. Madison."

"Tell me about her."

I hesitate. My mouth feels sticky, cloyingly sweet. "Can we wait to talk about her?"

Julie swings the camera out of my face. "I know this is tough. But Madison's the reason we're here, right?"

You're the reason we're here, I think, but it's hard calling bullshit on the only person I've ever truly talked to about this. The FBI agents and revolving-door shrinks don't count. Sitting in my dorm room, night after night, Julie and I didn't just rehash the unsolved vanishings in Locust. We talked about my broken life, my sense of never belonging. And when that got too intense, we connected over music and popcorn movies, easygoing laughter. Didn't know how much I needed that until she sought me out.

So, I nod. Sure, we're here for Madison.

"That's my girl. Let's introduce her to the world, yeah?"

The camera returns, and I swallow.

"Madison was thirteen. All bony legs and long stringy hair. Kind of a loner, clever. *Daring.* She wore thick cat-eye glasses and loved reading by candlelight up high in our attic. Halloween was her favorite season, the only time she could be anything she wanted. That last year, she was the sorceress from one of those ratty leather books she always carried around. Antler crown and a long purple cloak. I'll never forget the swish of the velvet. She had it on when she saved my life."

Julie peeks over her phone, offers a thumbs up. "Saved you, how? From what?"

But I've never been able to say.

Glimmers, echoes. The shadow in the center of the road.

Standing here now, a warm hand curls softly around mine and squeezes.

I don't dare breathe, don't dare move, don't dare allow Julie's followers to see inside the private theater of my astonishment. Can this be real?

The phantom fingers tighten. Slick but firm, waxy as candy corn, just like Madison's grip when she tugged me to safety all those years ago.

It's too much. I glance down, I can't help myself.

But like this town, my hand is empty.

"YOU'RE DOING GREAT!" Julie has me pose for B-roll shots in the road, then finally, *too soon*, we follow the final mile into town.

Here the weed-choked pavement crumbles down the centerline. That familiarity from earlier sinks into a pit of unease. A strange vertigo zigzags through me, a tumbling sense of being both lost and found, of racing fast as I can, backwards in time until we round the final bend and find the picturesque ruins of Main Street, USA.

The Texaco peeks from the trees first, antique gas pumps wrapped in brambles and a patina of neglect. We creep past a hardware store with a sunken roof, then the splintered husk of a mom-and-pop diner. Vandals, or the passing seasons, have shattered almost every window. Paint peels off the buildings, hoary wooden beasts shedding time-weathered skin.

"Wow, festive." Julie zooms in on the diner. A tattered cheesecloth ghost still haunts one window, stained yellow by the elements. "My fans are gonna eat this up."

Outside the post office next door, a plastic skeleton in decaying overalls slumps on a bench. I knew the town would be like this. Even so, a sickly-sweet chill invades my veins. Remnants of Halloween linger everywhere. From the purple-and-orange light bulbs strung like cobwebs between the buildings to the crooked marquee of the Rialto Theater announcing Locust's annual costume parade:

FR1GHTS BEG N AT T E STROK3 OF 7!

"Should've brought my vampire teeth," Julie quips.

"Yeah," I agree with a dry throat, "left my Snoopy costume back on the road."

Something flutters in my rearview mirror.

I hit the brakes and twist in my seat, heart rioting, squinting back through the windows of the passing diner. This time of year, they used to serve pumpkin pancakes with whipped cream and candy corn. I remember just now. A three-stack, that was Madison's favorite.

"Did you see that?"

"See what?" Julie whispers, and I feel the close-up zooming in on me.

Late afternoon sunshine ripples my vision. A flutter of purple velvet? Where did it go? "Someone ducked inside the diner."

"You're kidding." Julie peers over her phone. "Reagan, there's nobody there."

I watch the space between, uncertain.

She's right. Nothing moves in or around the restaurant.

It's nerves, gotta be nerves. Phantom hands and make-believe velvet. I loosen my vice-grip on the wheel, and my palms tremble, nervous to be empty, nervous to be tugged again.

"Hey?" Julie touches my shoulder. "You okay?"

"Maybe I shouldn't be driving. It's all a little much. Can we get out and walk?"

"Whatever helps. I know this is intense."

I abandon the driver's seat, and Julie follows. "So, million-dollar question. Anything look familiar?"

"I mean, looks like it did when the FBI brought me back *afterwards*."

"Sure, but anything *new* sparking?"

Glimmers, echoes. Madison's high-spirited laughter leading the parade.

Farther down, there'll be a modest clock tower, then a drugstore, followed by a shotgun blast of homes spread throughout the woods. My family's Victorian-style house waits just beyond those oaks, with its castle eaves and Madison's book-lined attic. I'm certain. Between the FBI tours and the tabloid photos that pop up this time each year, I've mapped everything.

I shake my head. "Can I have a few minutes? Before we dig in?"

"Anything you need. I'll just shoot some intros." Julie fluffs her hair, then flips the phone mercifully on herself. "Okay, my little gravediggers, it's Mistress Julie with *True Tales from After Midnight*, and the moment you've been dying for is now. It's the 31ˢᵗ of October, two hours until sunset, and I'm standing inside the cold, dead heart of Locust, Maine..."

Careful to keep Julie in my side-eye, I wander the leaf-littered sidewalk. Dozens of dark stains grease the pavement where jack-o-lanterns once rotted to fly-infested pulps.

"It's been called a modern-day Roanoke," Julie goes on. "Good people, hardworking people, family people. Where did they go, and what took them there? They abandoned everything: vehicles, homes, cherished possessions, beloved pets. Some even left mid-supper, half-eaten meals later found rotting on plates. Only thing they didn't leave behind were signs of a struggle. No corpses, no bloodstains, nothing out of place. Whatever happened here, happened peacefully…"

Did it? I wonder.

Glimmers, echoes. Madison wailing my name, shrieking for me to *run, run, run, little sister!* Fast as I can…

I approach the Rialto and peer into the grimy, spider-laced ticket booth. An ancient bag of candy corn slouches beside a roll of tickets for a midnight creature feature that never played.

Like nausea, the memories keep coming back up. Or have I always known them? Hard to tell for sure. The sun shines so bright.

Second only to her attic books and Halloween, Madison worshiped scary movies, I remember that. She couldn't get enough—the suspense, the bloody make-believe. Nothing frightened her. "Monsters can't hurt monsters," that was her motto. No matter what came at her—bullies, grown-ups, the deepening darkness—Madison was never afraid.

Not until our final moments together.

Alongside the town's buzzing silence, the ghost-echoes of Madison's shouts ring in my ears. *Run, little sister, run!*

"…And wow, folks have cooked up some wild theories over the years…" Julie's voice carries. "Mass hysteria, mass hypnosis, cults and ritual sacrifices, evil government experiments, and my absolute favorite: alien abduction…"

"Can you just stop?" I rasp, feeling breathless.

I've heard this trash my whole life, and just now it's all piling up. A dump truck of too much. Never should've let Julie talk me into this, no matter how broke and lonely I've been. The urge to dash to the car and get the hell out of town overwhelms every nerve. I inch away from the Rialto, suddenly afraid if I turn my back on Julie—my only friend—and her followers, even for a heartbeat, she'll vanish like all the others. Like a swish of purple velvet, Locust will take her.

Madison's long-ago voice shrieks inside my head. *Run, run, run!* Only…

Only, it's not inside my head anymore.

And that's not my sister who's shrieking.

Somewhere in this departed town, a telephone rings.

"WHERE IS IT?" I cry. My sneakers scrape a dizzy circle, and the town twists around me. From somewhere, faint but determined, a phone bell *rings, rings, rings!* If we don't find it soon, whoever's on the other end might hang up.

"There!" Julie tugs my elbow, aims her camera. "The drugstore!"

We chase the sound past the silent, sun-splintered clock tower, past telephone poles with frayed and fallen lines. As we reach the drugstore, the phone shrills louder, on and on, racing my pulse. The only entrance is a plate-glass door, motion-triggered. Without electricity, it doesn't budge, and the place probably has the only windows in town that aren't broken.

Mind spinning out, I tug on an iron trash barrel, heavy as sin, scraping it across the sidewalk. "Help me! It might be Madison calling!"

Julie stares like I've lost my grip, then hastily props her phone against a lamppost, a hasty but all-seeing angle.

Together, we hoist the trashcan and ram the door. It takes three tries before a cobweb crack appears and the glass shatters. I rush inside, leaving Julie behind as she fetches her phone.

Run, run, run!

The ringing pulls me through a maze of aisles to the pharmacy in the shadowy back. I scramble over the counter and fumble for the wall phone.

"Hello? *Hello?*" I strain to hear past the blood rushing through my brain.

The line crackles.

Someone takes a breath. Not me.

"Oh, thank the Lord," echoes a voice from beyond, faint, ephemeral, *familiar*. "I've been calling for ages. Was afraid nobody would answer."

"Maddie?" I gasp, though my heart's already twisting. "Where are you?"

"I'm looking for my sister," the voice says. "She lives in your town, but I haven't been able to reach her. Please tell me you know her? Eleanor Morris?"

My heart finishes its icy plummet, chills ripple through me. Eleanor Morris was my mother's name.

"Aunt Bethany?" I whisper. Aunt Bethany who died of a heart attack last December.

A warm hand closes on my shoulder, and I jump so hard I drop the phone receiver. It clatters to the linoleum.

"Who is it?" Julie asks as I squint into her phone's flashlight.

I scramble for the fallen receiver. "Hello? *Hello?*"

Dead silence. Not even the ghost of a dial tone. Almost as if…

I shake my head. "It was my aunt, my *dead* aunt. Please tell me you set this up? A little trick for your followers?"

"I wouldn't do that to you, Reagan." Julie sounds hurt. "And I don't invent content—"

A specter of purple flutters behind her.

I shove past, chasing afterimages down the aisle. Someone's here, hiding behind the fossilized cough syrup. The flowing edge of their cloak peeks into the aisle.

Madison? I reach for a fistful of purple velvet.

Metal hangers rattle.

The cloak swings empty.

Part of a sales rack of children's costumes.

Cold relief. I pull the cloak loose and hold it up to the pale sunlight beaming in from the front of the store. The cloak is flimsy moth-eaten velvet. *Scary Halloween Witch*, according to the label. A cheap version of Madison's. Her cloak was heavy and buttery, much lusher that this, much more majestic and commanding.

I put the costume back and freeze. Next on the rack is Snoopy. White cotton onesie, with a red collar and floppy black ears. Same costume they found me wandering in.

Julie brushes up beside me, whispering into her phone, "This place is a total time capsule."

She shines her light at the fully stocked shelves. Styrofoam gravestones, trick-or-treat buckets shaped liked cauldrons. And bags of candy corn. Shelf after shelf of it, nothing but candy corn.

"Yuck." Julie wrinkles her nose. "This town had a serious thing for the devil's earwax."

I swallow thickly. It was Madison's favorite.

With an easy chuckle, Julie fishes the costume rack and holds up a candy-apple-red vampire cape, poses for a live-action selfie.

"Is it me? Whatcha think, my little gravediggers?"

I stare at her. I think I haven't heard my aunt's voice in ten months. I think something's terribly wrong with this town. "We should go."

Run, run, run, little sister…

A sound erupts from the silence outside. Like a thunderclap, but *not*.

Julie startles, swings her phone toward the front of the store. "The hell was that?"

The sound erupts again, low, dented, discordant. Eerily familiar, like candy on the tip of my tongue.

When it sounds a third time, I gasp.

"The clock tower."

The bell clangs again, crooked, inharmonious, but louder, a clock winding up. The sunlight in the drugstore dims. Clouds passing over the sun?

I count a fifth gong, then a sixth. With each toll, the sunlight fades.

"I think someone's covering the windows! C'mon, let's catch them!" Julie grabs me and pulls me toward the front of the store as the seventh bell tolls and the darkness consumes us.

"Seven o'clock," I say.

Her light cuts a path between the cash registers. "My phone says it's only 3:33."

But when we burst out the front door, we stumble into a nightscape.

"Where's the sun?" Julie gasps.

Between the rooftops, stars and the full moon glow against an indigo backdrop.

"Where's the sun? *Oh God, where's the sun?*" Julie aims her phone skyward with a shuddery reflex of hand, recording the impossible starry darkness, gasping panic eclipsing her showmanship. But a strange surreal calmness overcomes me, an inevitability. We should've left when we had the chance.

"Julie, look." I point, but she's too busy gawping skyward, mumbling nonsense to her followers. I shake her and point again. *"Look!"*

Jack-o-lanterns.

Hundreds of them, maybe thousands.

They line Locust's sidewalks, shimmery orange firelight and serrated smiles, lighting the way for the Halloween parade that, after all these years, is finally about to begin.

"HOLY HELL, HOLY fucking hell," Julie trembles, phone sagging in her hand, screen aglow with fire-grin pumpkins. "I think the show's over. Reagan, we should go."

"But don't you wanna know?" I say, drifting forward.

Except for the jack-o-lanterns, Main Street remains dark, dead of electricity. But farther down, nesting beyond the oak trees, I spot the candlelight glow of Madison's attic window.

"Where're you going?" Julie cries. "Reagan!"

And it's funny, strange, I'm not afraid anymore. I'm done running from this town.

"I'm going home."

Julie chases me. "Are you insane? What's wrong with you?"

"Can't you hear their voices?"

"Reagan, you're freaking me out. Voices?"

"Madison's voice. And the whole town." Yes, there. Distant, soft. Whispers between the silence, like late-season katydids lost inside autumn air, buzzing with the magic words that bring Halloween to life.

"We need to leave! Now!" Julie grabs my right hand.

But invisible fingers close around my left hand. Smooth, waxy, tugging me…

I follow. A rancid sugar lump twitches inside my throat, and I follow.

No more running.

"Reagan, please," Julie begs, hand straining. "I'm your friend, I was wrong to bring you here. Please, I'm scared we—"

Her voice cuts off, her hand slips away. A choking, sputtering scream shreds the haunted fabric of the night.

I whirl.

But where my only friend stood a heartbeat before, the road shimmers with emptiness.

Julie is nowhere. Vanished.

The invisible hand tugs me onward. My sister's hand.

IT'S ONLY A short walk to my family home.

The jack-o-lanterns and my big sister's translucent grip lead the way.

The house rises from the trees like a Victorian fairytale. Rounded balcony, castle eaves, white-frosting trim. And, of course, a tower attic with a candlelit oval window.

Nothing looks familiar and everything does.

Wooden stairs lead to a sprawling porch clotted with jack-o-lanterns and a cobwebbed Halloween display. Tombstones, skull-faced zombies, black cats with arching spines, all the dime-store clichés.

At the front door, I take a split-second to feel afraid, to hope it's locked.

The knob turns and fate swings inward.

I cross the threshold into a parlor lit with more jack-o-lanterns. Furniture and knickknacks stand in limbo. Memories of my parents must cling like dust to every surface—memories of my childhood self, too—but as I trace my fingers along forgotten edges, I still don't recognize us.

I climb a long, twisted staircase, navigate hallways and more staircases through a pumpkin-lit haze. I don't bother peeking into bedrooms. What's the point when she won't let me remember myself? The house holds its stale breath as I approach the attic door. Arched, bewitching, closed up tight.

I hesitate. Madison always hated when I disturbed her. She'd throw curses and hard-edged books at me.

I touch the doorknob.

Someone on the other side knuckle-knocks.

Rap, rap, rap—then a flurry of childish giggles, whispers.

Run, run, run!

"Madison?" I open the door.

"Trick-or-treat!" cry the voices. Hundreds of them—1,312 if I had to guess. The missing citizens of Locust cluster in the attic, holding candy buckets out to me. Skeletal pirates, bloody scarecrows, headless horsemen, they watch me expectantly.

The one who got away.

Sweet bile rises. "I—I don't have any candy."

And with a trick, not a treat, the costume parade begins.

In a riot of laughter, the citizens of Locust march through the door, strangers all. If flesh still mattered, they'd knock me down, trample me. But they've become something else now. Their gossamer bodies graze right through me, shoulders and elbows and masked smiles blowing past my hollows like leaf-scattered wind, emerging on my other side as if I was never here. My skin chills and electrifies, but I resist the pull of their current.

On and on, they march. Grown men and women and children, all lost, all carrying candy buckets and canned laughter down the stairs and out onto the road, until only stragglers scurry down this attic hallway. At last, I recognize a real face in the doorway. A gauzy young woman costumed in plastic vampire teeth and a candy-apple-red drugstore cape. She brandishes a camera phone, aims it at me, but only for a heartbeat.

"Julie?" I reach for her.

She passes through me without even flinching, mist and glowing phone, following the others, a gliding puppet documenting the parade for an all-new graveyard of followers. Footage I fear nobody outside Locust will ever see.

"Julie!" I waver on the attic threshold as she disappears down the stairs. What do I do? Chase my only friend? Or truly meet my sister?

I face the attic beyond.

An impossibly cavernous space, alive with glimmering pumpkins and hallowed leatherbound books stacked to the high-arching ceiling. On the center floorboards, lines of candy corn form a thirteen-pointed star, and trick-or-treat buckets overflow with sacred Halloween offerings.

Poison apples, wings of bat, plastic spiders, and candy with glinting razorblades.

Madison's favorite grimoire sits open on her altar, brittle pages scribed in blood and mystic handwriting. A big wish, a powerful spell:

TO MAKE THE DAY ETERNAL

A velvet silhouette rises inside the flickering attic shadows. A lushly cloaked sorceress, with striped socks and a crown of mystic antlers. She watches from the murk with glinting cat-eye glasses.

"Hello, Maddie," I say. "You always did love Halloween."

"And you always hated candy corn. Remember, little sister, how you used to spit it out?"

"Not so little anymore." I tremble, standing taller than her now. "Let them go."

Madison cackles, echoes, cuts a quicksilver smile. Thirteen years old and boundless, she flicks her mystical hand my way.

A sudden lump squirms inside my throat, sickly-sweet. The devil's earwax. I clutch at my neck, choking it up. The candy corn clatters to the floor, jitters, then sprouts gruesome insectile legs and leafy green wings. With a long katydid chitter, it scurries into the shadows.

"Remember now, *little sister*?"

I'm already backing down the hallway when the memories overrun me.

Glimmers, echoes, an entire town clawing at their wriggling throats, green katydid legs protruding from their mouths, but they couldn't spit the candy out. Madison's spooky wistful magic infested them all.

But not me.

I always hated Halloween. Hated the scary costumes and shadowy identities, hated the wickedness blooming like corpse flowers inside my big sister.

Madison swoops from the darkness and snatches my hand, purple fingernails digging in—just like all those years ago. She tries to pull me.

Not to safety.

But back into her clutches, her spell, her endless Halloween dreamscape.

I jerk away and stumble down stairs and hallways until crisp nighttime air breaks against my face.

Run, run, run, little sister, try to run away, try to escape me if you can…

I chase the pumpkins, chase the otherworld parade of citizens, dizzy, tumbling, sweet katydids buzzing. When I reach Main Street, Locust stands whole again. Crowded, bustling, the never-ending march. Purple-and-orange lights float overhead and shimmer in every window, and all those tattered decorations phantom back to gaudy, witchy life. The marquee outside the movie theater glows, announcing a new creep show, coming soon:

TRUE TAL3S FROM 4FTER MIDN1GHT

Hosted by Mistress Julie and myself, no doubt, and introducing my sister in the role of the monster.

I shove through the ethereal chaos, past stranger after stranger, until I spot a candy-apple-red vampire and her faithful camera phone.

"Julie!" I block my friend's path.

Plastic fangs, smile shining as empty as a jack-o-lantern, she holds me in the eye of her camera, but she doesn't truly see me.

"We have to go!" I grab her phantom arm, expect to pass right through, but reality takes hold or drops away—*poof*, confetti—shattered.

Because look at that. My hands are small.

Wearing a costume of sudden impossible flesh, I cling to Julie with the tiny, trembling fingers of a five-year-old.

I gawp down at myself, shrunken, dressed as Snoopy once again, floppy black ears, red collar. Somewhere between home and escape, childhood recaptured me.

"Julie, we have to run," I beg, voice high and innocent, one final tug.

Julie's camera reels me in, ever-recording, and her hand clamps down on my own like a possessed bear trap, locking me in place. I try to jerk free, but I'm too little, there's no fighting it.

"Trick-or-treat!" cheers the town.

Down the road, between the jack-o-lanterns and Halloween sparkle, the parade parts like a festive sea, clearing a path for Locust's witch queen.

Madison strides toward me in a flourish of cloak and glee. The antlers of her crown stretch to the sky while candy corn twitches inside my throat. Majestic and ruthless and eternal, my big sister eclipses the moon as she welcomes me home to her eternal Halloween.

One last time, I turn away. I implore Julie and her camera, praying her little gravediggers see this, knowing they won't. My sugary little voice oozes, buzzes.

"It's the 31ˢᵗ of October in Locust, Maine, and this time, I didn't get away."

SALTING THE MEAT

Monday, July 7, 3:13 a.m.

McCarran International Airport

Las Vegas, Nevada

I STAND BEHIND you in the security line, darling, with only the cheap sugar of your perfume and fate between us. We've never once made eye contact, though I can't stop staring. As we snake through the line, I sample your sunburned skin from different camera angles, different reflective surfaces, different cuts. Currently, your plain, unseasoned face pixelates on the security screen above the TSA station. The camera loves you, but this one doesn't do you justice. You wait awkwardly but pleasantly while an agent in blue rubber gloves examines your return ticket and state-issued ID. Your God-given name appears on both, just as it appeared on your room service receipts and your luggage tag.

And now my heart.

Moving ahead, you slip off your backpack and cheap plastic sandals, tucking them obediently in the designated security bins. An extra-large bandage covers the sole of your left foot, and I suck my teeth as you limp through the metal detector. Ouch, darling.

You disappear in the direction of Terminal A as I hand over my ID and a one-way ticket to your home city. Across the country, across the years, ace detectives have invented countless tabloid nicknames for me: the Wichita Butcher, the Midnight Mutilator, the Sacramento Jackal, the Eastside Cannibal, the Shadowman… That last one's my favorite, though this morning, I'm simply Sherman Nobody Henderson. Mediocre build, unassumingly handsome, a balding business-class grunt on the path to middle-aged. The agent in the blue gloves waves my ID under his black light then stamps my ticket and sends me on my happy way.

A model citizen, I remove my loafers and my laptop. My blood thrills as my personal belongings disappear inside the TSA's all-seeing machine, to be examined for implements of terror. They need only search the anthology of home videos saved in plain sight on my laptop's hard drive. Though, naturally, they won't. I don't fit the profile for their brand of extremism.

I catch up with you at gate A33. Our flight is on time and will board in twenty-three minutes. The terminal echoes with the last-chance jangles of slot machines, and has a handful of open seats. You sit cross-legged on the floor in a corner, hunkered down as far from the red-eye bustle as you can get.

I purchase a large hot chocolate from the coffee shop, then choose a chair that faces your reflection in the predawn window. I don't usually have a sweet tooth, but for you, I'll make an exception. Hot chocolate was your beverage of choice out on the Strip, even though you've been old enough to order booze for two years now, darling.

I sip my drink and angle my phone and hit RECORD. Anyone walking behind me will see a guy playing a bland game of solitaire. I tell you, darling, it's astounding, there's an app for everything. My camera watches you read the same tattered fantasy novel you clutched like a battle shield all weekend. *Damsel Rising.* The day I first caught your scent, I googled a detailed synopsis. The story's a trite little slice of make-believe about a cowering nubile maiden who faces off against a dragon and transforms into a fierce knight. Are you getting to the good part yet, darling?

I know I am.

When the boarding attendant announces our flight, you bolt to your feet, eager to be rid of this city of sin. Sadly, budget ticketholders don't get herded onto the plane until last. I take my rightful place behind you and follow you into the throat of the plane.

You hold the ticket for 37E. Our flight is barely half full, but some weekend warriors have already crammed your overhead compartment with their carry-ons. You struggle to fit your backpack inside for about two seconds before your tender face flame-broils with embarrassment. You give up and take your center seat with the bag cradled in your lap.

I bite down on my amusement, taste blood, imagine it's yours.

"Hi there, darling. I'm right beside you. 37D." I flash you my ticket, too fast for you to read, then take the aisle seat to your immediate left, caging you in, nestling my elbow onto our shared armrest. And, darling, I breathe you in again. Your pulse points throb with the promise of warm vanilla. I reek of Old Spice and uncomfortable conversation.

You lean away from me, clearly desperate to claim the relative seclusion of the vacant window seat. The only other warm bodies seated in our row are the elderly couple in 37A and 37B, across the aisle. They lean weary heads against each other, ready for a nap before the flight attendants even point out our emergency exits.

"In Vegas for work or pleasure?" I ask as we wheel toward the runway. Naturally, I already know the answer.

"Neither." You wince and unsheathe your paperback.

"Better stow that bag of yours under the seat, darling. Don't wanna get on the ugly side of these flight attendants. I once knew one who could scream louder than a jet engine."

Especially when I used the pin of her flight wings to pry her fingernails off, one by one.

You obey, just like I knew you would, and shove your backpack under the seat. Though, not before fishing out an ancient MP3 player. You smile politely, then plug your ears with music. Between that and *Damsel Rising*, you become a living, breathing DO NOT DISTURB sign.

My favorite kind.

I wait until we get into the air before I tap your knee.

You startle, practically jump out of that sunburned skin. Unplugging an earbud, you regard me as if I'm about to inform you the plane is going down.

I hold your reluctant eye contact until I feel you squirm, then brandish my laptop. "Mind if I watch some home videos?"

"Go ahead," you say without a heartbeat of thought. I feel you longing for that vacant window seat. Most girls these days wouldn't hesitate to move, claim that personal space. But, darling, you're too polite to scoot away. You're a dying breed.

"I'm something of a home video enthusiast," I tell you. "Can't record enough of them. Especially now that every device comes with a high-def camera and a microphone. When I die, they're gonna find thousands of home videos on my computer and wonder if I spent my free time doing anything else."

"That's nice." You flash another quick, well-mannered smile. Before I can tell you more, you re-plug your earbud and retreat behind your paperback.

Alright, darling. Let's play.

I hit RECORD and tuck my phone in the far right of the seatback pocket so we'll both be in frame. Next, I crack my laptop, and my veins thrill, my mouth waters, a Pavlovian wolf drooling over the hundreds of video files that clutter my desktop.

I didn't lie to you. One day, perhaps when I grow old and sloppy and leave evidence of myself behind—or perhaps when a young damsel such as yourself turns knight and slays me—the proper authorities will discover my laptop and the meticulous documentation of my escapades.

In fact, darling, I'm counting on it.

It'll be the job of several lucky agents to sit in a tiny windowless room and watch videos stained red with flesh and intrigue, and wails for a mercy that never comes. They'll watch my videos on repeat, over and over, logging every exquisite nuance of my craft. Like how I select my prey, how I move unseen through the background of all your private places, grooming your vulnerability, testing your limits, ensuring that subtle but ever-growing terror salts your meat. They'll watch every last video and connect the dots from kill to kill, jurisdiction to jurisdiction, and realize their nastiest offenders—the Butchers, the Mutilators, the Cannibals— are all the same remarkable monster.

The same legend.

On my laptop, each tiny folder bears a victim's name typed in all caps. Famous names, darling, if you watch the news or follow true crime. Of course, even the most well-produced crime scene reenactments don't capture the raw intensity of those final moments quite like I do.

Those last flailing struggles, that final shuddering gasp, the sudden wetness of it all.

I stroke the video files with my fingertip.

Your name hangs high in the top right corner of the screen, where you're most likely to notice it.

Instead, you reach the heroic conclusion of *Damsel Rising*, then flip immediately back to those first pages where the damsel is weak and meek, utterly determined not to engage me or my screen.

That's okay, darling. Your self-seclusion positively rings my dinner bell. You absolutely refuse to see me coming.

I double-click your file and hit PLAY, start the show. Too bad you didn't bring popcorn.

The screen shimmers with a sprawling shot of hotel palm trees and an oasis of poolside sunbathers. Row after row of economy lounge chairs, colorful overpriced drinks, and half-naked bodies greased in coconut oil from the gift shop.

The camera pans past all that artificial fun and follows a path of bloody footprints stamped across the wet concrete.

Footprint after bloody, limping footprint.

They lead to the lifeguard's chair and a mousy young woman hiding behind a towel and a self-conscious one-piece. That's you, darling. See yourself?

The shot holds on your ever-reddening body. You hug your arms across your bathing suit, standing in a small puddle of your own blood as if it might be possible to fold inward and disappear. But you can't disappear, not from me. You're no showgirl, but you display nice lines, a generous flank.

Here on the plane, close enough to almost hear your heartbeat, I don't bother containing my predator's smile.

Will you catch me watching you?

In my video, you show the lifeguard your sliced and bleeding foot. You try to warn him about the broken shot glass in the shady, quiet corner behind the cabana. But you're not like the buoyant, bouncy girls he craves. To him, you're pathetically drab. The irresponsible asshole snorts and tells you glass beverages aren't allowed inside the pool area—*you* must be mistaken. Your doe eyes drop, instantly defeated, and you apologize for bothering him. You stain the wet concrete with your bright red footprints as you slink away.

That's the moment, darling, when I knew you were the perfect cut.

Now, I side-eye you in 37E, relishing our primal game of predator and prey, hoping to catch you catching yourself on-screen. Hoping to turn you into a frozen deer—a slab of sweet, wide-eyed venison turning salty in my high beams. What will you do if you catch me? Will you summon the courage to speak up? I bet not.

Problem is, you're glued to those futile storybook pages.

Fascinating, really. How you treat fantasyland as if it provides a sturdy shelter for you. A cowering maiden transformed into a fearless knight? Sorry to tell you, it never happens that way in real life. But maybe one day, I'll give your tattered paperback a vigorous once-over.

A snowstorm of static slashes across my screen. Your poolside image hard-cuts into a midnight shot of five vibrant young ladies in short glittery dresses. The middle one wears a white pageant sash: THE BRIDE.

You're not with them, darling, not in this shot—though you were a few hours earlier.

In fact, I learned a lot about you during that short-lived bachelorette dinner you spent with them. You and I sat back-to-back in adjoining booths. There's a reason they sometimes call me the Shadowman. You didn't even know I was there, just like the laughing, celebrating bridesmaids at your table barely knew *you* were there.

You're merely the sister of the groom. I know, because you explained this to your waiter, and then again to the busboy who served your hot chocolate. You, darling, explained yourself to the minimum-wage help as if apologizing for your very existence.

Poor thing. You barely spoke the rest of the meal, except to answer the maid of honor when she asked what exactly it is you do. *This and that*, you mumbled. Luckily, your future sister-in-law, in a gallant act of face-saving pity, cut in with your truth.

I captured it all on audio.

You, darling, want to be a writer. A *fantasy* writer. And isn't that sweet? You want to *express* yourself. You even rented a cute little cabin up in the mountains outside your home city so you can attempt your first novel in peace and solitude.

How utterly, deliciously quaint.

Not that it mattered to anyone. You didn't even make it to dessert before announcing that you'd booked an early flight home and needed to hit the hay. The other bridesmaids barely paid attention when you mumbled your awkward farewells—but I saw you.

You slunk off all alone on that gashed foot of yours

I have the footage of that, too—your long, lonesome limp back to your hotel—but I've saved it for last. It makes for a more intriguing final appetizer: you all raw and tender.

I caught up with the bridal party later on—followed them for hours, in fact—but I promise you, darling, only after I saw you safely to your elevator.

Now, they stagger across my computer screen on teetering stilettos. The camera follows immediately behind them as they wander the Vegas Strip, their snarky cackles polluting the open air. They barely spoke to you all night, but suddenly they have plenty to say *about* you.

They're worried for you.

Well, not really. Your almost-sister-in-law jokes about how your big brother worries about you living all alone in that gloomy cabin. The others mostly comment on your bad hair and maladroit cocktail orders. Bitches, truly. I'd hate for you to hear them speak this way about you.

But, of course, you *don't* hear. Your earbuds are crammed too deep.

I hold my finger on the volume, maxing out their voices: *...seriously, you're a saint for letting that freak show tag along. Did you see the way she chewed her food?*

The girls cackle at that, naturally they do. You're *their* prey, too, darling. Their wicked laughter carries, but only a couple of seats before the drone of the plane disguises it.

Still, I get zero reaction from you. Fine. I lift my elbow from our armrest, and oh so innocently tangle the chord of your left earbud. It pops out and whips into my lap.

"Forgive my clumsiness, darling." I pinch the earbud between my fingers, holding it just out of your reach, out of your comfort zone.

"Be nice, you guys, he's genuinely concerned." Your almost-sister-in-law's voice floats between us. I smile wetly. This is the part I so badly want you to hear. *"She's always off in her own little world..."*

But if you register the sound of her voice, you're a ninja master of the blank expression.

"That's okay," you say. We almost make eye contact, then your entire focus narrows to your earbud, desperate to reclaim it with as little social interaction as possible. You hold your hand out, not daring enough to pluck it from my fingertips.

"Her own little world?" the maid of honor snorts from my lap. *"What, like Mars?"*

No reaction from you.

"I enjoyed recording the Strip." I tilt my screen your way. Perhaps you think I'm angling to show you porn or something sleazy because you stone-cold refuse to look. Your polite smile tightens, and finally you reach for your earbud. I consider pulling it playfully out of reach, but you're adorable when you finally get assertive.

I reward you. I let you have it.

It slips back into your ear, and you disappear again. Into your own little fantasyland. Such a dangerous place. Why else would big brother worry so?

I keep my computer angled your way and FAST FORWARD past the bridesmaids, sealing them in a mental doggy bag, saving them for later. The maid of honor might make a nice quick morsel some midnight—after all the authoritative fuss about what I'm going to do to you dies down.

I hit PLAY on your big scene.

On-screen, you wander through a gaudy maze of shops and casinos, trying to escape the massive hotel where you chewed your dinner so awkwardly. You get lost almost immediately. Your corduroy skirt and plastic sandals don't adhere to the trashy sequin dress code worn by the surrounding crowds. Everything must feel like it's closing in.

Soon enough, you panic and double back. Head down, you almost crash into me and my upraised phone. To you, lost in your own little world, I'm just another starry-eyed tourist.

"Do you know how to find the monorail?" you mumble.

You don't notice my camera winking at you. You, darling, are tender perfection, so easy to sculpt and carve and season. I point you in the wrong direction through the smoky, flashy casino. The chaotic excitement of a thousand giddy tourists surrounds you. By the time you glimpse an exit, you're practically running. The shot jitters as my camera hurries to keep up, bursting through the tinted-glass door just a few steps behind you.

This isn't the monorail.

The monorail is far, far away, on the opposite side of the hotel. You have a return ticket, but from where you stand on the vast, light-bright Strip, you can see the shiny, golden top of your hotel just down the boulevard. Doesn't look that far, does it? Of course, there's zero chance you'll return to the humiliation of searching for the elusive monorail.

You do what I knew you'd do and walk.

But everything in this plastic city is deceiving, especially for girls who are easily lulled into fantasylands.

In reality, your towering budget-hotel stands almost two miles away on the seedier side of the Strip, where the sidewalk herds thin away, where the shadows pool in the gaps between tasteless rundown casinos.

Such a walk—and on that injured foot of yours.

You regret your decision about a quarter-mile in and start glancing over your shoulder. You don't see me, of course. I blend in like cigarette smoke on the horizon. All you see are the hulking hotels and how far you haven't come.

Your left sandal fills with fresh blood around the half-mile mark.

Gets quite juicy.

The camera tracks your bloody half-moon footprints down the cracked sidewalk. You limp and limp and ouch, darling. When a dark alley opens up between two discount souvenir shops, you slip in and rest a moment, whimpering in the shadows. Worst weekend ever, right?

Just wait.

The footage here turns a bit grainy. My camera only captures the fish-pale sliver of your left leg and the plastic ankle strap of your bloody sandal. All alone, so vulnerable. I could've taken you then—a quick, gasping meal. Behind a dumpster, or even in your hotel room.

But why rush it with such a lovely unseasoned specimen. So empty with possibilities. I have so many recipes in mind for you.

Seated here in 37D, I swallow deeply, imagining your unique mouth-feel. Pulsing vanilla seasoned with introversion and notes of awkward dreams.

I side-eye you in your seat, and for a rabbit-quick heartbeat, I catch you!

Watching yourself!

As soon as my head tilts, your eyes streak away, back to your paperback. Your face burns a mottled bright red. But are you blushing because I caught you watching my private screen, or because of what you saw there?

Did you recognize yourself, darling?

The question tingles the tip of my tongue. My blood goes wild with the adrenaline of the hunt. You're a gazelle finally glimpsing the lion in the grass. You spent your entire meek existence hiding from what the big, bad scary world thinks of you, but you've never really seen yourself through someone else's eyes.

You're beautiful, truly. Plain, as yet uncured, but there's so much you can become. So much I can help you become.

I don't take my eyes off you. "Like what you see?"

I know you hear me, even with that earbud jammed in your ear. I sense you trembling, smell the salty sweat of unease mingling with the vanilla of your jugular and your—

"Beverage?" The flight attendant rattles into our little fantasyland with her drink cart. Our flight is over halfway complete, but they always serve the budget rows last.

Quickly, smoothly, I hit PAUSE.

The image of your leg and blood-filled sandal freezes on the screen.

Sensation spikes, and times slows to a wonderful surreal crawl. Your eyes widen on the flight attendant and her impatient smile. You look from me to her and fill your lungs.

Hell, even fate holds its hoary breath.

What will you do?

Will you transform into the daring knight and rat me out to our flight attendant?

I leave my computer open, all the proof you need glowing in my lap. The bloody sandal on the screen and the sandal on your foot are a perfect Cinderella match.

You have me by the balls, darling. I like that grip.

Now, will you twist?

"Do you want a beverage?" the attendant asks again, practically tapping her toe.

I smile with upstanding teeth, and demure to you. "Ladies first, darling. Go ahead. Tell her."

You swallow, glance at me again, glance at her, hesitate. "Hot chocolate?"

Oh, darling. My shoulders slump for you.

"Make it two," I command.

She sloshes lukewarm cups at us, then rattles down the aisle, disappearing into the galley.

Your frozen image glows on my screen, a beacon to pull you into my darkness. I raise my cup and force a toast. "To those sweet oblivious moments."

You nurse sip after sip, busying your conversation-hole with chocolate.

I take a long gratuitous swallow, then hit PLAY and watch you arrive at your hotel elevator. I could've stepped inside and journeyed up with you.

But it's like I said, you're a rare breed. So dreamy. Something to savor.

Once you finish your hot chocolate, I take your cup and flash my finest concerned-stranger smile. "You should visit the little girls' room, darling. We're about to land."

You blush and take my advice, just like I knew you would. I close my laptop and enjoy the braised heat of your sunburn as you squeeze past.

Craning in my seat, nibbling the tip of my tongue with gentle canines, I watch you go. The anticipation alone is delicious. Will you find our flight attendant? Tell her what you saw on my computer? Will she pay you any mind, you meek, silly thing?

You head straight into the bathroom.

I choke up a hearty laugh, can't help it. Beginning to think you really didn't notice yourself limping across my screen.

Shame, shame, darling, you should pay more attention to your surroundings.

I glance at the slumbering elderly couple in 37A and 37B, then drag your backpack out from under the seat. Your toothpaste, your change of underwear, I fish through it all until a small treasure jingles in my hand.

Your house key.

The one that opens the door to that secluded cabin of yours. I slide a tin marked "lip balm" from my pocket and press your key into the clay inside, creating an imprint of each side. I take my sweet time double-checking the address on your ID. It's the same one I found online when I booked this flight and the cozy motel just down the mountain from you.

When you return from the restroom, all our personal items are stowed and ready for descent. You feeling hungry, darling? Because I've never been more ravenous.

You and I land without incident. I hit RECORD and press up against you as we depart the plane, last in line with the usual slow shuffle. Inside the terminal, you ride the moving walkways to the designated exit. Just before you escape outside, I close my hand on your tender sunburned shoulder, savoring the deep red you turn when you see it's me.

"Lovely meeting you, darling," I say, holding up my phone, framing you in a close-up.

"So long." You duck your eyes, duck your shoulders. You don't look back, and the space between us fills with the fresh air of dawn.

But don't worry.

You'll see me again, and my camera, too.

That secluded fantasyland of yours is a tempting unspoiled place, but it's not healthy to shut out the world.

About time you had a visitor.

And who knows, maybe with my midnight guidance you'll rise up and become that fierce knight. Maybe you'll be the true crime damsel who slays the Shadowman and exposes my legendary career to the world.

Not likely, darling.

But either way, I lick my teeth, eager to capture our happily-ever-after on video.

MEDUSA WITH THE HEADS OF MEN

JOURNAL OF HISTORICAL MEDICAL SCIENCE

September 2013

"Mythological Beings as Early Marvels of Xenotransplantation"

Dr. Jameson V. Knox, MD, PhD, DVM, MS

Providence Institute of Human Advancement

Abstract: Beyond their fantastical elements, the mythologies of ancient civilizations can offer modern insight into the prevailing social orders and daily practices of bygone eras, including ethical standards and practical biomedical applications. An intersection exists between these legendary stories and contemporary medical science that suggests mythological beings, such as the snake-coiffed Medusa and the three-headed Cerberus, represent early instances of xenotransplantation. Employing a multidisciplinary approach, including biomedical and veterinary sciences, bioethics, comparative mythology, and historical anthropology, this study examines the symbolic connections between chimeric narratives and the historical evolution of global medical practices. Building on existing literature, which often overlooks the medical dimensions of myth, this approach strives to fill a notable gap by demonstrating that surgeons of antiquity, unhindered by ethical outrage, successfully engaged in proto-xenotransplantation. Evidence of such could bolster modern medical progress in similar fields and strike down existing bioethical barriers.

MediGenix Organics
www.medigenix.com

ORDER #BIO333713

Date: 12/23/2017

Bill/Ship to:

Dr. Jameson Knox
Providence Institute of Human Advancement, New York

[off-site address on file]

Quantity/Description

Three (3) Canines
Type: German Shepherd (*Canis lupus familiaris*), Female
Purpose: Bio-enhancement research
Condition: Living

Thirty-Three (33) Ophidians
Type: Eyelash Viper (*Bothriechis schlegelii*), Female
Purpose: Bio-enhancement research
Condition: Living

One (1) Simian
Type: Bonobo (*Pan paniscus*), Female
Purpose: Bio-enhancement research
Condition: Living

**** All living subjects are ethically sourced and meet the required minimum standards for research purposes. Please ensure proper care and ethical treatment during the course of your research. ****

THE HARBORFIELD GOSSIP

Serpent Siege! Controversial Surgeon's Gala Crashed by Protesters

HARBORFIELD, NEW YORK—October 13, 2018—The ten-year wedding anniversary of notorious surgeon and self-made millionaire Dr. Jameson Knox and his wife—acclaimed starlet, artist, and blonde bombshell Mia Doukas-Knox—took a slithery turn when the couple became the target of protesters. During the champagne toast inside the luxurious Harborfield Grand Ballroom, members of the animal rights organization EARA (Ethical Animal Research Advocates) stood on balconies and rained three hundred live milk snakes onto the power couple and their black-tie guests.

Gala attendees who fled to outdoor gardens stumbled into a makeshift 'graveyard' erected by protesters. Seventy-seven cardboard headstones memorialized the test animals known to have been used in Dr. Knox's research. Anonymous representatives of EARA issued this statement: "Beyond what's already known about the appalling nature of Dr. Knox's experiments, we have mounting evidence that his current medical trials severely violate the Animal Welfare Act, most notably the requirement for researchers to minimize the pain and distress of test subjects."

Dr. Knox founded the Providence Institute of Human Advancement in 2010 and garnered attention in 2017 for groundbreaking experiments in which he successfully grafted regenerative snakeskin onto bonobos with third-degree burns. Despite his advancements in the field of xenotransplantation (cross species tissue and organ transplantation), the controversial surgeon has faced fierce ethical scrutiny by his peers, and has been compared both favorably and unfavorably to Vladimir Demikhov, a mid-twentieth-century Soviet transplantation pioneer notorious for creating a viable two-headed dog.

Knox's wife, Mia Doukas-Knox, is a one-time Hollywood starlet known for her sizzling role as the femme fatale in the critically acclaimed 2003 film *Hot Night in Sin City*. She is also the accuser in the high-profile 2006 sexual assault trial in which her producer/director Herbert Bridgestone was controversially acquitted for her rape. After subsequently bowing out of Hollywood, Doukas-Knox has since become a respected victims' rights advocate and a multi-medium surrealist artist whose work routinely appears in posh New York galleries. These days, she uses her creative talents to make performative social commentaries—most notably, her much anticipated "Divine Retribution: Not All Snakes," an interactive art installation scheduled to appear this month on the Bowery.

Dr. Knox and Doukas-Knox first met on the red carpet at the 2008 Met Gala and were married three whirlwind months later.

When asked about EARA's grievances against her husband's research and their disruption of her anniversary party, Doukas-Knox, seen post-gala with docile milk snakes coiled around her arms, answered, "I pray no living beings were hurt during tonight's ordeal. This one night of the year was meant to celebrate love, not the unfortunate avenues of my husband's career."

In turn, Dr. Knox also made a public statement regarding the serpents in his midst. "My marriage is of little consequence. My research, however, will change the world. These animal-hugging fanatics will find themselves on the ignorant side of history."

FROM: MiaDoukas@PegasusRisingArt.com
TO: administrator@EARA.us.org
SENT: October 14, 2018, 11:15 a.m. EST
SUBJECT: many thanks

Hello new friends,

The gala met my every expectation! Thank you for granting my sham marriage the symbolic send-off it deserves. Jameson is indeed an obsessed, venom-hearted man. I'm happy to help you shatter his reputation. As discussed, I'll search for key cards and passwords to his most sacred private laboratory. But I have one final condition: once I find a way in, I intend to go with you. I deserve to witness the atrocities he sacrificed his integrity and our marriage for.

—Mia

MANHATTAN POST

Two Pop-Up Art Installations Subvert Ancient Greek Myth

by Jake Phoenix, Culture and Arts Correspondent

NEW YORK CITY—October 21, 2018—In Ovid's *Metamorphoses*, we first meet Medusa as a lovely kind-hearted mortal with golden ringlets. As a devoted priestess of Athena, the chaste goddess of war, Medusa captured the lustful attention of her goddess's bitter rival, Poseidon. Dripping toxic masculinity, the god rose from his sea to seduce Medusa, but the virgin priestess fled in terror to the temple of her goddess. Poseidon stormed inside and raped Medusa right there on Athena's sacred altar, then exited with a smile. Furious to find her temple and priestess defiled, Athena turned her divine retribution onto Medusa. She blamed Medusa for making herself too tempting, then cursed her with an insidious headful of snakes and a gaze which froze mortal men into stone. Medusa's first stony victim was her loving best friend and would-be hero, who heard Medusa weeping and rushed to her side. Devastated, cast out as a monster, Medusa fled to the ruins of a temple where the gorgon remained isolated until the day she was beheaded by the 'hero' Perseus. A divine retribution that proves a woman being blamed and punished for her sexual assault is a practice as timeless as Greek mythology.

Now, two pop-up art installations in the Bowery seek to subvert this trope through modern expressions of classical art.

"Divine Retribution: Not All Snakes" by renowned feminist artist Mia Doukas is an interactive installation that allows victims of sexual and domestic assault to write messages to their attackers on rubber snakes and nail them to the oversized decapitated head of a mouthless man. The head stands 6'4"—the same height as Herbert Bridgestone, notorious Hollywood producer and director who Doukas accused of rape in a 2006 trial. In a verdict that has become all too common, Bridgestone was acquitted after DNA evidence contained in Doukas's rape kit was deemed inadmissible. Doukas's rape kit was one of seven hundred contaminated kits thrown out due to improper storage in an outdoor police evidence shed.

For years after the trial, Doukas faced public blowback in which she was accused of being a liar and openly chastised for her strikingly attractive appearance. These disturbingly viral trends too often encourage other assault victims to remain silent. Doukas's installation gives voice to the countless victims of this ever-pervasive rape culture, bolstering modern movements like #MeToo. And what an empowering vision it is! A mere three nights after its debut, the decapitated head of "Divine Retribution" already has over three thousand snakes attached.

"Medusa with the Head of Perseus" by Italian sculptor Luciano Garbati is also on display on the Bowery. This nude bronze was inspired by the sixteenth-century sculpture "Perseus with the Head of Medusa" which depicts the 'hero' flaunting the gorgon's decapitated head. In Garbati's sleek reimagining, it is Medusa who walks proudly with the severed head of Perseus. *[continued on page 33]*

FROM: MiaDoukas@PegasusRisingArt.com

TO: JPhoenix@ManhattanPost.com

SENT: October 22, 2018, 10:37 a.m. EST

SUBJECT: your recent article

Hi Jake,

We've never met, but I feel like we have. I'm Mia Doukas, the artist you wrote about in yesterday's newspaper. Thank you for your kind words. Your summation of the Medusa myth was refreshing. Hers is indeed a sympathetic story, as is the plight of women across the ages. I've read several of your other articles and determined that not only do you have a keen eye for film and art, you're also a much-needed victims' advocate. Unfortunately, there are still those with boorish voices like my husband who prefer to mine mythology for their own insidious gain. Keep up the empowering work, Jake!

Your newest friend,
Mia

FROM: JPhoenix@ManhattanPost.com

TO: MiaDoukas@PegasusRisingArt.com

SENT: October 22, 2018, 5:43 p.m. EST

SUBJECT: re: your recent article

Hi Mia,

What an honor to hear from you! I'm a huge fan of your work (from Hollywood silver screens to the galleries of New York!), and I admire your own feats of advocacy. I'm also, unfortunately, well-versed in your husband. His papers on xenotransplantation and chimera myths exhibit a shocking hubris, never mind his blatant contempt for ethical standards. In my line of work, I hear things—unsettling things. Forget Greek mythology, Dr. Jameson Knox reads like something out of Shelley. I was frankly surprised to discover you're married to such a man. He must possess some wondrous virtue that remains absent from public eye. Do enlighten me.

Delighted to be your newest friend,
Jake

FROM: MiaDoukas@PegasusRisingArt.com

TO: JPhoenix@ManhattanPost.com

SENT: October 23, 2018, 5:33 a.m. EST

SUBJECT: re: re: your recent article

Hi Jake,

As your newest best friend, needless to say, this is off the record—though perhaps not forever. Your question kept me awake all night. I suppose once I loved *something* about Jameson, but for the life of me, it feels like a dream I made up. He must've once been fun, compassionate, attentive, a lover of the arts, a women's advocate, or why else would I marry him? Certainly, he's a brilliant surgeon, but could that have swayed my heart? Odd how present-day disgust obscures past love. And yikes! Talk about an overshare. We haven't even met in person and here I am burdening you with the pre-echoes of my imminent divorce. Let me cut to the good part, Jake. I'll be visiting a gallery in the city this week, perhaps we could meet for coffee?

Your friend,
Mia

BIG BILLY'S PIZZERIA

Security video surveillance, 10/27/18

Timestamp 12:37: Overhead view. A bustling lunch hour, the pizzeria sits at full occupancy. A woman with long blonde hair and a short black dress approaches a two-top table in the corner, occupied by a dark-haired man in a handsome suit jacket. The man stands. The two smile and shake hands for 7.7 seconds before sitting across from each other. They peruse menus, place their order, then lean toward each other, consumed in instant conversation. Audio unavailable.

Timestamp 14:37: The restaurant stands near-empty, though the corner table remains occupied. The dark-haired man has repositioned his chair beside the blonde woman. They duck their heads over the man's phone, scrolling through a screen that isn't visible from this angle. Occasionally they share a laugh or pause to meet the other's gaze, but as they continue reviewing something on the phone their expressions darken, appearing progressively troubled.

Timestamp 16:37: The pizzeria is filling up again. Finally, the couple stands. After shaking hands and exchanging goodbyes, the woman starts to walk away, but the man says something that makes her stop. She turns and they lock eyes. Appearing breathless, she hurries back and kisses him on the mouth. The exchange is very cinematic. The kiss lasts 13.7 seconds before she ducks back and hurries for the exit. The man remains a minute longer, smiling in stunned paralysis before exiting the pizzeria himself.

FROM: MiaDoukas@PegasusRisingArt.com

TO: administrator@EARA.us.org

SENT: October 29, 2018, 8:55 p.m. EST

SUBJECT: re: re: many thanks

Hello friends,

I've made a new friend who champions our cause and has the connection to Jameson we've been praying for: a disgruntled assistant with VIP access to Jameson's hallowed private lab. The man can't go public because Jameson forced an NDA on him, but he's got key codes, passwords, and intel for us. Since your attack on our anniversary gala, Jameson has grown increasingly paranoid and plans to purge his security team. This reset will leave the laboratory blind and vulnerable in the coming days. Be ready for my green light.

—Mia

#IPHONE VIDEO FOOTAGE

10/31/18, 3:21 a.m.–3:37 a.m.

Video opens on the wooded, eastern edge of the Providence Institute of Human Advancement, a stately building with Corinthian columns and zero windows. Security cameras nest in high corners. Two masculine figures in ski-masks cross into view, circling around the side of the building. The cameraperson speaks off-screen.

VOICE OF MIA DOUKAS-KNOX

That's his private entrance down there.

The camera view judders down a nondescript stairwell toward a basement entranceway with a red-glowing key card reader. As the shorter of the two masked figures produces a key card, the taller figure faces the cameraperson.

TALL UNKNOWN MALE

Sure you wanna follow us inside? It's likely to be pretty monstrous.

DOUKAS-KNOX

I lived with the man for ten years. I know all about monstrous.

The key-card reader buzzes, red to green. The steel door opens to a darkened hallway. Igniting pen-lights, the men proceed inside. The camera follows.

Three steps in, motion-triggered lights flood the hallway. Everyone freezes, caught in the swivel-gaze of security cameras.

DOUKAS-KNOX

He's seen us. We've got less than fifteen minutes.

SHORT UNKNOWN MALE

Until what? You said he fired his guards.

DOUKAS-KNOX

He did. And he won't call police. He'll come himself. We should hurry.

(The taller figure blocks the hallway.)

TALL UNKNOWN MALE

I won't put you in danger for this.

DOUKAS-KNOX

That's sweet, but I'll put myself wherever I choose. Clock's ticking. You wanna waste it playing hero? I'm not the one who needs saving.

The shorter figure crosses the hallway to another key-card reader. The security camera follows their movement. Another light flashes, red to green. Steel gears whir and unbolt, and doors open to a sterile room lined with computer terminals and med-tech stations with equipment that blurs with the camera's swift-passing motion.

SHORT UNKNOWN MALE

I'll hack his database. You two rescue the animals.

The adjacent room is a large, octagonal surgical chamber with a steel operating table, currently unoccupied, surrounded by monitoring equipment and tripod video cameras for documenting surgeries. Everything appears pristine and unused. Another door stands nearby.

DOUKAS-KNOX

The animals should be through here.

Beyond is a large animal holding facility lined with steel-bar cages and oversized glass aquariums. Everything appears pristine and unused. Displaced silence amplifies their footsteps as the camera peers into cages. Food bowls and water bottles occupy every domicile, but the cages stand vacant of animals.

DOUKAS-KNOX

Something's wrong. They should be here.

TALL UNKNOWN MALE

This place doesn't smell like it's been used.

SHORT UNKNOWN MALE

There's nothing on the hard drives. This place is a decoy.

The camera rattles and spins, and the masked camera operator swings into view. Her mask pulls away, revealing a fall of blonde hair and the movie-star features of Mia Doukas-Knox, famous green eyes and high cheekbones. Incandescent with rage and ready for her close-up, she films herself stepping toward the eye of the nearest security camera. She glares into it with slitted eyes.

DOUKAS-KNOX

Jameson, you sick, mad monster! Whatever abominations you're hiding, consider this our demise! I want a divorce!

(She pivots toward the taller masked figure, tugs his mask above his mouth, and kisses him with the fury of the Gods.)

BAKER COUNTY GAZETTE

Mysterious Animal Remains Discovered in Field Blaze

SMITHTOWN, VERMONT—November 5, 2018—A suspected arson fire occurred this morning in a field on the abandoned Thompson Cattle Ranch. Around 5 a.m., distant neighbors smelled smoke and called 911. Firefighters and community volunteers rushed to the fire that by then had consumed nearly three acres of long-grass.

After extinguishing the flames, firefighters investigating the blaze's point of origin discovered the charred remains of dozens of animals, including what is believed to be dogs, snakes, and monkeys. Due to the extreme heat of an accelerant, the remains appeared to be fused together.

One volunteer described the blackened bones as "eerily chimeric." County experts, including the coroner and a veterinarian, are collaborating to identify the animals, hoping to provide insight into this bizarre act of arson. The presence of human remains has been ruled out. Please contact Smithtown's Sheriff with any information about this incident.

MediGenix Organics
www.medigenix.com

ORDER #BIO333983

Date: 12/23/2017

Bill/Ship to:

Dr. Jameson Knox
Providence Institute of Human Advancement, New York

[off-site address on file]

Quantity/Description

Thirty-Three (33) Ophidians
Type: Eyelash Viper (*Bothriechis schlegelii*), Female
Purpose: Bio-enhancement research
Condition: Living

*** *All living subjects are ethically sourced and meet the required minimum standards for research purposes. Please ensure proper care and ethical treatment during the course of your research.* ***

FROM: DrJamesonKnox@ProvidenceInstitute.health

TO: MiaDoukas@PegasusRisingArt.com

SENT: November 7, 2018, 1:57 a.m. EST

SUBJECT: I AM EVERYWHERE!

Wife—

There exist no secrets between a husband and his wife. There's nothing you do that I don't know about. No sabotaged galas, no seduction of journalists in pizzerias, no plots to defile the sacred altar of my laboratories. I am all-seeing and all-powerful. Even this last week, as you attempt to misdirect me with credit card charges to the Broadway Hilton, I know your true location is the one-bedroom love nest of Jacob Quinn Phoenix, 133 16th Street, #4B. I can also tell you his blood type, his SAT scores, and how many cavities he's had… But I won't bore you with pedestrian facts. Are you still curious, Wife? Would you like to witness the scientific miracles I've been perfecting? All you ever had to do was look me in the eyes and ask. This offer stands. There exist no secrets between a husband and his wife.

—Your Husband and God

DR. JAMESON KNOX

Private security video surveillance, 11/7/18

Timestamp 4:37: The full-color HD surveillance screen is bisected into four sections. The first view shows a nondescript elevator door set inside a weathered wooden wall. The second view features an operating theater with a polished surgical table. The third, an animal holding facility, focuses on a large aquarium piled half-full with squirming eyelash vipers. The fourth pans the marble foyer of a posh residence. The front door swings inward. Mia makes a dramatic entrance, fists balled, blonde hair swinging in a thick braid. She glares into the security camera, then crosses the foyer toward a grand staircase.

MIA

Jameson, you nasty bastard! Show yourself!

Timestamp 4:38: The camera switches angles, following as Mia rushes upstairs, then down a hallway, yanking open double doors. The view changes again as she storms the luxurious master bedroom. Jameson sits propped on the king-sized bed, cocksure in silken pajamas, laptop open, screen showing this real-time surveillance feed. Without lifting his eyes, he watches Mia approach.

JAMESON

Always charmed to see you, Wife.

MIA

I'm here to see your lab.

JAMESON

It'll be my greatest pleasure. But first, a farewell kiss?

MIA

Are you insane? You make my skin crawl.

Timestamp 4:39: Jameson sets his laptop aside and stands, one hand bulging in his silken pants pocket. Mia backs away.

JAMESON

Am I so vile? You once worshiped me, your brilliant leading man. Recall the feral stink of our sex, the way I slicked you up with Met Galas and red-carpet premieres…

MIA

Hearts change. Yours has mutated.

JAMESON

One kiss, then I'll show you my altar, you'll witness every hidden power of your God.

Timestamp 4:40: Jameson grabs Mia's ponytail and thrusts her head back, exposing her throat. He plunges his mouth against her, violating her with kisses as she thrashes wildly against him. He pulls a bubbling yellow-green syringe from his pocket and stabs her thigh, depressing the plunger. She immediately falls limp and slumps back onto the bed. Jameson follows her down, pressing his weight atop her, licking her throat. Seconds later, he sneers at the camera. Not every God likes to be seen.

JAMESON

Camera, cut to darkness.

Timestamp 4:41: The fourth camera auto-shutters to black, leaving only the first three views glowing. In the third screen, the eyelash vipers writhe in their glass prison.

HARBORFIELD POLICE DEPARTMENT
MISSING PERSON REPORT

Date of Report: 11/9/18

Reporting Officer: Wayland, Badge #3235

Name of Person Filing Report: Jacob Phoenix

Relationship to Missing Person: friend

Missing Person's Full Legal Name: Mia Doukas-Knox

Date of Birth: unknown

Last Seen: Phoenix residence, 133 16th Street, #4B

Date Last Seen: 11/7/18

Time Last Seen: approx. 2:30 a.m.

Circumstances: Mia Doukas-Knox is currently separated from her husband, Jameson Knox, who has an alleged history of abusive behavior. At approx. 2:00 a.m. on 11/7/18, Knox sent Doukas-Knox an email stating he's been spying on her. After receiving the email, Doukas-Knox and Phoenix fell back asleep. When Phoenix woke, Doukas-Knox was gone. Phoenix's attempts to reach Doukas-Knox at the residence she shares with Knox have been unsuccessful. Phoenix worries Doukas-Knox is in mortal danger.

Additional Notes: Officer Wayland visited the Knox residence on 11/9/18 and was invited inside by husband Knox. Knox wrote and signed an affidavit stating he hasn't seen his wife and believes she is somewhere having a 'salacious tryst' with Phoenix (see attached document). Knox invited Officer Wayland to search the residence. There was no sign of Doukas-Knox, nor evidence of an altercation.

DIGITAL VIDEO LOG

Proto-Gorgon Trial #3
Timestamp 11/13/18, 3:27 p.m.–3:43 p.m.

Footage displays a blood-splashed operating theater. A surgical table sits center-screen, occupied. Mia lies supine, wearing a surgical gown and a stained turban of pulsating bandages. Her skin bares a bruised, yellow pallor and her labored breathing rasps around tubes. More tubes sprout from bandages, cycling acidic-green liquid. Consciousness glints inside slitted eyelids.

VOICE OF JAMESON

You're awake. You must feel haggard. My last few test subjects barely survived past thirty-six hours.

(Mia rolls her head, attempting to speak around tubes.)

JAMESON
Allow me.

Jameson reaches into frame, yanking tubes free, leaving Mia choking on bile and raw panic. She gropes the writhing bandages atop her head.

MIA
W-what…did you do?

JAMESON

What you deserve. Females, animals, objects, you exist to serve your God. Yet you wasted no time, Wife, seducing your little journalist. You drip sex like venom. Even now, you ache for love, don't you? Makes a man wonder if the allegations you made back in Hollywood were even true.

MIA

You're a monster.

JAMESON

And what're you?

Jameson begins unwrapping Mia's bandages, around and around. A trembling forked tongue flickers from beneath.

JAMESON

I'm curious, Wife, what did your little journalist say to you in that pizzeria? To make you turn back and kiss him? The video I saw didn't have audio.

(Mia smiles dimly, wetting chapped, scaly lips.)

MIA

"Turned her to hideous shapes. Yet if she please… She can boast unrivaled grace in these…"

JAMESON

We'll see.

Mia's bandage uncoils and a viper drops loose, limp, and hissing its dying mortal breaths.

DIGITAL VIDEO LOG

Proto-Gorgon Trial #3

Timestamp 11/14/18, 3:07 a.m.–3:21 a.m.

Unbandaged, Mia sits propped up on the surgical table. Slitted eyes, parched and scaly skin, shaved head. Jagged, half-dead eyelash vipers dangle from her inflamed, infected scalp, stitched with crooked sutures. Forked tongues flicker dimly. Jameson steps into screen and grabs a fistful of snakes, uses them to hold up Mia's slumping head. She weeps in pain.

JAMESON

Look at yourself. Maybe I should be merciful, sever your glorious head? Present my trophy to your lover. How's that for "Divine Retribution"?

MIA

Go to hell.

JAMESON

Ladies first.

Jameson thrusts Mia away and flees the screen, footsteps vanishing behind the sound of elevator doors. Alone, Mia stares into the camera, absorbing her serpentine reflection. Limp, beady-eyed nightmares frame her face with florescent colors and spiked superciliary scales.

Mia weeps prayers under her breath, the names of countless victims and their countless monsters, brittle poetics, unintelligible curses. She sinks ever deeper into the toxin-bruised gaze of the woman she's become, into the gaze of all women. And in the space between, inside mortal sockets and serpentine skulls, her eyes ignite with a diabolical light.

One by one, her snakes twitch and thrash, revivified, rising in waves like static-kissed hair, hot bloodlines and cold bloodlines mingling in discordant harmony. They curl in on themselves, sinewy, divine. Their fangs hook her exquisite cheekbones, her all-seeing eyelids, dripping venom, infusing her with the outrage of the ages. Sibilant hisses swell ever louder, dozens, then hundreds, thousands, haunted voices striking at the air. Green static crackles across the video screen. Something hideously lovely glows within Mia, radiating indignant fire. Peering into the camera, she stretches a gorgeous rictus smile and hisses her husband's name.

IPHONE VIDEO FOOTAGE

Timestamp 11/14/18, 4:23 a.m.–4:36 a.m.

The video opens on a misty predawn field of charred long-grass. Hulking silhouettes of a barn and farmhouse loom in the near distance. Faint green light emanates from the barn. Footsteps crunch as the cameraman hurries across the field.

VOICE OF JAKE PHOENIX

If found, give this video to the police and the *Manhattan Post*. This is Jake Phoenix, searching for my close friend Mia Doukas. She's been missing for a week. I've traced receipts for the purchase of live snakes and reports of arson to the abandoned Thompson Cattle Ranch in Smithtown, Vermont, what I believe is the off-site laboratory of Mia's husband, Dr. Jameson Knox. I believe Mia is being held against her will and is in mortal danger. There's a light ahead.

The scenery jostles as Jake rushes toward wide-open barn doors. Ancient cattle corrals form the barn's dilapidated wooden innards. Nearby, a glowing green doorway leads to what was once a feed storage room. Inside, a green light bulb illuminates a nondescript elevator door and a key-card reader.

JAKE

I knew it.

Muttering a prayer, Jake swipes a key card through the reader. A buzzing pause, then the reader clicks, red to green. The elevator door slides open. Jake steps inside, camera view aligning toward a control panel. One button points up, one points down. Jake chooses down.

JAKE

Coming for you, Mia…

The elevator opens, revealing a shadowy operating room and a surgical table splashed in blood. Nests of golden hair litter the floor.

JAKE

The aftermath of some kind of surgery, or slaughter. Holy good God…

Across the lab, another doorway glows green. The camera approaches, hesitates on the threshold. Beyond, an animal holding facility floats in soupy green light. Steel cages and glass aquariums line both walls. The camera zooms inside an aquarium, glinting off the twisting emerald curves of snake-shaped statues. The haunted light flickers from the far corner, where the camera catches blurry movement behind the cages.

JAKE

Mia? Is that you?

VOICE OF MIA DOUKAS

Don't look at us!

Mia's words resonate oddly in the camera's microphone, creating echoey, hissing feedback, casting the impression of many voices speaking at once. Static fizzles the screen.

JAKE

I'm here to help you.

The camera drifts closer to a feminine silhouette standing backlit in the corner, facing the wall. Long shadows twist the laboratory and firefly pinpoints waver around her head—tiny, glowing eyes bending toward him.

MIA

Stay back! We're our own hero. We have to be.

JAKE

What did he do to you?

MIA

What men do. Condemned us for his barbarism.

JAKE

I'll take you to a hospital.

Jake's hand appears, reaching for Mia as the camera view dips toward her bare feet, toes pointed toward the wall. The hissing rises.

MIA

Sssstop! You're smarter than this. Look around you. Truly look. There's no undoing what's been done to us.

JAKE

"Yet if she please… She can boast unrivaled grace in these…"

MIA

You're a noble friend, Jake. Don't die in this temple tonight. If you want to help, then amplify our voices…

JAKE

But, Mia—

MIA

Go!

Mia's bare feet begin a slow-twisting turn. The scenery blurs as the camera backs away from the insidious tendrils of her silhouette, flaring neon-green before fizzling to black.

DR. JAMESON KNOX

Private security video surveillance, 11/14/18

Timestamp 7:58: The footage is bisected into four sections. The first three hiss with slithery green static. The final view holds on a marble foyer. The front door bursts inward. Mia enters wearing a sleek gown of iridescent scales and a magnificent crown of vipers. Tangled muscles, forked-tongues, her snakes cascade past slender hips. She holds her heavy head high, radiant gaze hidden by a living blindfold of serpents. Still, she walks boldly, guided by grace and myriad interconnected eyes. Static zigzags the screen as she glides toward the staircase.

Timestamp 7:59: The camera sizzles neon-green, flash-cutting to a view of the staircase. Mia glides upward, framed by her halo of serpents, fluid voices reviling countless names in one.

MIA

Jamesssson…

Timestamp 8:00: In the upstairs hallway, the double-doors blow inward. The screen crackles, shifting again as Mia invades the master bedroom. Jameson stands bedside in bloodstained scrubs, one hand thrust deep in his pocket, one cradling an iPad. He tightens his oily smile, watching this surveillance feed with a male gaze, keeping his eyes downcast, refusing to look directly at Mia. Refusing to see what he created.

JAMESON

What took you so long, Wife? Grieving your lost hero?

MIA

We see you, Jamesssson… We see what your kind does to us…

JAMESON

You did this to yourself.

Timestamp 8:01: Mia's vipers roil, a tempest of furious susurration. Casting wavery shadows, she glides across the bedroom. Jameson sidles away, measuring his distance, keeping his head down, performing his own slithery dance. Mia and her snakes expel a chorus of forked-tongued laughter, a multitude of sibilant voices.

MIA

Little, slippery man, cowering behind shields… Like the countless many who slithered before him…

(Jameson continues backing away.)

JAMESON

You think I fear you? I created you in my image. Look at yourself! Perfectly phallic!

MIA

No, look at you! See inside us, feel what we feel…

Timestamp 8:02: Electricity jolts across the bisected screen, emblazing every panel with tendril-surges of jagged neon. The fourth screen vibrates. Mia's ophidian silhouette blooms, elongates, hissing open like a hand of too many fingers, reaching for Jameson. The man's smug expression pales. Still, he refuses to look up at her. Mia glides closer, divine extensions of herself poised to strike, prey becoming predator. Jameson shrinks, thighs bumping the mattress. His hand shifts inside his pocket.

JAMESON

You belong on your knees!

Timestamp 8:03: Jameson yanks a bubbling syringe from his pocket. Mia's vipers lash out, hooking fangs into his wrist and coiling around the syringe, immobilizing his vile, groping hands, sinking venom and voices into his unctuous soul. Thousands, millions, billions, rising up as a furious chorus of one. *Note: The audio here is vastly layered—attempts to isolate individual narratives reveal a staggering stratum of voices, each unique, each conveying its own trauma, but each pierced with the same through-line.

MIA and INESTIMABLE VOICES OVERLAPPING

Your reign ends now!

Timestamp 8:04: Amid a writhing nest of static, Mia faces Jameson, dragging him closer, piercing him, contorting his smirk into a scream, transmuting him from the inside out. The serpents unwind from Mia's eyes and her furious gaze blazes open. Jameson tries to twist his head away, tries to squelch his eyes in blind shame, but snakes force his chin up and needle-fangs pierce his eyelids open, poisoning him with the agony of eons. He stares into Mia's collective, reflective gaze, seizing on his own toxic atrocities. The bisected security screens, those omnipresent leering eyes, flare an acidic green, and all four surveillance feeds blister away and cut to black, scorched by divine retribution.

MANHATTAN POST

Vigilante Viper Strikes Again! Seventh Acquitted Man Found Petrified and Headless, Neurotoxin Present

by Jake Phoenix

NEW YORK CITY—February 14, 2019—The Vigilante Viper's seventh victim was discovered in his apartment Wednesday night. What remained of Victor Reynolds, 46, was a headless corpse posed in a state of extreme calcification.

An autopsy revealed significant amounts of an ophidian-derived neurotoxin in Reynolds's system. Known colloquially as the Medusa Toxin, when administered via several injection sites (similar to snake bites), the neurotoxin acts as a paralyzing agent, calcifying living tissue and hardening muscles and organs. Reportedly, Reynolds's stony skin displayed a scaly jewel-toned appearance. His decapitated head has yet to be recovered. Investigators theorize the Vigilante Viper collects them as trophies.

While searching the scene of Reynolds's death, police discovered other trophies: explicit Polaroids linking Reynolds to a 2007 date rape case for which he was acquitted. This continues a palpable trend in these murders. All seven of the Vigilante Viper's targets, seemingly unrelated and diverse in background, share one disturbing detail in common.

They were acquitted of sexual assault.

In all seven cases, the accusers' rape kits were deemed inadmissible due to improper police storage. The kit in Reynolds's case was one of seven hundred kits thrown out in Mariposa County alone. The mishandling of rape kits and stigmatization of assault victims is unfortunately a widespread trend throughout the country.

The case of the Vigilante Viper's first target, Herbert Bridgestone, was no exception.

The producer and director of *Hot Night in Sin City*, Bridgestone was accused of sexually assaulting his lead actress after drugging her beverage during a private pre-screening of their movie. Despite the rape kit being inadmissible, evidence against Bridgestone included photos of his accuser, taken post-assault, that depicted graphic bruises and patches of scalp where her hair had been torn out. Regardless, Bridgestone was acquitted. Many who opposed the verdict speculated that his high status in the film industry won him favor with the jury. Like Reynolds and the Vigilante Viper's other targets, after his death, evidence was found in Bridgestone's Manhattan vacation penthouse which retroactively pointed to his guilt, including bags of the date rape drug Rohypnol. Bridgestone's calcified, headless corpse was discovered in November 2018, after he failed to appear on the *Late Show* to promote his latest movie.

Despite an increased police presence and bristling unease amid a certain breed of male, the Vigilante Viper's pattern of brutal attacks has shown no sign of slowing. Police remain on high alert, hoping to protect further men from similar gruesome fates. Several local men, with and without criminal backgrounds, expressed everything from severe anxiety to an enraged sense of injustice. One man, wishing to remain anonymous, said: "I've never met a dude who'd harm a woman. It's a witch-hunt these days. All that #MeToo propaganda. We live in a society where all men are now guilty until proven innocent."

Conversely, the sentiments from local women run along opposite spectrums. When asked how they felt about the Vigilante Viper remaining at large, women living near the attacks expressed relief.

"The Viper's a shadow in the darkness," said Melanie, 29. "And for once, that darkness is working in our favor."

"It's maddening how many of these perpetrators go unpunished," said Zahra, 22. "But the Viper sees them."

"The justice system wasn't created to honor women's safety or respect victims," said Sonya, 33. "This is about reclaiming our power."

"Every woman has a story," said Vera, 47. "The Viper is helping us rewrite the ending."

Investigations into the Vigilante Viper's identity remain ongoing, and authorities implore anyone with information to come forward. Until then, it seems countless men will sleep a little less easy tonight. Check back daily for more details as this story continues to unfold.

STATION 99

THREE WEEKS AFTER my big brother ditched out on me, I raid his bedroom. Screw him if he thinks he can abandon me in this hell-house with nothing but stale memories and our asshole dad's absentee parenting. I pick Theo's lock with a paperclip and invade the ghost-weed funk of his private domain. Bikini posters, his ghetto blaster, his collection of heavy metal mixtapes. I haul it all down to my basement bedroom and heap it atop the cobwebby boxes of our dead mom's things. I even snag Theo's 13-inch black-and-white TV, with the tinfoil bunny ears.

He warned me if I ever touched it, he'd knock my teeth through my skull. Supposedly, if he tweaks the knobs and bunny ears just right, he can dial in the Playboy channel. I've personally only ever seen him manage a staticky sitcom. But whatever. I swipe the TV anyway and set it on a cardboard box near the foot of my bed. Its bulky glass-and-steel weight bows the cardboard, but that's cool. Maybe part of me *hopes* it'll collapse and smash to pieces. Just like Theo shattered our whole stupid brotherhood.

I mean, he didn't even say goodbye.

I pop a knob on the television, and a static snowstorm fills the screen. *Click, click, click.* No matter how far I twist the dial, no *Playboy* channel appears. Not even a bad sitcom. Just static—and I know what happens to morons who stare into staticky TVs. I've seen *Poltergeist*, I'm no scab. I've caught every ghost show, freak show, creep show there is, thanks to our favorite late-night horror hosts.

Svengoolie, Dr. Creep, Elvira, Mistress of the Dark.

Theo and I used to watch them together. Not on this crappy black-and-white heap. But on the TV in the family room, years ago, before Mom went drunk driving and Dad stopped paying the cable bill. Theo loved the cheesy slashers, and I dug anything with zombies.

Frustrated, I snap his television off. It's getting late, and *I've* still got school tomorrow. My usual lonely routine. I nuke a TV dinner, then crawl into bed with the dismal taste of meatloaf in my mouth. I shed my eyeglasses and sink into the basement's boxy cobweb shadows, staring foggy-eyed out the window. Where's Theo crashing tonight? Somewhere in the city on some rock star wannabe's couch? Some sleazy hotel with his headbanger girlfriend?

Who knows? Dad doesn't care. Wasn't even gonna report Theo missing until I threatened to do it. Then he badmouthed him the whole time—shitty grades, no respect for authority. The cops agreed, runaway punks were a dime a dozen, Theo and his crush were typical rowdy seventeen-year-olds. They said he'd come home when he got hungry enough, or cold enough, or bored enough.

But three weeks and not even a secret phone call while Dad's working graveyard to tell me he's fine, having a blast. Not so much as a postcard swearing to take me with him one day.

I grit my eyes closed, ignore the pit in my guts until darkness drags me into empty dreams. Painless nothingness.

Feels like a thousand hours later when Theo calls my name.

"Jeremy, dammit, wake up!" His voice crackles.

I grunt into my pillow, pulling myself up from the muck of unconsciousness. Theo brought a lantern, like when we used to camp in the woods behind our house. My bedroom flickers with dull gray light. I fumble for my eyeglasses, but the nightstand's empty.

"Jeremy, it knows us…"

What knows us?

"Dad's gonna pulverize you," I mumble, sitting up, bangs mopping my blurry eyesight. "Where've you been?"

Theo doesn't answer.

I squint at the foot of my bed, at the greasy fog-light of his lantern.

Only, it's not a lantern. His television is on.

Oh balls, I'm dead. "Look, Theo, I'm sorry. You were gone so long…" The excuse fizzles. I squint at the flickering shadow-shapes of my sunken bedroom.

"Theo?"

"Jeremy!" Voice metallic, echoing from the television. *"It gets inside…"*

This has to be a nightmare.

Shadows swirl inside the TV's buzzing light. Blurry-eyed, I practically press my nose to the glass. Static lightning-bolts across the screen, manifesting an eerie smooth-faced creature. No eyes, no mouth, no nose. Just bony limbs and spiky shoulders hunched like an emaciated gargoyle over a white-neon station logo.

Station 99.

The gargoyle-thing tilts its head as if locking that faceless gaze on me.

"Stay tuned for the *Video Macabre*, Jeeerrreeemmmyyy…"

I jerk backwards at the growl of my name. Static rushes the screen, flickering oblivion, and Theo's voice shouts out, crackling, filling with static. *"She's dead… Collette's dead… Blood everywhere…! Jeremy!"*

Before I can unchoke my idiot terror long enough to scream, *What's happening? Where is he? Who the hell is Collette?*—the television sparks and cuts to black.

"STATION 99?" HEATHER Gibson says the next day. We're ditching sixth period, loitering in the ancient tennis courts behind the high school. She flicks a cigarette at me. "You're full of it. Cable channels don't go that high."

"Didn't say it was a cable channel." I lean against the chain link fence, bone-deep exhausted from thinking about this. But I can't stop. "It was something else. A prank. I don't know. But that was Theo's voice. I know it was."

"Maybe he rigged a VCR?"

"There's no VCR. It's just a clunker, some off-brand TV from like the '60s."

Heather scrapes spiky pink bangs aside and lights another menthol. "What about airtime on public access? You said Theo wants to be a rock star."

"A lead singer, yeah." I cough out a laugh. "He's not really any good. But, yeah, maybe that's it."

"Totally. A trippy hardcore opening to some rock video." Heather sucker-punches my arm. "Don't look so gloomy. Your brother's practically famous."

"I guess."

Awkward silence descends. I stare at her steel toe boots. She's cute, in an edgy way. Kinda punk rock and stylish like the girls Theo dates—like girls on MTV. We've hung out off and on since freshman year started, almost three months now. Some days, I get the feeling she likes me, like in *that* way. But I've never made a move. Too afraid to blow it. Afraid if I did, Theo would rib me for shooting above my horizons. Stupid to care what a guy who became a dropout thinks.

"So," Heather says, "who's Collette anyway?"

"His girlfriend, I think."

"You don't know his girlfriend's name?"

I shrug. "He has so many. Anyway, Collette isn't the one he ran away with. That's Amy Sanchez. I think… I think Collette might be Collette Johnson. Some of Theo's friends told me she went missing two nights ago. Her parents went on the evening news and everything."

"Wait, what?" Heather stops smiling. "If she's with Theo, you gotta tell the cops."

"I don't know for sure she's with Theo. It's just something my television said."

"Your television said she's dead. Dude, Jeremy, this is too freaky."

"Maybe I dreamed it."

"Still freaky." Heather flicks her cigarette. "I gotta get to last period."

"That's cool." Wishing I was edgier, wishing I was someone else, I adjust my glasses. Found them under my bed after Theo's television went black. "But hey, will you ask around? See if anyone's heard of Station 99?"

"Or the *Video Macabre*?" Heather does her worst Svengoolie, then clears her throat with an apology. "I'll see what I can find out."

NINE O'CLOCK. EVERY light in my empty house blazes. My TV dinner congeals on the coffee table in the family room. Should've manned up before sundown. Except, the second I got home, I swore I felt Theo's television in the basement, waiting for me. My bones locked up like picture tubes and steel. All I had the balls for was uneaten meatloaf on the couch, television dark.

Now, I force myself to confront our 32-inch color Zenith. There's a remote, but I think Station 99 prefers dials. I hit the power. Color ignites the screen, a rerun of *Family Ties*. I twist the dial, watching the station numbers flicker past. Without basic cable, ghost-static ices the higher channels, but I keep twisting.

67... 73... 78...

Heartbeat rioting... 81... Static buzzing... 83...

The Zenith cycles back to channel 2.

The nine o'clock news.

I'm about to keep going, one more spin around the tilt-o-whirl of madness, but a familiar name stabs my ears.

"…missing Chester High senior Collette Johnson was discovered this afternoon beneath a city offramp. Police aren't disclosing the nature of her death, but witnesses describe disturbing amounts of blood… *Blood everywhere…*"

The newscaster's voice buzzes surreal between my ears.

I stagger into the kitchen and rip the phone off the hook. But who do I call? Heather? Never asked for her number. Dad at his graveyard shift? The cops? And say what? Theo's freaky, possessed television predicted this?

They'll blame him, and Theo didn't do this. No way. *No way*.

I end up pacing the kitchen, back and forth until exhaustion blurs my brain. Need some sleep already.

I approach the basement stairs, chewing my coward lip. The stairwell stretches like a jagged nightmare-throat down to the dank belly of my bedroom. I swipe the light switch. The light bulb hanging at the murky bottom stays murky. Of course it does.

I push my glasses higher. Longer I stare, the more I think I see the dimmest ghost-flicker of gray light down there. Theo? …*Collette?*

"Screw this." I slam the basement door. I'll crash on the couch tonight.

"JEREMY, WAKE UP!"

Theo's voice crackles along the shadow-sticky edges of my mind. I sit up, blinking against murky gray light, and fumble for my glasses on the coffee table.

Only, I'm not on the couch. Where—

My hand knocks my bedside lamp.

It topples, but the gray light remains. The light at the foot of my bed.

Theo's television. Glowing with black-and-white smudges, voices buzzing like corpse-flies. *"Blood everywhere…!"*

"Theo? Where are you!" I skitter closer, jam my blurry vision against the screen.

The gargoyle-thing station logo lurks in a test-pattern sea of starless night.

Station 99.

Please stand by...

The words echo my gummy vision.

The gargoyle-thing straightens from its bony crouch.

Static zigzags, and a rolling movie reel fills the screen, counting down... 3... 2...

The gargoyle-thing reappears.

Looks almost 3D now, live-action. Fish-pale, bald, facing the camera with its featureless face. That fleshy void gapes at me. No mouth, no nose, ribbons of 35mm film blindfold its eyes.

"Welcome back, Jeeerrreeemmmyyy, to Station 99's *Video Macabre!*"

It spreads sharp-nailed hands, and the camera pans out to reveal a haunted graveyard soundstage. Fog-machine mist swirls between balsa-wood coffins and Styrofoam tombstones. Skeletons bask in dangling cardboard moonlight. Just like the campy, low-rent set-ups used by Elvira and Svengoolie.

"Now, lonesome fright fan..." The gargoyle-thing's chin bobs, a muffled meat-puppet voice. "I bring you the blood-soaked conclusion to *Camp Slash-Away*, starring Theo Romero and Amy Sanchez!"

Theo? *Camp Slash-Away*? But I know that movie.

The one about Claw Face, the undead hiker maniac who got mauled by a grizzly while his fellow campers escaped to safety. For revenge, dude shreds every teenager in his woods with steel bear claws.

In a lightning-slash of static, Station 99's graveyard soundstage cuts to a forest. Trees careen past the camera, the shaky perspective of someone running for their life. A smear of log cabins, an archery range. I know this scene! Theo and I watched it a hundred times. This is where the last camper standing runs to the boathouse and grabs the harpoon. She's gonna spear Claw Face's eyeball with it—then with a ropy twist and yank of optic nerves, she'll rip out his undead brain! We used to cheer every time. The gross-out effects freaking rock.

But as the camera hard-cuts to the boathouse door slamming open, something's off. The wall of rusty tools and the old rowboat creaking on the water are the same. But the lean-mean camp counselor with the blood-matted blond curls and the shredded Camp Wickery Woods T-shirt isn't any of those things.

She's Amy Sanchez.

Even in black-and-white, I recognize her. My brother's girlfriend. Spiky Joan-Jett hair, heavy tear-streaked eyeliner. Instead of yanking the harpoon off the wall, Amy climbs into the rowboat.

"Amy, no!" I shout at the television. "You gotta get the harpoon!"

She doesn't hear me. She grabs an oar, not realizing the boat is roped to the dock, not realizing oars are no match for Claw Face.

A hulking shadow fills the boathouse door.

B-movie moonlight spotlights inky bloodstains on hiking boots and jogging shorts and the meaty scars streaking the maniac's twisted face.

My *brother's* face.

I grip the television, but shit! I jerk away—the metal is red hot!

On-screen, Theo surveys the boathouse, steel bear claws glinting from both fists as he steps inside.

He takes his time stalking toward Amy.

"Theo, what the hell?" I cry. And so does Amy.

"Theo!" she begs, trying to wave him off with her oar. "Fuck's sake, snap out of it!"

He catches her oar mid-swing and yanks it away. Violins shriek as he tosses it aside and slashes out with his claws, inches from Amy's horror-struck face.

"Theo, stop!" I shout.

"Jeremy...it knows us!" His ghost voice echoes the air-waves, but his mouth never moves. Flat, expressionless, a meat-puppet silently calling me. He swipes at Amy again. She recoils, screaming, rocking the rowboat. This time his blades graze her chin. Dark wet gashes.

This has to be a joke. A public access *gotcha* he cooked up to torment me for snatching his things.

"Jeremy..." His voice crackles, static-choked inside my spiraling ears. *"Station 99... It gets inside..."*

"Somebody!" Amy turns in a frantic escape-crouch, aiming to dive into the water.

Theo overshadows the rowboat, spreads his arms, and punches both bladed fists into the sides of Amy's throat.

A slash of Technicolor-red paints the screen.

Impossible gore, impossible color. Blood sizzles against the glass. This can't be real, I fumble the coal-hot television knobs, trying to dial back my sanity.

Click, click, click...

Every station is Station 99.

Theo hoists Amy from the boat, clamping her between his claws. She gurgles, gagging up neon blood before slumping into the boat with a grisly splash.

She's dead! *Blood everywhere!* This can't be real!

I punch the on/off button—again, again. Nothing happens.

Theo's television won't turn off!

I tumble off my mattress, skitter toward the outlet, reach for the plug.

"Don't unplug it!" Theo's voice again. At least, I think it's Theo's voice. Strangled vocals, choking on static. *"That's how it gets you..."*

I drop the plug and confront the TV. "What do I do? Theo!"

But the station logo is back. Not black-and-white, but grisly red. The gargoyle-thing hunches over Station 99, watching me without eyes. *Knowing me...*

It twitches, starts to stand.

I back away, letting my crappy eyesight fog the screen.

A feedback screech of laughter fractures the glass, hatching gruesome light into the real world.

High up, the basement window shatters.

A faceless shadow crouches inside.

MY BONES LOCK up, icy steel, frozen picture tubes. I watch the nightmare shadow crawl through my window.

"Little help?"

I exhale a ragged, gut-deep breath. "Heather?"

"Sorry about the window." She kicks away teeth of broken glass with her steel-toe boots, then dips her face back in the gap. "Looked you up, saw your light on. Swear I only tapped the glass. To get your attention."

She has it.

"You gonna help me down or what?"

"Oh, yeah." I snap from my daze and scramble over. She spreads her leather jacket across the jagged window edge. Heather freaking Gibson. Any other night this would be the wildest dream come true.

I grip her midnight-cool hands, then absorb her weight as she pops down, landing like a punk-rock ninja.

She ruffles the hair out of my eyes. "Did I wake you?"

"No, I was just watching—oh hell, Heather, *look*. Channel 99..."

But Theo's television stands dark.

Dark, silent. Screen uncracked.

"Shit." I fiddle the knobs, but the television stays dead. "I'm not messing with you. Feel, the screen's still hot. I swear, it was just on."

I tell her everything. The faceless gargoyle-thing, *Camp Slash-Away*, Amy and Theo with his dripping steel bear claws. Let it all gush out like a hacked-up jugular. I sound deranged like in the movies, those loopy town drunks nobody ever listens to. But if I don't puke it out, it'll fester inside, and Station 99 is already taking up so much space. It gets inside...

"Holy shit," Heather says when I'm done.

"I get it if you don't believe me."

"No." She stares at her lamplit reflection in Theo's television. "I think I might. Listen, Jeremy, Collette Johnson is dead. Like, *really* dead."

"I know." I swallow miserably. "Saw it on the news."

"I asked around," she says. "Station 99 and the *Video Macabre* were dead ends. Not even the geeks at the video store have heard of it. But there *is* something. A girl I know in Collette's art class told me Collette said she needed to get a jacket back from one of her exes. That was two days ago. What if she meant Theo? What if she came here, and Theo intercepted her somehow?"

"No. *No.*" I jerk to my feet, start pacing. "Theo wouldn't do that."

"He's no rock star," Heather says. "What if he decided to be a movie star instead? Only something went wrong. He tried recreating his favorite horror movie, but a death scene got out of hand. After that, maybe things just snowballed."

"You're wrong, you don't know him. Theo wears a hardcore shell, but he'd never hurt anyone."

"You just watched him rip out Amy Sanchez's throat."

"That wasn't him. It was…"

"Who? Claw Face? *Reel Head?*"

"Who?"

"Reel Head." Heather winks at the TV. "The station mascot with the 35mm blindfold? We gotta call it something."

"Yeah, I guess." I swallow thickly. "Theo said it knows us."

"Knows you *how?*"

"Not sure…" The television's square eye gleams at me, reflecting our silhouettes. "Like when you look into it, it looks into you."

Heather folds her arms, tries to conceal a shiver—or a laugh. "Listen, before we get all slippery with theories, we need proof Collette even came here."

"Proof how?"

"Where's Theo's bedroom?"

Upstairs, we pick the lock on Theo's door. Heather hits the light, and I cringe, half-expecting to find Theo sitting in the dark. The room's empty.

"Maybe Collette snuck through the window?" Heather creeps inside, wrinkling her nose at Theo's heavy metal residue. "He just left it like this?"

"Didn't even take his mixtapes." *Station 99 doesn't let you pack...* But I don't say the crazy part out loud. This surreal MTV dream girl, stealing my breath with her friendship and keen, smoky eyes, already thinks I'm bonkers enough.

Atop Theo's dresser, a dust-free square marks the spot his television occupied just two days ago. Nearby, Heather pokes her toe through tangles of dirty laundry and unearths a jacket. The collar sparkles with purple sequins. "Guessing this isn't Theo's?"

I stare at it, vision throbbing with invisible static. "Doesn't mean anything. Maybe it's Amy's or...or... *Dammit!*" I hunch over, fighting a gutful of sick. Not every night your dream girl proves your brother's a psycho killer.

"Hey, it's cool..." She rubs my back. "We're both a little freaked."

"Yeah." I straighten, try to look less spineless. "So, what now? Rat him out to the cops?"

She holds my eyes, doesn't let me flinch. "You think that's why I'm here?"

Isn't it? Our awkward silence again, dreamlike, invading Theo's bedroom like static on a television, growing bigger, buzzing my heartbeat, stealing my voice. Heather bites her lip.

Oh hell, what am I doing? I shadow in and kiss her.

And she kisses me back. I swear she does. Soft but with bite, tastes like cherry lipstick and X-rated daydreams. Except suddenly, she's shoving me away.

I start to apologize for being an idiot, for shooting above my horizon, but she clamps my chin between spiky fingernails and angles my face toward the bedroom window.

Red light sprays the glass, then a splash of blue.

Red, blue, red, blue.

The cops are out there.

SOMETHING'S HAPPENING IN the woods behind my house. We watch in eerie silence from Theo's bedroom window, our bleak faces pulsing with a red-blue heartbeat.

Cops use yellow tape to cordon off the trees where Theo and I used to camp. While Heather squeezes my sweaty hand, a coroner's van pulls between the cop cars, stopping slantwise in the weeds. Officers escort the rubber-aproned coroner into the forest, and soon camera flashes ignite the skeletal silhouettes of trees. They're photographing the crime scene. Can't see the body from here, but we both know.

It's Amy Sanchez.

"They're gonna come looking for him," I say. "Any second now, they'll knock on my door. And what do I say? I saw it, Heather. I saw him kill her."

She squeezes my hand. "We tell them the truth."

I cough out a sick laugh. "What truth? That Reel Head made him do it?"

"C'mon." She tugs me back down into the dim throat of my bedroom. She kneels between my bed and the cardboard box propping up Theo's television. Tiny hesitation, then she punches the button. The screen erupts with static. "Looks like it's working now."

"What're you doing?"

"What do you think?" She twists the knob, station after station of snow. With every *click*, my spine shivers, my nerves turn brittle.

"Maybe you should stop," I whisper, like it can't already hear everything we say and think and are.

"Stop?" *Click, click...* "If I witness Station 99, too, we'll have a solid lead. It's gotta be airing from a soundstage somewhere, right?"

Still sounds like she wants to turn my brother in. But that's cool. Feels like I checked out hours ago, just a morbid spectator watching all this from the comfort of unreality. Heather thinks Station 99 is a place the cops can just *find*? Like with K-9s and SWAT teams?

She wheels through empty channels... *click, click, click...* like Russian roulette.

Nothing happens.

I listen for Theo in the static.

Click, click… A combination lock she just can't crack. *Click-click-click!* Growing hectic. Are those faces in the snow? Faceless faces, seeking eyes to fill?

"Stupid thing!" Heather kicks the cardboard box.

The ancient, rotted cardboard crumples, and Theo's television pitches face-first onto my concrete floor.

The screen shatters, sparks, dashes of lightning, a thousand glass pebbles scatter outward like cockroaches.

"Theo!" I cry. A bat-shit reaction, and I know it. Heather backs away, crunching broken glass as I hoist the shattered TV upright.

"God, sorry," she says. "Guess I don't know my own—"

She cuts short.

The television's fine.

We both saw it shatter, can still see the evidence scattered across the floor.

But the television gleams at us, good as new.

The Station 99 logo glows inside phantom static.

Please stand by…

WE PERCH ON my bed, knee to trembling knee, waiting for who the hell knows what.

Heather decided we shouldn't stare directly into the Station 99 logo, so now she grips my clammy hand and side-eyes the basement clutter. My dead mom's boxes, shadow-deep, littered with Theo's abandoned things. "This is where you sleep?"

I shrug. "Theo and I used to share a bedroom. He grew out of me, that's all. It's not so bad."

"It's just…" Heather chews her lip.

"Just what?"

"Your whole identity seems buried down here."

I flinch, can't help it. "Sorry I'm such a faceless nobody."

"That's not what I meant."

"Yeah, but you're right. It's like with everyone gone, I don't know who I am."

The static glow ripples across Heather's gorgeous, accepting face. I still can't figure out what she's doing here, middle of the night, with a haunted television and a killer on the loose, manifesting like an apparition I wished for and got.

"You're my dream guy." And she kisses me, lips red velvet. *Heather Gibson kisses me.*

This time, there's no wondering if I overshot.

We clutch each other and go deep, cherry lightning, letting tonight's tension unravel with every kiss. Wild gravity pulls us to the mattress and—

"Welcome back, Jeeerrreeemmmyyy, to the *Video Macabre!*"

Wide-eyed, Heather and I sit slowly upright. The gargoyle-thing with the 35mm blindfold waves hello from Station 99's graveyard soundstage.

"Holy shit." Heather grips my arm.

"Told you."

"Your old pal *Reel Head* here," it says, flesh-mouth twitching. "Back from the shattered grave to continue tonight's dreadful double feature! You just witnessed the throat-gushing new conclusion of *Camp Slash-Away*. Now… Which *fright*-mare from the void will thrill you next?"

"Reel Head?" Heather says. "I just made that up."

A wheel of misfortune appears on-screen like a game show. A different movie title labels each spiderweb spoke. "Ready for a spin?"

A thrust of Reel Head's bony hand, a black-and-white spiral. *Click, click, click…*

The wheel slows.

The Blob… Chopping Mall… Ghoulies…

Click…click.

Night of the Headbangers.

The one where toxin-dosing zombies infect a rock concert—I used to love this one.

Reel Head claps its pale bony hands. "Ladies and not-so-gentle-men, I give you *Night of the Headbangers*, starring Jeremy Romero and Heather Gibson. Live and *in pieces!*"

"No, *no way*." Heather jerks to her feet. "This is fucked up, Jeremy. Turn it off."

I try, just to show her I tried, punch the on/off button again, again. But it won't turn off. Is this how Theo and his girlfriends felt right before Station 99 took them? An electric sort of inevitability. It crackles in Heather's frantic gray eyes.

She lunges for the power cord, and I grab at her. Theo said to never unplug it, but she does anyway.

Blood-splashed lightning cracks like broken glass, zigzagging the basement. Heather shrieks my name.

She goes light-bright and skeletal.

Everything snaps to white. The air crackles. Thickens. Dims. Ears ringing, head twisting. The Station 99 logo sears my vision, then fades to ghostly afterimages.

All I sense is the concrete floor, a gray blur of movement. *Heather?* My mouth tastes meaty and metallic, coppery, like under-nuked meatloaf.

Somewhere nearby, Heather screams my name.

Lots of people are screaming. Movement. Chaos. Fog. Are the cops here? I blink again, and the patina of static clears. I raise my head.

Not cops. A rock concert.

I see Heather now, up there on the stage in the spotlight, hoisting an electric guitar.

A freak in a shredded concert T-shirt rushes the stage. Rushes Heather! She winds back and swings the guitar like an axe. As his grayscale head explodes in a pulp of neon red, it hits me. Oh hell.

Night of the Headbangers.

My mind bolts upright, sharpens. Rafters line the stage, and spotlights explode electricity, illuminating the toxin-dosed headbangers below. I've seen this scene a hundred times. Soon, a mob of frothing, gnashing zombies will storm the band and trap them backstage. Doesn't end well for them. Only the drummer and a groupie survive...

Because they climb the rafters instead!

No time to freeze. I have to get Heather up there, save her, break us out of this Station 99 hellscape. I shoulder past twitching, foaming headbangers, and scramble onstage. Every metalhead's dream. I angle for Heather, but the lead singer slashes my line of sight.

Alive, uninfected, and swinging his microphone stand like some off-brand Ozzy.

"Theo!" I try to scream it, but my voice froths with static.

But it's really him, and inside I expel a ragged sob.

My brother. Live and in person!

I rush over, reaching for him, barely noticing the toxic-black veins infecting my arms until I shadow Theo's spotlight and take hold.

"Jeremy, what the—" he cries, finally noticing me as I sink my teeth in. "Stop!"

Don't make me do this!

But Station 99 knows us… It gets inside.

And it makes me do it. Like a bony hand lodged gut-deep, protruding up through my throat, flapping my jaw, snapping my frothing, undead teeth.

Unable to stop, I chew out my brother's vocal cords with a meaty *rip*.

Blood sprays the black-and-white stage, staining the scenery red.

Blood everywhere.

Theo collapses in a gushing heap, a string-cut puppet. Tendons and meat. Will the cops match his wounds to my dental records? His unbelieving eyes lock on me as I crouch over him, ravenous, *so ravenous*. And I can't stop!

I devour. Even after the light snaps to black behind my big brother's eyes. Gnashing, frothing, screaming inside.

"Jeremy!"

A steel toe boot connects with my head, shatters the picture tube inside.

I pitch sideways, then lift my dripping maw, flesh lodged in my teeth. My toxin-sharp vision shivers, narrows on my brains-and-leather dream girl. Hate for her to see me like this.

I wanna wipe my mouth, but my arms don't respond, except to reach for her.

"Snap out of it, Jeremy! You know what Reel Head does." Heather cocks the gore-stained guitar overhead. "Damn it, Jeremy, fight it!"

"*I'm sorry!*" I try to scream, choking on static, teeth clicking. I can smell my mangled brother, my idol. The same blood infecting my veins pools around his head. I wanna spit.

This isn't who I am.

I shamble to my feet. Heather backs keenly away, wild to swing. Reminds me of the girls who survive gory movies. I hope she's seen this one. Hope she knows what she's gotta do.

"Jeremy? Please! Don't make me!"

Station 99 tightens its hold, bony fist flexing deep.

I try to fight its B-movie toxins—just like Theo tried. Closing in for one last kiss, meat-puppet teeth clicking, voice shouting on mute.

I was Heather Gibson's dream guy, I think as the guitar shatters my vision.

Blood, lightning. Static fills me.

My midnight creep show hard-cuts to black.

ATTACK OF MELVIN

AT 4:37 ON a Friday afternoon, deep in the basement laboratory of Elroy von Griffin, between plumes of indigo smoke and dazzles of lightning, the pink-and-blue goo inside his beaker achieves consciousness.

"*Glub-glub*," bubbles the pink-and-blue goo, which in Pink-and-Blue Goo translates to: "Hey Daddy-O, call me Melvin."

Having yet to pen the *Pink-and-Blue Goo to Human Translation Journal*, Elroy doesn't understand Melvin's gurgled hello. He taps the beaker and leans in close, and his jagged carrot-top fills Melvin's glass sky like bizarro lightning.

Eager as a newborn chick to impress his creator, Melvin sprouts a sticky tentacle and high-fives the glass.

Elroy—secretly known as Doctor von Vex ever since he started plotting diabolical revenge—sloshes the little guy around his beaker, whipping him into a gooey tornado, curious what he's got here. More tentacles squirt out and Melvin clings to the glass in a lousy attempt not to go all twisty-dizzy. The laboratory blurs into a whirl of wood-panel walls and sparkling elixirs and hazy, flickering light bulbs.

"Glub-glub," Melvin bubbles and burps, Pink-and-Blue Goo for: "Yikes, Daddy-O, not digging the whirly ride."

Doc rolls his eyes. "Not much of a terror, are you? No way is a little snot like you gonna intimidate my chem teacher." His disappointment haunts the laboratory—a saggy aura that absorbs deep into Melvin's effervescent pores.

In fact, all sorts of nifty tidbits about his creator have sunk in so far. Like how Doc longs to be feared and admired by all the rat bastards in town who spread vile rumors about his missing grandfather. And how, lately, he sits at his bedroom window and watches for footprints to dent the lawn—footprints that never appear. Melvin knows that three months ago, Gramps drank a frothy experimental serum then vanished from sight. *Poof! Eureka!*

That first invisible evening, Gramps paid a visit to the police chief and the mayor, made them think their closed-door meeting had a poltergeist. Spilling glasses of rare cognac, flipping furniture, taunting them with disembodied laughter. Hell, that night, Gramps paid haunted visits to several high-ranking mouth-breathers.

But he *didn't* sneak up and drown the high school lunch lady in a vat of secret sauce like Doc's half-baked chemistry teacher, Ivan Blackwell, claims. As evil super geniuses aiming to one day conquer the town—then the world!—Doc and Gramps only want the stuffed-shirt crooks and megalomaniacs to fall from grace. Melvin knows that doesn't include murdering the lonely old lunch lady in the middle of the night, bless her sloppy-Joe-making heart.

Another thing Melvin knows: it isn't normal—or particularly polite—to absorb secret knowledge from, *poof*, out of nowhere. But abnormal or not, Melvin can't help himself. Just like he can't help seeing without eyes or hearing without ears. Melvin wonders if this might be his evil super power.

He sure hopes so.

He's always wanted an evil super power.

Doc's an expert thanks to the antique film reels Gramps left behind after Blackwell and his mob hunted him into hiding. The creatures in those movies come jam-packed with evil powers. Enviable stuff like rising from the accursed tomb, wielding the strength of ten men, transforming into hideous beasts!

Not that absorbing secret knowledge isn't the cat's meow.

But having teeth and claws would be swell, too. Then Melvin would be able to wreak loads of havoc on Blackwell like Doc envisioned.

Deeper in the laboratory, a wolf howls. *"Ah-wooooo!"*

"Hey, it's the best part!" Doc grabs Melvin's beaker. "C'mon, you little ankle-biter, at least we can watch some flicks together."

The source of that shimmery, flickering light floats into Melvin's view.

"Gramps's movie projector," Doc says proudly. "This used to be his laboratory. While his serums brewed, we'd kill time watching old movies."

Melvin knows Gramps used to chatter on obsessively about his experiments, sometimes over the best parts of the flicks, but Doc never minded. Gramps taught him everything he knows.

"And this..." Doc plops onto Gramps's ratty old couch, giving Melvin a primo view of the screen. "This is *Claw of the Werewolf*. One of the first talkies ever made."

"Glub-glub!" Melvin suctions against his beaker, riveted by the old-fashioned gentleman who appears on-screen. The man wears a ruffle-necked shirt and clutches a severed wolf's paw. Above him, cottony storm clouds part like theater curtains, revealing a full moon. In stop-motion flashes, the claws on the cursed paw sharpen and elongate, and the gentleman rakes them across his chest!

"Watch this!" Doc leans forward. He always enjoys a good monstrous transformation. The movie screen jitters as stop-motion fur sprouts from the gentleman's hands and—

Something clatters deep in the laboratory.

Doc startles to his feet.

"Gramps?" Hugging Melvin's beaker, he squints past the projector at the antique crates near the back. A broom lies toppled on the floor nearby. "Gramps...?"

Nobody's there.

At least, it *looks* like nobody's there.

But Gramps is see-through, after all.

That first invisible night, minutes before Blackwell's mob swarmed their doorstep, Gramps announced himself by slamming Doc's chemistry book and spinning his soda bottle off the table. Gramps stood there, invisible but half-dripping in secret sauce. But before Doc could chuckle in amazement, Gramps clamped a cold, invisible hand around his wrist and started muttering about murder.

Truth is, that first invisible night, Gramps had snuck into the high school to spy on the secret serums and experiments of his arch nemesis, Ivan Blackwell. Instead, he stumbled upon everyone's favorite science teacher holding the limp lunch lady's head in a vat of spicy tomatoes. Gramps tried to help her and ended up painted in sauce. Blackwell wasted no time, ran shouting into the streets, pinned his two-faced crime on the incredible vanishing man and his dripping red hands.

Nobody believed Gramps was innocent on account of all his invisible mischief and schemes to rule the world. Even Doc's parents were fooled. Gramps cursed himself for flaunting his invisibility with frivolous pranks and swore he'd return to prove his innocence the instant he invented an antidote.

But that was three months ago.

"Gramps?" Doc studies the empty basement air. "I'm searching for an antidote, too. No luck yet—except *this* boogery little side effect." He swirls Melvin's beaker. "But I'm getting closer. Blackwell's gonna pay. Gramps…?"

Melvin stretches his sticky awareness throughout the basement and beyond. He senses the Friday evening drone of Doc's nuclear parents, upstairs. Doc's mother fusses over supper while his father smokes a pipe in the recliner. Both worry vaguely about the endless hours their teenage son spends in his madcap grandfather's laboratory instead of attending wholesome high school events, like the sock-hop his chemistry teacher is chaperoning tonight.

What they don't know is that Blackwell under-his-breath threatened to frame Doc for random crimes against humanity if he dares show his genius face tonight. Or any night.

As for Gramps? Melvin concentrates but detects zero sign of the incredible vanishing man.

"*Glub-glub,*" he burbles, sorry to give his creator more disappointing news. Bad enough Melvin makes such a lousy monster.

The laboratory door groans, and Mrs. von Griffin calls down, "Elroy, supper time!"

Doc groans, lifts Melvin to eye-level and stares in at him. Melvin bubbles attentively. "Sorry, little booger, you're on your own for a bit. Maybe later we'll work on transforming you into something more ferocious."

"*Glub-glub!*"

"Elroy, your meatloaf's getting cold!"

"Coming!" Doc sets Melvin in front of the projector light, then rushes upstairs.

And wowza, here's something straight outta coolsville:

As that flickering movie-scape shines through Melvin's effervescent insides, all seven ounces of his gooey persona light up with fangs and fur and moon-glow—all the wonderful wisdom *Claw of the Werewolf* has to teach him. Feral hunger, snarling chaos, mortal screams from those pesky pitchfork villagers…

The movie's gentleman—now a beast to be feared—rises from a crouch with meat and mayhem lodged between his teeth. "*Ah-wooooo!*"

Bubbling, bloating, sprouting spines of fur, Melvin's glowing pink-and-blue cells multiply at mutant speed. He fills the beaker to bursting, and the glass cracks like lightning. The beaker shatters and Melvin gushes outward, landing on the floor with a chunky *splat*. Writhing, squirming, he pulses and stretches into a veined membrane of furry flesh. Bones take shape, hardening into spine and legs and snouted skull.

The projector shines with the ferocity of a full moon.

And Melvin rises from a crouch and unleashes a gurbly howl.

"*Ah-wooooo!*"

THE FOREST RUSHES past. Shadowed fog parts in plumes before his snarling snout and loping speed. The full moon's gravity commands the tides of his lunacy, compelling him forward. His skull echoes with the meaty, beating dinner-call of hearts at dance beyond the mossy trees. He's forgotten his mission—he only wants to bite and snap and bray at the moon!

And here's something else unexpected:

Deep inside his wolf-torn physique, way back in the cowering corners of his jittery, gooey mindscape, Melvin's not so sure he digs being a wolf-person.

No offense to wolf-people, but they seem to lack self-control.

Sure, this beastly form has its perks. There's no denying his rabid animal ferocity. And all around, woodland creatures scurry in abject horror as he tears past.

But these woods are new to Melvin, haunted with curiosities. He'd love to absorb it all, stop and smell the wolfsbane. To the west, the trees stand against a lively prismatic back-glow. What marvelous phenomenon could be creating such colorful light out here? Melvin extends tendrils of perception westward just as his apex nose hones in on meat to the east. He pivots from the light, breaking through the eastern tree line onto a fog-drenched blacktop.

The parking lot of Mossy Forest Senior High.

The moon floats between wispy gray clouds, and a glowing rectangle marks the open door to the gymnasium and the sock-hop boppin'-and-a-rockin' inside. Poodle skirts and bow ties and juicy throbbing jugulars.

Melvin throws his head back. *"Ah-woooo!"*

Jaws slavering, he lopes forward. Behind the school, a group of tenth-graders hold their tickets out to the chaperon at the door—a two-faced killer with a greaser hairdo and test tubes rolled into the sleeves of his lab coat.

Ivan Blackwell in the flesh!

Melvin's wolfish, snapping appetite turns ultra-ravenous.

At once, he absorbs the chem teacher's murky aura. Cold-hearted charmer, failed biochemist, petty-minded fiend who concocts chaos and siphons joy. Like when he reduced the beloved lunch lady to leftovers after she glimpsed his chemical dark side. Like how he covets super geniuses with adoring grandsons and town-conquering schemes that are way more clever than his own. He enjoyed showing up on the von Griffins' doorstep with that frothing-mad mob—but he still grinds his teeth when he thinks about how Gramps escaped his clutches. If Blackwell ever catches him, he'll drain the invisibility serum straight from the old fart's veins and use it to commit even more heinous crimes in Gramps's name.

And all the while, the town saps will go on believing he's a swell guy.

Melvin realizes Blackwell already *has* a serum bubbling in his veins: a daily infusion of wickedness, because he's too lame to be evil on his own.

This monster wouldn't know a proper evil plan if it tore his throat out!

Melvin explodes from the fog, trying his darndest to direct his meat-lust at Blackwell's throat. But it's awkward, controlling his toothy trajectory. He leaps wildly at the ticket line.

Mid-pounce, everyone turns to gawk at him.

Tenth-graders scream and scatter. Blackwell yowls and barrels away, shoving teenagers to the pavement in a mad coward's dash for the gymnasium. Melvin undershoots and clamps frothing teeth around Blackwell's ankle. He tastes like bitter envy and inferior serums. Yuck! Melvin gnashes his teeth, snarling and snapping and gagging deep inside.

Overhead, shadow-clouds slither across the edge of the moon.

At once, Melvin's lunar powers wane and his teeth turn squashy. Blackwell lurches free and stumbles into the gymnasium.

Howling, Melvin tears after him into a colorful blast of confetti and rockabilly.

The sock-hop erupts!

Jitterbuggers shriek and stagger out of Melvin's path across the dance floor. Blackwell dashes toward a cluster of cheerleaders, figuring he can outrun the skirts.

Outside, the clouds thicken, swallowing half the moon.

Inside, Melvin's skeleton softens to jelly as he leaps for Blackwell's spine with balding paws and vicious, viscous claws.

The last of the moon vanishes behind the clouds.

Melvin's teeth snap and squish and melt.

He *splats* to the gymnasium floor.

Stunned to be his tiny pink-and-blue self again, Melvin jiggles and trembles. From way down here, the confetti-filled gymnasium seems cavernous.

Snickering wickedly, Blackwell looms enormous above Melvin and nudges him with a steel-toed boot. "What do we have here?"

"Glub-glub!" Melvin sprouts tentacles and lunges with all the ferocity of a garden slug.

Even so, Blackwell recoils and staggers outside, bellowing, "Don't just stand there, you letter-jacket morons! Help me find a pickle jar…"

Oh, yikes! Melvin whimpers tiny bubbles. He knows he should slime his way out of here, but without teeth and claws and loping speed, the parking lot seems vast and dangerous.

Some monster he's turned out to be.

Yet, the marvels of the night don't cease. Out in the parking lot, the fog swirls and parts in the shape of a man. Muddy footprints appear on the gymnasium floor and rush toward Melvin.

"Come along, little friend," whispers a voice of thin air. "You don't wanna be here when that scoundrel returns."

In a flubbery whoosh, Melvin glides upward, oozing between the fingers of an invisible hand.

"GUESS WHAT HAPPENED at my school tonight!" Doc grabs Melvin's beaker and peers in, starry-eyed with mayhem.

"Glub-glub!" Melvin bubbles, because wowza, does he have a story to tell!

But Doc talks excitedly over him. "A werewolf crashed the sock-hop! At least, that's what they're calling it. They say it was all lumpy and malformed, but definitely had fur and teeth. The best part: it attacked Mr. Blackwell! They're scouring the woods right now, probably with pitchforks and silver bullets…" Doc trails off. He tilts his head, lifts the beaker higher, then arches an eyebrow at Melvin. "What the…?"

Hastily, he retrieves a pair of tweezers.

"Sorry, this might tickle." He plunges the pinchy end into Melvin's goo-filled center and extracts a square of foil confetti. It shines in the open moonlight, and Doc suddenly realizes why the laboratory feels breezier tonight. The high window is shattered. Melvin's fault from when he crashed outside to chase the blood moon. Doc looks from the window to the confetti to Melvin, then to Gramps's projector and the *Claw of the Werewolf* reel. Quick, he dashes to his chalkboard and scratches out complex monster formulas and movie equations, making Melvin's lunar-wolf hangover throb with awe. Finally, Doc cries "Eureka!" and faces his creation.

"You're full of surprises, you little booger."

"*Glub-glub!*" Melvin gushes, because there's still more super astonishing news Doc doesn't know.

But Doc starts pacing in front of Gramps's movie collection, his evil-genius-brain-wheels spinning as he imagines all the monster mayhem Melvin can unleash on Blackwell.

A vampire to vex him, a gill-man to gut him, a—

"Wait a second." Doc halts mid-thought.

Finally. A smudge on the floor near the window catches his eye. A muddy footprint.

"Gramps was here? Gramps was here!"

"*Glub-glub!*" Melvin bubbles. "That's what I've been trying to tell you, Daddy-O!"

"Gramps?" Doc sweeps the air but comes up empty. His heart cracks with a million uncertainties, but one question asks them all: "Why did he leave again?"

Melvin wishes he knew. The incredible vanishing man didn't say much on the walk home, and when Melvin tried absorbing his aura, all he sensed was a whole lotta nothing. As if Gramps's invisible skin had turned his soul invisible, too.

"We have to find him!" Doc cries. "If he's in the woods while Blackwell and his mob are hunting your wolf-thing, they might catch *him* instead."

Hope bubbling, Doc devises a plan, then reaches for the perfect movie reel. He feeds the sacred 35mm film into the projector, and lively, flickering light fills the laboratory.

"Ready, little booger?" He sloshes Melvin's beaker affectionately.

"*Glub-glub!*" Melvin bubbles. "Go ape, Daddy-O, I was born ready!"

Doc sets Melvin in the projector light then steps back to watch his creation truly come alive. *Alive!*

Tonight's special feature: *Curse of the Pharaoh's Tomb*.

Shimmering movie light and pyramids and sandstorms blast through Melvin.

He bubbles, gurgles, bloats, and his beaker swirls to the brim with ancient bandages.

THE IMMORTAL POWER of Anubis, god of mummification, guide of lost souls, flows through Melvin's sandy veins and bends to his kingly will. Conqueror of death, enchanter of the desert— or in this case, the mossy woods. So far, it's no contest: Egyptian curses are way niftier than the lunar ones.

Melvin lurches forward on stiff legs and brittle bones, trailing bandages like ragged party streamers. Out among the fog-haunted trees, distant flashlights cut the nightscape, and fevered mob-voices echo all around.

"Is Gramps out here?" Doc whispers, tiptoeing in a crouch.

Melvin wishes he had better news to report. Every time he extends tendrils of perception, he only senses the agitated glee of the monster hunters. Blackwell riled them up something nasty. They wield pitchforks and seething dispositions, just as Doc predicted. Farmers, teachers, the sheriff, the mayor, all manner of men brainwashed by Blackwell's two-faced scams and manipulations.

Melvin senses Blackwell out there, too. He carries a rifle loaded with silver bullets—only he's not here to fill the wolf-blob-thing full of mystic metal. He's placed bear traps all over these woods, silver-plated jaws wicked enough to take down a Sasquatch. He plans to capture Melvin alive, imprison him inside his science lab, and perform insidious experiments in order to extract his evil super powers. Same thing he hopes to do to Gramps.

And speaking of Gramps…

His aura remains as invisible as the man himself.

"*Hhmmm-mmm,*" Melvin moans with vocal cords withered and papery from four thousand years inside the tomb.

"Don't say that! He's gotta be out here!" Doc shout-whispers. He can't fathom why Gramps would escort the little goo-booger home only to beat feet without even saying *hello.* "Something's wrong. Call him again."

Melvin nods and summons the power of Anubis deep into his heart and lungs—or rather, into the linen pouches of myrrh, cassia, and other burial spices crammed inside his chest cavity. His heart and lungs currently rest inside canopic jars somewhere in an Egyptian tomb.

"*Come to us…*" Melvin rasps, an invocation so dusty and ethereal it's only audible to the mind. "*Come to us…*"

In *Curse of the Pharaoh's Tomb,* the mummified pharaoh uses the powers of Anubis to find his lost queen and mind-warp her into returning home to the pyramids. Sadly, Melvin's attempts to mind-warp Gramps don't seem to be nearly as effective. In fact, he's a tad worried that all these ancient invocations might be luring Blackwell's mob their way.

Man-oh-man, he's sorry to disappoint his creator like this.

Melvin aims his attention westward, toward that mysterious kaleidoscopic light beyond the trees—same one he noticed during his wolfy rampage. The lively glow reminds him of Gramps, so he crosses his crumbly finger bones and intones:

"*Come to us, Gramps… Like, lickety-split!*"

"Look." Doc points.

Up ahead, a low branch snaps on its own, and the fog parts.

"Okay, okay, I'm here already," whispers that voice of thin air.

"Gramps!" Doc doesn't waste a heartbeat. He races forward, lab coat fluttering. "Where have you been?"

"Where have I been? *Where have I been?* I've been a *monster.*"

"I'm not afraid of monsters," Doc says. "In case you haven't noticed."

Standing at his creator's side, ghastly with bandages and dry rot, Melvin moans in agreement.

But Gramps mutters on. "Never casting shadows, never being seen, it's dissolving my very soul. I've vanished from within, don't you see? *Don't you see?*" He cackles morosely, and his voice roams the trees. "I thought I could discover an antidote, but I failed you. I can never come home like this, never prove Blackwell is a fiend. I—"

BANG!

A silver bullet whizzes past Melvin's skull.

"Elroy von Griffin, you chem-flunking dunce—I should've known!" Blackwell calls out from deep in the trees. "Always causing trouble, now inventing monsters to destroy our beloved town. A menace, just like your dear old grandpappy!"

The scattered mob rallies toward Blackwell fifty trees away, dozens of flashlights constellating together.

"We better make like a tree and leave," Doc whispers.

Dutifully, Melvin faces the monster hunters, keen to give Doc and Gramps a head start.

"*Leave us…*" he rasps. "*Leave us…!*"

But maybe a person has to have a mind in order for it to be warped, because instead of leaving, Blackwell fires a second shot.

The bullet strikes Melvin's myrrh-stuffed chest with a *puff* of ancient dust. Melvin staggers back, but remains upright. Pink-and-blue goo oozes from the bullet hole.

No biggie. Silver doesn't kill mummies.

"Little booger, don't just stand there!" Doc waves at Melvin from the edge of the woods, backlit by that mysterious polychromatic light. "Get boogieing!"

Melvin lurches after him, stiff-legged and awkward. He almost makes it to the edge of the woods when—

SNAP!

A silver-plated bear trap clamps his foot.

The metal teeth bite straight through his ankle, separating dusty foot from splintery leg. His foot dissolves into pink-and-blue goo.

Well, dang.

Melvin jerks free of the trap and steps forward onto his stump. He wobbles, but remains upright and takes another footless step, then another. A snail-trail of bandaged slime unravels behind him.

Another trap snaps, and Melvin hits the dirt with a *splat*. Pink-and-blue goo explodes from between his bandages.

"Gramps, careful!" Doc shouts as the incredible vanishing man crashes back through the branches. No monster left behind! Melvin still can't sense Gramps's aura, but he's sure about one thing: this man definitely has a soul.

Gramps scoops Melvin into his invisible hands and retreats through the trees. At the sight of Melvin gliding through air, Blackwell's greasy mind sharpens like a switchblade. Two for one! The wolf-mummy-blob-thing *and* the invisible pain-in-his-ass.

Wobbly and disoriented and wishing he could swallow Blackwell whole, Melvin clings to Gramps's arm like a melting marshmallow on a stick.

"Whoa, easy there, little friend," Gramps says. "You've got bite in you, after all."

Gramps's invisible skin tingles like a mild acid-burn everywhere Melvin leeches onto him. Melvin tastes faint pinpricks of blood, and in those droplets, he finally glimpses Gramps's lonely, regret-ridden aura. Gramps misses Doc as much as Doc misses him. He watches over Doc often, but is too ashamed of his failures to let himself be known—not even during lonely, sleepless nights when his grandson calls out to him.

At last, they burst through the trees and that mysterious prismatic light pulls into view.

Melvin can hardly believe his eyes—and not just because he doesn't have eyeballs. He's never seen anything so extraordinary.

"Quick, to my secret hideaway," Gramps whispers to Doc. And together, they race toward the glimmering Technicolor glow of the drive-in movie theater.

"THIS WAY!" GRAMPS leads Doc between shiny convertibles and pick-up trucks stuffed full of fellow movie-lovers in 3D glasses.

The silver screen stands taller than the trees and shines with fantastic colors and out-of-this-world action. Starships and lightning beams and a magnificent neon-green creature with electric stitches and the strength of ten earthmen.

Outer Space Frankenstein!

From what the moviegoers have seen so far, Melvin knows it's the tale of a starship that crashes in the desert, and the super genius who reanimates the stitched-together remains of the alien creature inside. Sounds nifty!

Melvin clings to Gramps's acid-tingly arm, bubbly with antic-ipation as they race toward a concession stand with a projector booth above it. Melvin knows Gramps lives in the storage cellar below the building, but that's not where they're headed.

A ladder stretches to the roof.

With Melvin wobbling around Gramps's arm, he and Doc start climbing just as Blackwell's mob bum-rush the ticket booth. They spread out between the parked cars, their pitch-forks clashing garishly with the hep chrome and Technicolor.

"There they are!" Blackwell shouts as Doc and Gramps reach the popcorn stand's low roof and pass in front of the projection window.

Gramps sits up here sometimes to watch movies and reminisce about his grandson while his botched antidotes brew. These space-age films aren't as fearsome as the classics, but Gramps thinks Doc would enjoy them. But right now, there's no time for popcorn flicks.

"This is your moment, little friend." Gramps holds Melvin out.

"We're counting on you!" Doc agrees.

"Glub-glub!" Melvin tentacle-swings off Gramps's arm and suctions to the projection window. On the big screen, starships and space-lightning bubble over with a bloating pink-and-blue goo. A crack of lightning later, and a hulking shadow manifests in the center of the light.

Melvin.

He steps forth.

Furry limbs and claws of the wolf; bandaged-wrapped torso of the mummy; topped off with a neon-green head and one heck of an intergalactic brain pan. All of it held together by stitches of zip-zapping lightning!

"It's an abomination! It'll destroy us all!" Blackwell shouts at the gathering mob. Innocent moviegoers flee their cars, scrambling for the exits.

Melvin glares at Blackwell with large insectile eyes and roars in some spooky-stellar alien language. *"You're cruisin' for a bruisin'!"*

Savage as the wolf, he leaps from the roof and lands in the center of the mob.

They recoil, every face foggy-eyed and foaming with the lies Blackwell tells about monsters. Can't they see who the *real* abomination is?

Melvin's spine tingles, and he senses Blackwell aim the rifle a split second before the silver bullet explodes through his bandaged shoulder, kicking up another puff of ancient dust.

Melvin whirls on Blackwell, flexing out-of-this-world strength, ready to lash out with claws, to curse him with ancient magic, to—

A pitchfork stabs Melvin's shoulder.

Right between his flashing electric stitches.

With a meaty yank, his entire wolfy arm flies off, smacking a Chevy with a pink-and-blue *splat!*

Should've seen that coming, but it's no picnic keeping track of an entire rowdy mob.

Blackwell fires another shot. This time the silver hits home, dissolving Melvin's furry leg. He topples onto his back with a dusty *oomph*.

"It'll destroy us all, eat our children!" Blackwell bellows, stoking the mob, whipping their auras into a rabid, monster-crazed froth.

They descend upon Melvin.

Stabbing and forking him apart at his seams until he's nothing but a tiny, quivering puddle of goo.

"Glub."

Wearing a rictus of delight, Blackwell looms over Melvin with a greasy popcorn bucket. "You're mine now."

The bucket drops like a cage, and the movie light disappears.

"Little booger!" Doc cries. Gramps tries to silence him, to pull him back into rooftop shadows. But it's too late.

The mob whirls and hoists their weapons.

Inside the popcorn bucket, Melvin burps and whimpers and feels around with tiny desperate tentacles.

Meanwhile, Blackwell takes gleeful aim at Doc's wily carrot top, cackling. "The invisible man surrenders now, or the punk eats silver!"

"What kind of pathetic, tantrum-minded, half-baked evil genius threatens an innocent chem student?" Gramps calls out, prodding Blackwell's inner fiend.

"Tantrum-minded?" Blackwell's neck veins bulge around the bait. The jealous contours of his face darken. His eyes turn sunken and demented. "Half-baked?"

"And witless, and unimaginative, and a real wet rag!" Doc taunts.

"You slime-hugging flunky—*I'm* the only mastermind here!" Blackwell roars, teeth showing yellowed and crooked, toxic glee boiling his filthy aura. "I should've offed you fools when I marinated that snooping, pearl-clutching lunch lady!"

The mob gasps. Dozens of frenzy-mottled faces turn in shock, horror-struck by the confession of everyone's beloved chemistry teacher.

Insane with hell-sauced abandon, Blackwell squeezes the trigger.

The projection window explodes an inch from Doc's head.

Beneath the popcorn bucket, Melvin seethes and gurgles.

And here's something nifty that Melvin's new intergalactic alien wisdom teaches him about himself: Gramps was right. He's got bite in him. It's dark under here, but he doesn't need a flickering movie projector to transform into the monster he was always meant to be.

Gurbling and burbling, Melvin's pink-and-blue cells double and triple and expand with the cunning symbiosis of an alien mind, the savagery of the wolf, the immortality of the mummy, the loyalty of Doc and Gramps as they've nurtured his gooey soul.

The popcorn bucket bursts and Melvin blubbers outward, lumpy and pulsating and ravenous, like a massive inside-out stomach.

He swells to the size of a Buick, acidic with fury.

Bigger and bigger, a full-grown BLOB!

He creeps and leaps and—before Blackwell can squeeze his trigger again, before he can kill and thrill and wreak more ugly havoc on the true evil super geniuses of Mossy Forest—Melvin surges upward, whips out a dozen pink-and-blue tentacles.

And swallows the tyrant whole.

SLURP!

Repugnant to the end, Blackwell cackles and writhes inside Melvin's caustic bite-y center, flesh melting, eyes bulging, face elongating and dissolving around his grinning skeleton. But who's laughing now!

The mob drop their pitchforks and scatter.

As Blackwell's bones fizzle to sludge, Doc and Gramps rush down to greet Melvin in his full blob-errific glory.

"Cool beans!" Doc cheers. "You did it!"

"My friend, you are a devourer of magnificent proportions. Utterly remarkable!"

"Glub-glub!"

"What's more, look at this," Gramps says. "It seems your wondrous properties of manifestation are proving to have quite peculiar side effects…"

Gramps holds up his arm—the same arm Melvin clung to back when he was pint-sized. It's slightly pink like a sunburn, and wrinkly because Gramps is old.

It's also visible!

"Gramps, I can see you!" Doc exclaims. "Well, part of you, anyway."

"Yes, Doc, my boy. I best take a peek at that secret formula of yours. I believe this town's monsters might find a happy ending, after all."

"*Glub-glub!*" Melvin agrees. "Right-O, Granddaddy-O!"

As they head for home between the mossy trees, Doc grins at Melvin, bursting with gooey pride. "You know, little booger, we still gotta get you a name."

"*Glub-glub,*" Melvin bubbles—but they can worry about penning the *Pink-and-Blue Blob to Human Translation Journal* some other night.

First, they've got an antidote to create.

TRICKSTERS

8:57 P.M.

I linger on the steps of my front porch, hugging the candy bowl with a heaviness in my chest. The last of the trick-or-treaters crunch down my leaf-littered lawn, returning to the shadows of the sidewalk. Teenagers, tricksters, they jostle each other, hooting and whooping it up—and good for them! I'd join them if I wasn't seven decades north of my childhood. I shuffle past my clan of shakily carved jack-o-lanterns. I'll keep the candles burning a while longer. Maybe there will be stragglers. The gang of candy-bag ruffians I ran with back in the day never went home before midnight.

Grinning at antique memories, I settle into the creaking wooden bones of my rocking chair, hidden deep enough in porch shadows to give any visitors who tiptoe up my walkway a nice healthy scare. If there *is* anyone left to scare. The street beyond my oak trees rests in moon-dappled peace. But an old man can hope, can't he? One more glimpse of sneaky mischief, of snickering monster-shaped shadows streaking through front yards. This was the hour when the old gang used to switch out pillowcases full of Pixy Stix and Atomic

Fire Balls for sacks of soap and toilet tissue pilfered from our mothers' powder rooms.

Ah God, do I miss those guys. Squares by day, hellions by night. Good old Emerson with his giddy sense of humor and out-of-this-world throwing arm—he could chuck a roll of TP higher than any kid I knew. And sweet-tooth Charlie, who belly-crawled through yards and giggled like a ten-year-old madman at every prank we pulled.

These days they're elderly men in their graves. Emerson ended up the butt-end of a heart attack, and Charlie got suckered by a stroke. Death snuck right up on the poor bastards, only nobody was laughing in the end.

Of course, back in the day, we thought we'd laugh forever, live forever. Hell, some Halloweens it seemed as if the good times might just roll on and on. Treats and scary stories and tricks. Hot damn, the mischief we caused! And me as our mastermind, always one prank ahead, hip to every trick in the bag.

The neighborhood never saw us coming—not even dressed as spacemen and masked cowboys and skeletal grim reapers in inky, glittery robes. They'd wake up November 1st to find their windows soaped and foggy, their trees and yards haunted with slow-wavering streamers like the tattered remains of bed-sheet ghosts. And Halloween would last another day.

Somewhere down my street, a young lady shrieks. Sharp and sudden—maybe at a goblin or a vampire leaping out at her from behind a parked car. It's the perfect goof for when the walk home turns spooky.

I listen for a second scream, for bursts of laughter, but the spiced autumn air settles back into silence.

With a sigh, I balance the candy dish on the porch railing and flip the switch on my transistor radio—same model I had as a kid. Another tradition, I dial in K-103's annual Halloween radio drama, already in progress. The gang and I used to live for these old shows—crackly and creepy over the airways—my radio clipped to my belt as we capered through sleepy yards and blackened streets.

Tonight's story is a classic: the proverbial escaped maniac on the loose with a mask and a hook—the kind who terrorizes nubile couples necking in backseats. They're even playing it as breaking news, complete with buzzing police bulletins. I chuckle. Might fool the kiddies, maybe even spook some folks into locking their doors. But old pros like me are wise to the gotchas of the season.

As the newscaster interviews snappy police detectives and weeping survivors, I indulge in leftover chocolate bars and watch pumpkins and porch lights blink out across the neighborhood. One after another, signaling the time for treats has expired.

Somewhere closer, comes that second scream. A high-pitched shriek, it echoes between the houses.

On the radio, the newscaster's brisk vocal fry darkens in tone: *"In the interest of public safety, please, Miss, tell our listeners what you saw tonight…"*

A melodramatic pause darkens the staticky airwaves, then: *"We were driving home from Lookout Hill,"* says a voice reminiscent of poodle skirts and strawberry phosphates. *"There was someone lying in the middle of the road. My boyfriend pulled over, and we got out to help. But it was just a scarecrow. Someone's idea of a joke. We dragged it off to the side, then climbed back into the car. But the keys were missing from the ignition! That's when we heard the most awful sound… A tap-tap-tapping on the undercarriage. Someone was hiding beneath the car! My boyfriend and I slammed our doors just as a dark shape crawled out from underneath us and rose up outside my window. A tall, gangling man with a machete!"*

Chuckling again, I shake my head. In my day, it was a hook.

"He wore a tattered burlap sack over his head, same as the scarecrow he left in the road. Black stitches for eyes and a crooked grinning mouth. He tapped his blade on the glass and tilted his head, as if to say 'Gotcha!' We weren't going anywhere, not without the keys. He was almost playful at first. Circling the car, tapping his sharp, steel blade along the hood and roof and windows. Tap-tap-tapping right up until he—"

My porch light blacks out. The radio buzzes to silence.

A power outage? Oh, good grief! And just when things were getting hairy.

Streetlights and glowing windows go black all down the block until the whole neighborhood rests in black-and-gray gloom and breath-held anticipation. The only light is the sallow, flickering glow from my jack-o-lanterns.

I throw a sideways glance at my dark and silent radio, and my pulse goes jagged. That radio runs on batteries, so how the heck did it—

A sharp sound cuts across the neighborhood.

Tap. Tap. Tapping...

The sound drifts along the street and through the oaks in my front yard, makes the hairs on the back of my neck prickle on end.

I creak forward in my rocking chair, squinting at the murky, night-stained lawn and the empty sidewalk where—

TAP-TAP-TAP! Someone knocks on my front door.

I startle, gasp, nearly fall out of my seat, heart clenching like a fist.

A short grim reaper cloaked in an inky, glittery robe stands alone on my welcome mat. The plastic scythe is his small pale hand is just like the ones they used to sell at the corner Five-N-Dime. The kid withdraws it from my door.

"Snuck up on me there, didn't you?" I laugh the laugh of old fools and clutch the candy dish against my pounding, hammering chest. The trick-or-treater turns to face me in my rocking chair. Beneath his reaper's hood, he wears a cartoon skull mask with an exaggerated grin and gleaming white-and-black eyes.

"Nifty costume, kid. Had one like it myself once." I haul myself up onto bony, uneasy knees and wobble toward him. Sweat prickles my forehead despite the crisp autumn air, and an eerie heaviness returns like a sack of tricks to my pounding chest. My left arm trembles, tingles, ready with the candy bowl. Lucky kid, I think I might dump it all into his pillowcase and call it a night. I just need those three magic words...

But the little reaper tilts his head at me, silent.

He reaches out with his plastic scythe and *tap-tap-taps* my breastbone.

"What the hay, kid?" I try to chuckle, but my voice has gone gravelly.

With a swish of his cloak, the kid rushes out into the yard—and *oh!*

My eyes widen like moons. The candy dish tumbles from my hands with a clatter.

Oh, how strange. How impossible and strange!

My yard is haunted.

Hundreds of gauzy, toilet-tissue streamers hang from the oak trees, tendrils of a simpler time. They sway in a lazy breeze and part like a veil to reveal the dark silhouettes of candy-bag ruffians watching me from the sidewalk. My heart pounds and pounds with sharp pangs of nostalgia.

The old gang.

Sweaty, icy awe prickles my spine and antique skin, and I stagger forward and grip the porch railing.

The old gang—these days, they're elderly men in their graves.

Yet I'd know those cowboy hats and space helmets and giddy Halloween troublemakers anywhere. They face my house with devilish, glinting eyes and sagging pillowcases full of treats.

Or is it tricks?

I clutch a hand against my pounding chest. *Pounding, pounding*, and the nightscape spinning. I need to sit down. But I'm afraid to look away from yesteryear, from the ethereal spectacle haunting my front yard—afraid if I turn around this living dream will end and darkness will sneak up on me.

Impish and gleeful, the tricksters disperse into my yard, boyish shadows sneaking through the ghostland of gossamer white streamers. Emerson in his space helmet tiptoes with slow, exaggerated footsteps, while Charlie in the cowboy hat drops down and belly crawls through the fallen leaves.

All the while, the pint-sized grim reaper looms on the sidewalk. He points at me with his cloaked hand and taps his plastic scythe against the pavement.

Tap-tap-tapping. The sound is surreal, it floats through the yard, echoing all around me.

Sneaking up.

I tighten my grip on my chest.

Tap-tap-TAP!

A machete bursts through my ribcage.

Blood sprays out, splashes the jack-o-lanterns, and my hand closes around the blade. I can't believe it. Razor-sharp steel. It slices through my fingers, but I try to hold on even as the jelly goes out of my knees.

I collapse to the porch, old meat and bone and nostalgia.

"Gotcha," the maniac in the scarecrow mask says and yanks his machete free.

Should've seen that coming. Of course, in my day, it was a hook…

Dying laughter wheezes through the frothing, ragged hole in my chest. With a playful tilt of his masked head—stitched eyes, warped burlap smile—the maniac steps over me and blows out my jack-o-lanterns.

It should all go black.

But instead of flickering to darkness, the nightscape flares around me. Misty and white, as if someone soaped the windows of my soul.

The scarecrow maniac stalks back into the night. *Tap-tap-tapping* his bloody blade down my porch steps, strolling past oak trees laced with spectral streamers and out into the neighborhood. Somewhere farther down, sirens rise and red-and-blues strobe against the houses. Help is coming, but that side of the street seems suddenly silly and far away—like how childhood was once long lost.

With the maniac gone, the coast is clear. Charlie and Emerson storm the porch around me, whooping and hooting and giggling like tiny madmen.

I try to protest as they grab my elbows and haul my old bones upright. My head droops, but as I squint down at what should be my slashed and ancient torso, cold awe tingles through my chest and bones and spirit.

Oh, how impossible and strange!

I stand cloaked in a robe of inky glitter, and my tiny, ageless hands grip a plastic scythe and a pillowcase.

All around us, those tattered gossamer streamers ripple and sway, never darkening or fading. Excitement and sweet terror swell inside my chest as I caper down the steps of my blood-splattered porch. Still can't believe I fell for that—a machete.

But I can only laugh.

The night is young again.

The neighborhood will never see us coming!

A gang of mischievous shadows, we jostle and jest and live it up, out here on the sidewalks of our endless Halloween.

ASHES UPON ASHES UPON ASHES

TO: SkyWatch3r333@cmail.com
FROM: benjamin_rhodes@retromail.com
SENT: 10/13/24 2:31 a.m. EST
SUBJECT: grim harbinger

Father is dead. There won't be a funeral. You and I will split the estate, but with stipulations—see attachment. He was never going to let us go easy. You'll have to come to Maine if you want your half. I'm not doing this alone, too.

TO: benjamin_rhodes@retromail.com

FROM: SkyWatch3r333@cmail.com

SENT: 10/13/24 6:46 p.m. PST

SUBJECT: re: grim harbinger

Really, Benji? You sniveling martyr. It was YOUR choice to lick our family's ashes off his feet all these years. You don't get to blast me with batshit demands. That dead bastard dangles some cheese and expects me to drop my hard-won life to perform one last puppet dance? Fuck his stipulations! And fuck you for being there for him when you knew who the real victims were. There's nothing in Maine I want. I'll never go back. You can keep everything. Knowing that sick twisted monster is dead is inheritance enough. Hope he fucking suffered.

TO: SkyWatch3r333@cmail.com

FROM: benjamin_rhodes@retromail.com

SENT: 10/13/24 10:59 p.m. EST

SUBJECT: re: re: grim harbinger

It has never been about what you want, blessed sister, not even when you ran away to sunnier coasts. You have no idea how unbearably horrific everything might have been without me here. Settling Father's estate isn't merely a matter of liquidating investments and sweeping out the manor house. As you very well know, we still have the east bedroom to contend with. Don't place this burden on me alone, or I'll be forced to release the old family movies to the police. The ones where you're the willing star. You cannot run from it forever, Margot. I expect to find you on Father's doorstep very soon. We will endure this together.

IT'S LATE WHEN I arrive. So late, the spruce and maples bordering the estate have grown thirty years taller, blocking stars that were once my only comfort. I slow my rental to a crawl, tires crunching gravel as I pass beneath the iron gates and follow the snaking woodland drive. The familiar twists and turns awaken the same gut-sick anxiety that haunted my later childhood, that ominous despair of returning home.

As Father's manor appears ahead, hulking wings of stone and glowing stained glass, snow begins to fall like the feathery slow passage of a dream. Except I know better, don't I? It's not snow.

It's ashes.

Flurries and whorls and drifts of ashes. To the east, between the dusted trees, I spot the endless flickering roar of the family fire pit. A ribbon of pale gray smoke stretches heavenward, anointing the starry sky. I shiver, stepping from the car, feeling the northeastern cold like a genetic stain in my bones.

A sallow gas lamp illuminates the arched entryway and the old sentry of stone statues—angels once, torsos now, broken limbs, shattered wings, collecting ash in every jagged crevice. I hesitate several yards short of the manor's mahogany and iron door. Last time I crossed that threshold, I was dripping blood, refusing to look back.

"Margot, you're finally here," calls a baritone voice it hurts to recognize.

A silhouette approaches from the eastern woods, a man who doesn't lose his shadows in the lamplight. My chest tightens. I recognize him by the bleak, overzealous eyes. Decades have mutated everything else, turned him gaunt and grizzled. What is he now—early fifties? Time has been kinder to me—softer on the outside, anyway. *You could've run!* I want to scream. *You didn't have to stay!*

But that's a lie.

"Look at you," Benji says.

"I'm here now," I reply, voice gravelly with resentment, or maybe guilt.

Ash dusts his thinning hair and smudges his forehead, vague sigils and shadows. He carries a movie camera, naturally—Father's

8mm handheld, ever-rolling, documenting every hideous day, just as Father wished. Benji doesn't dare hug me hello, knows there's no closing the gap between us. Instead, he aims the camera at the ash-swept ground, clears the smoke from his throat. "You've had a long trip. If you'll join me, I've prepared a late supper."

The night air wafts with the stench of charred meat. The stench of home. I glance toward the woods and the still-crackling fire pit.

Then I gather my baggage and follow my brother inside.

FATHER JOINS US for supper—dust and bone chips and horrid memories shoved into an urn at the head of the table. Benji sits across from me, too close for comfort. Eye contact is impossible.

Only the 8mm camera looks at me directly. Before supper, Benji propped it on a tripod as naturally as he laid out the silverware and the roast beef. Never asked my permission. Now, the incessant whirring fills our awkward silence.

"Is the camera still necessary?"

"We're documenting history, like the prophets of the past. Lens and celluloid instead of papyrus and iron gall ink…" Benji trails off, knows I've heard this before. He stares at the plate he prepared for me. "You've hardly touched your roast?"

"Not really big on charred meat."

"Right." He lowers a maladroit forkful to his plate. Despite myself, I regret my tone. At least he's trying. Would I prefer he be inhospitable? I glance around the dining hall, nauseous with something akin to déjà vu. Mahogany furniture and Mother's old handwoven tapestries, a host of wingless marble statues and loose ashes collecting in every vast corner.

"Everything looks the same," I offer diplomatically, nibbling a roasted carrot.

Benji half-shrugs. "Redecorating was never Father's priority."

"No, it wasn't."

Our silence returns, heavier.

"Forgive my curiosity," he says, "but what've you done with yourself, all this time?"

I swallow thickly. What? Besides hunkering down, watching the highways and the skies, waiting for the fires to catch up with me? "This and that."

"Always thought you'd be a ballerina. You were always twirling around in those poofy dresses Mother sewed."

"That was…" My heart gives a hard knock. "That was before."

"Right, guess that's the you I still imagine, but you were pretty young…" Benji hesitates. "Ever marry? Ever have kids?"

And there it is. I stare at my plate, shocked he even has to ask. "No, I managed to avoid those tragedies."

"Father was hoping you might've—"

"I know what that monster hoped," I snap, throwing my fork down, sitting back in my high-backed chair. "How about you? I don't see any little women running around, barefoot and pregnant. No cherub-cheeked heirs with your shifty eyes."

"No, *I* was busy overseeing other duties." Benji drops his fork. Takes him several ragged heartbeats before he sets his meat knife down, too. "Anything else you'd like to know?"

"Yeah, actually." I glare at the urn, feeling cold and ashen myself. "How did he die?"

Benji stares at me. "During a moment of weakness."

AFTER SUPPER, BENJI retreats without ceremony. "You know your way around…"

I do. And apparently, nothing's off-limits. Had I hoped it would be?

I'll be staying in my old west wing bedroom. I was sixteen the last time I slept there, cowered there. It's almost midnight, but other parts of the manor demand my presence—this discordant tug I've always felt, a macabre curiosity, a twisted responsibility. I suppose I owe Benji a debt. I'm just not sure how that debt should be paid.

I follow ash-clotted stone hallways past high-ceilinged parlors and antechambers, my old childhood maze. Moonlight shines through stained glass windows, casting prismatic shadows, fragmented shapes of saints and sinners. Every echoing footstep shrinks me into the terrified girl I once was, the girl who felt vital duty boiling in her blood, Wingless statues watch from every cobweb shadow. The angels belonged to Mother. I remember a time when they still had wings and adoring gazes. Now, everything in Father's manor whispers of ruin. I turn a final corner and the hallway before me telescopes outward, leading to a single mahogany-and-steel door.

The east bedroom.

The ashes in the hallway grow darker the closer I dare, shades of bone gray into sodden reds. I'm surprised when the bedroom door handle turns in my hand, unlocked, awaiting me. But I don't push inside. I hold my breath, hyper-alert to the resonant silence beyond. Something stirs inside, a wetness scraping.

Maybe the shadow-hiss of my name.

I recoil, ears ringing, unsure—unsure what I just heard. And, oh hell, please, I don't want to decipher it. I trip backwards, stumbling through the rat maze of walls and doors, electrified by old horrors, spinning out. But this time, I don't arrive outside in the cold, on the highway, at the bus-stop.

I slam through a set of padded red doors into Father's home theater.

A row of well-worn seats, a curtain-framed screen, a projection window, and a booth beyond. Once upon a time, Father built this room because Mother adored the dewy nostalgia of old home movies. Now in the center seat, a film canister looms with an ominous label:

FOR MARGOT

Strange, how I still recognize Father's squat handwriting.

My skin crawls. Whatever fresh hell he immortalized on celluloid for me to witness, I don't have the stomach for it. Instead, I follow a spiral staircase up to the projection booth.

The family archives.

I'm not prepared for this either, even though it's exactly what I expected. A sturdy antique movie projector and shelves upon shelves of 35mm film canisters, each labeled with consecutive dates. A film a day for thirty-plus years. How many is that? I juggle loose math, arriving at a nebulous thirteen thousand. Jesus fucking Christ.

"Oh, Benji…" I turn in a slow, gut-sick circle, digesting the full scope of Father's obsession. Who on Earth did he expect to survive long enough to watch all of this? And now I wonder if the bottle of lighter fluid stashed in my suitcase will be enough.

I drag my clammy hand along reel after reel, lost days mercifully passing me by. The labels grow yellower the further back I browse, rewinding the clock until Father's squat hand-writing becomes Mother's looping script.

These ones here are different. Our earliest home movies, only a couple dozen of them. The memories Mother recorded, the sunny footage from our childhood.

From *before*.

Numb—but maybe that's best—I select a random canister from Mother's collection and load the film reel into the projector.

APRIL 14TH 1982

Grainy footage opens on glittery streaks of sunlight and a quaint, red barn petting zoo. A happy family gathers around a rustic picnic table, waving at the camera with motion-blur hands—Mother and Father, both spry and dark-haired in their early forties, and little Margot and Benji, four and eleven, respectively. A homemade feast decorates the table—sandwiches, salads, a wild blueberry pie. Behind the family, a handsome black goat and freshly sheered sheep mingle inside a pen. Little Margot glances repeatedly over her shoulder, round-eyed and rosy, enchanted by the animals.

MOTHER

Smile pretty, my darlings. Ready to say grace?

Well-mannered, perfectly at ease with casual touch, the family links hands and bows their heads.

MOTHER

Bless, O Lord, this food of your servants…

As Mother prays, the black goat sniffs the air and nudges its horned head against the pen, unlatching the gate. Father and little Margot tilt their bowed heads, alert to the sparkle in each other's eye as the goat trots closer.

MOTHER

…bless us to thy service…

Father winks at little Margot, and the two unlink hands, opening a gap at the table. Thrilled, the goat helps itself to the wild blueberry pie. Benji and Mother both gasp, prayer abruptly forgotten. There's a moment of astonishment, then the family explodes in delighted laughter.

MOTHER

My goodness!

FATHER

Looks as though we've got a picnic guest, Mother!

BENJI and MARGOT

Can we keep him?

Blueberry gore dripping from its muzzle, the goat regards the family with eerie, rectangular pupils. Father ruffles the scruff between its nubby horns.

FATHER

And share all of Mother's pies with this piggish beast? I think not.

The children burst into more giggles, sunbeams washing out their eyes. Father dollops Mother's nose with berries, and Mother returns the goopy purple favor, indulging more laugher, almost children themselves. Father kisses her forehead and—

I STOP THE film dead, going cold inside. It's too surreal to watch, like beyond numbing, almost an out-of-body experience. A dream we all shared once. All of us faithful and picturesque and untouched by horrors.

Seeing Father that way makes everything worse, a travesty. He was a good man once, a whimsical father, a charming and loving husband. All of it rots inside me, festers that much deeper because I know the hideous future awaiting that family. Who gives a fuck how amazing Father used to be?

I don't bother re-shelving the film. Just toss the reel onto the floor, watch the celluloid unspool into ashy shadows. I glance over my shoulder, expecting to find Benji in the doorway.

I'm alone.

I return to the archives in search of another film. A specific film. Nothing unique about the label, nothing fortified about the canister. Odd how Father never took special care with it, odd how it blends in with all the other days. For the rest of the world, that's certainly true. But for me, it practically glows.

The date emblazoned on my soul. The first day of history.

MAY 30TH 1983

Night-grain footage opens on a cliff side, the shadow-cast maple woods to the left, the white-capped ocean to the right, the entire starry cosmos lit up beyond. High beams from an off-screen vehicle bisect the darkness, spotlighting three washed-out silhouettes. A man and two children dancing like exaggerated rag dolls. Lens flares zigzag the scenery as the camera moves closer, and crackling car speakers fill the night with a jazzy swell of trumpets.

FATHER

Mother's playing our song!

MOTHER

Shall we boogie?

Mother's slim hand appears, reaching out as her over-exposed children skip closer. Little Margot pirouettes in her tutu, ever-rosy and carefree, and Benji snaps offbeat fingers, a boy on the verge of his teens, shaggy but with a spit-polished potential. The camera sways with them.

FATHER

May I cut in?

MOTHER

Only you, handsome!

The children's faces smear, rhythmic blurs as the scenery turns. Father grins handsomely into the camera, and Mother's hand cups his shoulder as they whorl and tango. She squeaks in delight when Father dips her, falling into his arms while the camera-gaze glides skyward, capturing a glimpse of ancient constellations as they twitch and start to reform.

MOTHER

Oh, do you see that?

FATHER

What in heaven…?

The footage jitters as Father sweeps Mother upright, trees and headlights streak past. The camera-gaze sweeps skyward again, refocusing on the firmament with a tremble. A thousand pinpoints of light blaze brighter, and star by impossible star, the constellations quake and start to crumble. Oily lens flares glide across the screen as all the stars zip apart like fireflies.

FATHER

What is that? The hell is that?

MOTHER

Dearest Lord!

BENJI and MARGOT

(frantic cries, excited, terrified, inaudible)

The camera shudders. The stereo melts into a discordant groan. Off-screen, headlights explode into darkness and silence. Above, the stars spiral closer, vibrating, static fizzling.

MOTHER

Father, get the children!

Father's shadow streaks past as the stars cluster into a single strobing light. A hideous existential beacon. When it's not lit, there's absolutely nothing. It begins a vast cosmic descent, blinding the camera with alternating brilliance and void. Disquieting inky shapes take form inside the strobing radiance, boundless limbs, a bleeding silhouette reaching for the camera.

BOOMING METALLIC VOICE

(terrible thunderous static, inaudible)

MOTHER

I hear you! (heavy gasping, rattling, inaudible) I'm your vessel… (inaudible) My grim harbinger…

FATHER

Mother, don't!

BOOMING METALLIC VOICE

(terrible thunderous static, inaudible)

The sky beats like a heart. Inside the pulsing other-worldly radiance, the inkblot shape spreads vast wings and gyres downward. The camera rattles, dipping as Mother falls to obedient knees. Pebbles jitter around her. Something lurches, something jolts. At once, the pebbles shrink away and Mother's feet dangle into view as the ground sinks away below her. Jagged static. The top of the station wagon appears, the tops of her family's heads, then tempest-tossed treetops. It all shrinks away, and Mother's dress flutters, her legs kick, rising higher, higher…

BENJI and MARGOT

(frantic screams and shrieks, words inaudible)

FATHER

(receding)

Mother, tell it no!

MOTHER

(screaming, inaudible)

The camera-gaze shudders skyward, but there is no skyward. The sky is all around, the inverse of night, black stars shaking. Mother's sundress tears, her legs scissor open, and her wide eyes and prayerful screaming mouth appear, out-of-focus inside the white-shadow radiance. Immaculate light, flashing, thunderous, fathomless. And deep within the chaos, a glimpse, an epiphany, an oil-slick gleam of black feathers. Nebulous black wings fold around Mother like the beating hand of God. The camera loosens from her grip and plummets past stars, trees, family, everything reeling, earth rising. A final explosive jolt. Then merciful darkness.

I STARTLE AWAKE in the front row of Father's theater, feeling crushed, dropped from great heights. As I sit up, doorway shadows stir and Benji takes shape, my own grim harbinger. Was he watching me sleep?

The screen flickers with silent empty light. The reel ran out hours ago. Benji steps closer, his camera surreptitiously aimed my way. This early in the day, he still wears his bathrobe, fuzzy and worn, yet on him there's something ceremonial about it.

"Have you watched Father's last film?"

My head's too full for this, too feathery. Not that it's any of his business, but… "No."

"You really should."

"And why's that?" I snap, exhausted. "Don't say because Father wished it."

Benji pauses, as if no other answer exists. "Why are you here, Margot?"

"You blackmailed me, threatened to give our home movies to the cops."

"A bluff, and you knew it. What we do here is too vital to risk outside interference. On some primal level, you understand that. You fear what's coming, just like Father feared. That's why you never contacted the police after you ran."

A hollow pain eddies in my chest, like I could scream. But I don't. I lock eyes with Benji, make sure he sees me. "Because I was ashamed. For all of us."

"You shouldn't be," he says curtly. "The world should thank us."

"Never fucking say that to me! You don't get to decide what this world deserves. What *we* deserve."

"I'll ask again, sister. Why are you here?" From his bathrobe, Benji produces my bottle of lighter fluid. He went through my things? "Maybe watch Father's video before you burn it all to the ground. You know what's at stake."

I cross my arms, refuse to let him see me tremble. "How long will you keep doing this?"

"Long as I'm able."

"And what happens when you die? When I die? We've nobody to inherit this burden."

"Father was of a mind to take matters into our own hands. I'm still virile…" He stares at me, and gooseflesh is all I know. This sick fucking family. These sick fucking monsters!

Benji's wristwatch buzzes. He silences it and moves to leave. "You'll excuse me."

I narrow my eyes. "Off to save the world?"

No hesitation. "Yes."

I LURK INSIDE the ashy stone hallways, listening to the echo of Benji's morning rituals. A visit to the east bedroom, then outside to the woods to stoke the fire pit. He's right. What good is a bottle of lighter fluid?

I could run, just climb into my rental, get the hell out of here while he's still in the woods. Who are we to decide what's right for the world? But the lure of the film archives is too heady. Maybe I need one last reminder, one last glimpse of what I'd be running from.

Back in the projector room, I stand before the altar of reels.

Any day between *May 31st 1983* and my escape on *July 6th 1994* will feature the same sinister routine. What Father called "our duty." I select a random canister and load the projector. Closing my eyes, squelching them tight, I fast-forward to the end of the day. There's nothing before that final scene that I never want to witness again.

But I need to witness myself.

OCTOBER 1ST 1988

The east hallway smudges past, murky and shaky as the camera chases ten-year-old Margot. A harried girl, with twiggy limbs and stringy blood-greased hair, she carries a dripping bundle in her arms—a bundle that wails in gurgling tongues. Every shriek shivers the screen with static. Benji shouts from behind the camera, the baritone of a boy who's almost a man.

BENJI

Hurry, Margot, we must hurry!

Margot runs faster, bloody feet slipping on stone, twisting and blurring down the maze of hallways. A door crashes open, the night sky appears. Margot follows a well-worn path into the maple woods, ashes swirling around her ankles with every foot-fall. The family fire pit blazes ahead, sparking higher until it dominates the frame.

MARGOT and BENJI

Forgive us, Lord! Spare us!

Margot steps forward, and the heat of the fires inflames her blushing, devastated innocence. Firelight reflects off the fleshy bundle. A newborn grim harbinger, still slick with afterbirth. It twists its head, poisoning the camera with oily, lucid eyes, watching the watcher.

BENJI

Do it, Margot!

MARGOT

Forgive me!

Margot closes her eyes, squelches them tight, and throws the child into the flames.

SCREAMING OUT FROM my disemboweled soul, I rip the reel from the projector, let it unravel. Walls of films loom around me, closing in. Too many days! I tear cannisters off the racks, crack them open, spill their celluloid innards.

My head reels, countless hideous scenes playing simultaneously, looping over and over, an endless, discordant montage of fiery insanity. Because only fire terminates the grim-dripping fruit of apocalyptic conception. Doomsday after doomsday, ashes upon ashes. It's too much for one family to bear, too much for one little girl.

"I never asked for this!" I scream at the soundproofed ceiling, the indifferent sky, the unspooled guts of my broken family, celluloid twisting high as my empty womb. This must end with Benji and me.

But first, I have one final film to watch.

FOR MARGOT—OCTOBER 10TH 2024

The trembling footage snaps to murky life inside the east bedroom, a stone floor with a bloody patina. A voice, barely human, moans. The camera swings past motion-blur stirrups, tangled bed sheets, a fleshy writhing heap, a deflated belly, an afterbirth smear cradled in the cameraman's arm. An extreme, rattling close-up on Father. He appears ancient, corpse-like. His eyes betray the sunken burnt-out depths of his vile self-imposed duty.

FATHER

It's the final hour, has been for decades. Every day after endless day, her belly swelling full as the moon, trimesters passing in wicked hours, flaunting this grim miracle she allowed inside herself. I, at last, am ripe and ready for the destruction her child will bring. Who am I to stop the inevitable? Humanity rots, morality rots, her angel spoke the insidious truth. I need only look inside Mother to know that. Whatever survives the ruins of this world should remember what she did, like Eve in the garden. We had paradise once.

Father shakes his bedraggled head. Something crackles and pops off-camera.

FATHER

My fidelity completes its long rot. I told Benji I'd perform today's burning alone, but it ends tonight. History ends tonight. I appointed myself as savior, but I grow old, fatigued, spiritless. And Mother…

(sobs, hesitates) Mother must end, too. May the world forgive me. Tonight, I become the beast my daughter always imagined…

The grainy footage turns shadowy as the camera refocuses on the infant nestled in the crook of Father's arm. Tranquil, oily eyes burn into the lens, fathomless coal-fire depths capable of igniting cities. Its little bones crackle and crumble and reform, the sinuous rip-and-tear of growing pains. Looks like time-lapse, but it's not. Chubby limbs elongate, tiny hands sprout tiny claws, growing ever-dexterous, aging weeks in long minutes. Father hums Mother's favorite song. By the time the shouting fills the hallways, the newborn appears to be a baby of one year.

BENJI

(off-screen)

Father, what've you done? The sky! The stars are gathering!

In the hazy background, the bedroom door slams open, Benji stumbles in.

BENJI

Father, don't do this! Please!

Benji reaches for the child, and Father, despite his monologue, doesn't resist. He gapes at the quick-growing bundle, as if seeing it anew, cravenness destroying his resolve. The footage warps sideways as the child curls unforgiving fingers around Father's bottom lip. It screeches, flexes, and Father's jaw unhinges, ripping free with a jagged, dangling wetness.

BENJI

Father!

The camera swoons. Father collapses sideways, twitching and gushing, stains upon bloody stains. Benji rescues the camera, the world shaking as he grabs the baby by one chubby ankle. The child swings, chubby limbs splayed like a cross, clutching Father's mangled jaw like a rattle. The scenery quakes as Benji runs, rushing through stone hallways and doorways, out into the night. The camera catches a star-streaked glimpse of the ominous, turbulent sky, constellations spiraling out of alignment. Between the trees, the fire pit blazes into frame, closer, closer, fires rising up, crackling around the blackened char of countless tiny skulls. Skipping futile prayers, Benji tosses the giggling child into the flames.

I LET THE film play itself out, Father's final moments looping endlessly on the dark-side of the projector. Numb, entranced by newfound duty, I wander from Father's theater, a puppet re-knotting her strings. Stained glass hallways and wingless angels pass me by. Ashes upon ashes. If I find Father's urn, I'll dump him into the drifts. For now, I arrive at the east bedroom just as Mother's labor begins.

She writhes weakly atop the bed, her bruised legs in stirrups, the rest of her bound by chains of atrophy and insanity. An old woman, decades from the beaten middle-aged hostage I last knew. A haggard, white-haired spectacle of bedsores, stretch marks, brutal scars. Lightless concave eyes. If her once-beautiful mind still exists, it hasn't resurfaced since the late '80s. Her body has never been her own. Flesh sags off her skeleton in diaphanous wrinkles, though her swollen, distended belly looks ready to pop.

The camera whirs on a tripod. Clinical, cold, bedside manner of an alien, Benji approaches Mother, wearing Father's rancid scrubs.

"Did you watch Father's film?"

"Yes."

"And you saw what happens? You remember your duty?"

"Yes."

Just as Mother agreed to hers. But I don't say this to Benji. He and Father disregarded the sanctity of a woman's body, the divinity of our autonomy. Barefoot, bloody, kept in restraints. This is how they honor womens' work, these mock saviors. But what must be done has always fallen on the strongest among us. I understand that now. If only I realized it thirty years sooner.

And when, after the savageries of childbirth, my half-sister is reborn again, I meet her oily gaze and extend my arms. "My turn."

Benji allows me to take her.

Just like old times, a dripping bundle in my arms. Benji and his camera chase me through the hallways, through the woods, back to the fire pit. Overhead the stars rest easy, ever-watching, ever-waiting. Humanity will never be pure again. I will never be pure again.

The fire pit blazes but doesn't warm my gooseflesh. The child coos in my arms, tiny bones crackling, elongating.

"Hurry, Margot!" Benji edges closer with his camera, ready to yank our sister from me if I don't do what I must. "Hurry!"

So, I do what I must. I squelch my eyes shut, and with Mother writhing in my heart, with her winged Lord watching, waiting, I perform my duty. One final time.

I shove my sibling into the fire.

Benji's blistering screams are immediate and hideous and deserved, hot-spitting sparks.

I don't open my eyes until his voice and duty sizzle away, replaced by tiny gurgle-tongued giggles. My sister smiles up at me, watching with oily eyes and Father's 8mm camera clutched in her divine little hand.

END OF DAYS

A whir of shaky electric static. Crooked footage opens on a dash-view of the front and back seats of a rental car. Margot occupies the driver's seat, white-knuckling the wheel, starry-eyed transcendence bleeding across her face. A blanketed bundle slouches in the front passenger seat, pallid bone-slung features rocking in-and-out of periphery. In the backseat, a sky-clad child sits unrestrained, approximately five-now-six-now-seven years old. Strange sigils burn across her body like open wounds with inner embers. Smoke curls from her giggling mouth. Through the back window, the stained glass manor recedes into the distance and ash flurries swirl and rise. The sky draws into majestic view above the treetops. One by one, stars twitch and loosen from the void.

MARGOT

It'll be over soon, Mother. It'll all be over soon…

THE CLOVER CAFÉ

CONSCIOUSNESS RETURNS SEVERAL seconds before Sam opens her eyes. In this brief and cottony haze, she can still pretend.

She's home in bed, buried in blankets, stretching luxurious bones while the house stirs around her. Footsteps on the stairs, kitchen cabinets banging open. Any minute now, Claire is gonna smack her with a pillow or spray a whipped-cream flower on the tip of her nose. *Wake up, nerd, it's waffle-thirty.* She can practically smell the hot butter and cinnamon. They'll pig out on the couch and watch their parents' ancient stash of VHS movies all throughout the morning, quoting the cheese-ball dialogue and snickering into each other's shoulders. Sam in her ratty UCLA sweats, and Claire with no makeup and those goofy blue bunny slippers—and *gasp*, what would the cool kids say? Luckily, Claire's brat-pack friends won't be around to judge. Sunday mornings are just for sisters. Best hours of the week. Laid-back, cozy, and it sounds like rain today. Even better. With a lazy smile, Sam opens her eyes.

Claire stares back.

Half-lidded, vacant. Face bloodless and doughy, one cheek scrunched against grimy floorboards.

Claire?

Overhead, rain patters against an unfamiliar roof, the relentless tapping of ten thousand fingers trying to get inside Sam's head. Lightning branches outside a broken, stained glass window, flash-illuminating the splintery innards of the church and the pickaxe lodged in the back of her big sister's neck.

Claire!

Sam's mind throbs. She tries to sit up, but the last three days pile back in, crushing her with the weight of corpses. Literally. On top of her. The entire brat pack pins her down, sagging limbs and torsos: Shawnee, Brie, Jake. And Claire.

A surge of nausea rises from Sam's guts and exits in a scream.

She lashes an arm free. If she can reach Claire maybe one of them will wake up, a jump-scare in her bed, like the old movies they watch every October. But Claire is real, and so is the tender, cavernous gash in Sam's temple. Her hand comes away red. *He thinks he killed me.* She remembers now, her one semblance of a plan. Stay under the bodies where he left her, play dead, pray for help to come. Not that any prayers were answered this weekend.

Over the rain, another noise rises—scraping, urgent, the grave-work of a shovel.

He's out there.

Oh God. She whimpers, shrinks smaller. She wants to lie here, stay buried, *be buried.* What's the point without Claire? Claire was the fighter, the one who stood a chance. The one who helped her survive this lonely life. What else is there now but to sink into the floorboards and wait for oblivion?

Claire stares at her. Observes her spinelessness with dead marble eyes. Practically imploring her.

That fucker can't get away with this!

Everything hurts, her head feels gooey and soul-drained. But Sam shoves out, dislodging herself, sending corpses lolling to one side. *Oh God, oh God, I'm so sorry.* She wanted them out of Claire's life, but not like this. She was gonna steal her away to college. They were gonna be roommates and—*and now...*

Sam limps past their bodies, past the altar to the broken window. The bones in her right ankle crunch hideously, so she stands on her left tiptoe and peers out.

Gravestones haunt the driving rain. Vengeful angels, winged demons. And at the center of it all, the animated hulk of the priest wields his shovel.

Digging five graves.

Sam turns away. The church is a dilapidated husk full of weapons. Razor-shards of stained glass, iron shackles bolted to the pews, toppled candlesticks and crucifixes.

But something in here is much deadlier.

"I'm sorry," she whispers and yanks the pickaxe from the back of Claire's neck. The body lurches then slumps to the floorboards.

Don't think about it! Just go! Now! For Claire!

The front door releases a splintery shriek, but the rain is too loud, the rhythm of his shovel too satisfying. He doesn't see her staggering through the mud, savage determination twisting her once gentle face. The fucker. She'll only get one chance at this. With a silent scream, Sam raises the pickaxe and swings.

IT'S REALLY COMING down out there.

Even at full throttle, the windshield wipers can't keep up. Might as well be driving this old rig at the bottom of a lake. With a sigh, Big June flicks the switch for her chicken lights. The 18-wheeler's mounted high beams blaze to life and cut through sheets of passing rain. The road beyond remains a spectral gray ribbon. A lesser driver would've pulled over miles ago to wait out the storm. Not Big June. She cranks the gearshift and hammers down on the gas. There's a pick-up scheduled for 3 a.m. sharp, less than fifteen minutes away.

Big June never misses a pick-up.

Lightning splits the night with a flash of day. The rain turns white, and on both sides of the highway the desert reveals itself. Hard-baked terrain melting into rivers of mud. It's been a while since she's been on a run in these parts—and never in the rain, of all things—but she's not surprised. Her line of work lends itself to the middle of nowhere. Backwoods roads, sleeping neighborhoods, gone-to-seed summer camps… Sometimes all in one night.

No GPS signal way out here, but she checks her mileage. Getting closer.

She pops the CB from the cradle—more dead air. Typical for these runs, but force of habit keeps her honest. "Come back, Home Base, this is Big June. Getting greasy out here, but I'm coming up on the pick-up site, ETA three minutes. Will radio again once I'm all loaded up. Please standby."

She re-cradles the CB and looks up as a young woman dashes into the road: stark white in the high beams, bedraggled and waving a pickaxe. No time to stop!

A second before the *splat*, the figure lunges sideways out of the lights.

With a yelp and a prayer, Big June pulls the brakes. Air hisses, tires wail. The rig skids into a fifty-foot stop. Holy good God! She isn't sure if the poor soul made it until she catches her in the side mirror running the length of the trailer, screaming for a ride.

Three minutes early.

But Big June smiles.

She never misses a pick-up.

SAM DOESN'T REMEMBER climbing in. She's chasing the rain-drenched brake lights of an 18-wheeler, then she's in the passenger seat. It's that sudden. The interior swims around her, tracers of light from the dashboard, patter on the roof.

She drips all over, rainwater, tears, cries of animal anguish pouring from her mouth. The driver kneels next to her, blurring in and out: a grandmotherly thing, small-boned, long silver hair and an oversized trucker hat with a four-leaf clover. She drapes a blanket over Sam's shoulders.

"It's okay, sweetheart, Big June's gotcha now. You're not alone. Just breathe, let it all out."

But Sam's mouth is too full, the last three days too unending, everything trying to spill out at once. All she sees are Claire's empty eyes. "Call an ambulance!"

"Sorry, sweetheart, no signal out here. You know that."

"You don't understand. They're all dead! Please... *My sister...*"

"*Shhh...* I know, I know." A hand settles on Sam's arm, achingly warm. "Right now, we have to worry about you. Tell me now, this is important: did you get the bastard?"

"I..." Sam's fingers cramp around the pickaxe, startling her. She didn't even realize she still had it. The steel point rests against the dash, gleaming and bloodless. The rain must've washed away the hair and bone and—*don't think about it, don't!* A sick chill spreads through her, feels like a scream. "*I had to.*"

"*Of course* you had to." The woman tucks a sopping strand of hair behind Sam's ear. "By the looks of you, he had it coming in spades."

"He was gonna bury Claire."

"Claire?" The name comes gently. "Your sister?"

Sam starts to nod but ends up hunched over in her seat. She moans and cradles the pickaxe—Claire's final gift to her. She can still feel the sword-in-stone resistance as she wrenched it from her neck. *Oh God, oh God, I just left her there!*

"Sweetheart, I know it's awful. But I need you to sit back up. Your cut's still gushing."

Sam shakes her head, but the air shifts as Big June guides her upright. There's a soft tug as the old woman tries to slip the pickaxe free.

"Don't!" Sam recoils, jerking the weapon away.

Big June puts her hands up and sits back calmly on her haunches. "That's okay, sweetheart. Hang on to it if it helps." A first aid kit sits open at her knees. No sudden movements, she produces a roll of gauze and antiseptic. Just a kindly old woman. The priest was kind at first, too.

"Okay if I fix you up a little?"

Sam resists, but only in spirit. She shakes, racked with all-over sobs as Big June dabs the meaty parts of her temple. The antiseptic stings, but the woman's words are brutal. She tells Sam she's brave, she's strong, she's gonna make it through this. *It's not right!* Sam can still see Claire running from the church, the shape of the priest as he filled the candlelit doorway. How will she make it through anything ever again?

"Stay with me, sweetheart," Big June says from the driver's seat.

Sam blinks, her vision unblurs. Outside, the road streaks past, wet and silver in the headlights. *When did we start moving?* She touches her temple, surprised at the bandage.

"Where're we going?" She sits up straighter. "I can't leave her!"

"Somewhere they can help," Big June promises. "Just down the road."

"No." Sam's fingers tighten around the pickaxe. "There's nothing out here. We hiked this road for a day before he found us."

"It'll be there, trust me."

Trust you? But bone-heavy exhaustion pins Sam to her seat. The miles pass, fast and slow all at once. At some point, the rain starts to thin, and a hazy green glow appears in the distance. A mounted radio crackles with a distant, broken voice. *"Big June, this is… come back… that pick-up…?"*

Big June snaps up the handset. "Home Base, this is Big June. That's affirmative. Just crossing out of this darn storm. Got you on my horizon. ETA two minutes. Standby."

The radio voice responds drenched in static, some code impossible to decipher.

"Tell them to call someone," Sam says. "Tell them we need the police!"

"They already know, sweetheart. I promise. Help is coming."

Sam keeps one hand on the axe, one on the door handle.

With the final mile, the storm lets up. It's almost as if they drive right out of it. Rain gives way to dry asphalt and a nightscape blanketed in moving fog. That green glow at the end of the road pulls closer and takes form: a cheery little building with a jukebox sheen and a flickering neon sign.

THE CLOVER CAFÉ

Big June turns into the empty parking lot. Despite the middle-of-night hour, the place is open. Sam sees people inside occupying several booths and a long counter.

Before she knows it, she's limping across the parking lot with Big June as her crutch, cocooned in a blanket, clutching the pickaxe to her chest. They pass under the buzzing green neon. The café door opens with a jingle and the sweet aroma of a thousand Sundays engulfs her. Warm butter and cinnamon.

"Come in, Sam," the voice from the radio says. "We've been expecting you."

*"**WAKE UP, NERD.** First day of October, you know what that means."*

An M&M bounces off Sam's forehead. Eyes squeezed shut, she feels along her pillow, then pops the chocolate into her mouth. Three more plink off her head.

"Alright, I'm up, I'm up." She smiles and cracks one eye.

Claire stares back.

Face screwed-up, tongue twisted out, completely juvenile, irredeemably goofy.

Sunday mornings are the best.

Comfy-clad, they shuffle down to the rec room, carrying plates of Claire's world-famous cinnamon-butter-fried waffles and bags of Halloween candy to honor the month.

Claire plops down in front of their parents' sacred wall of VHS and selects three classics. She holds up the cover art for Sam's inspection. "Which one first?"

A wooded summer camp framed inside the silhouette of a knife-wielding killer.

A young woman terrorized in her bed by a bladed skeletal hand.

A skin-masked maniac waving his chainsaw overhead.

They all make her shudder, but Sam points. "That one. It's got the best ending."

"WELCOME TO THE Clover Café, Sam. We're so glad you made it. Do you prefer a booth or the counter?"

"I...?"

Sam squints against an assault of polished tile, immaculate countertops, shiny vinyl seats. The voice from the radio manifests before her as a trim, middle-aged waitress in a pale green uniform. Neat red lipstick, vintage platinum curls. She lingers inside the heaven-scented entranceway with a menu and a sly smile.

"They call me Goldie." She steps closer. "It's an honor to meet you. You're an incredibly brave girl."

Sam shakes her head. *An honor?*

"It's okay, sweetheart." Big June nudges her forward. "You're in good company. Miss Goldie runs this old joint. She'll have what you need."

"What I need?" Like that ambulance she asked for? That cop car? Transportation back to a life that's been forever gutted? What's the point without Claire? Surviving makes even less sense in the light.

"First things first." Goldie loops an arm around Sam, helping Big June keep her upright. "Let's get this wildcat off her ankle. I'd say a booth is in order."

Sam sobs. "You don't understand..." *Claire* would've wanted a booth; she'd stretch her legs out the length of the seat and flirt with the waitstaff, order fancy desserts she knew they didn't have. All Sam wants is a dark corner, somewhere she can crouch into a ball and scream. This place was here the whole time?

Customers dot the seats, amorphous bodies on the too-bright edges of her awareness. They talk in late-night voices, and somewhere, somebody goes on laughing. It's not fair. They've never watched someone they love slump to her knees. They've never been dragged away, reaching and screaming as the soul faded from her eyes! They shift in their seats and side-eye Sam's soggy bandage and the pickaxe-shaped lump inside her blanket. Chin down, she asks Goldie for the bathroom in a voice about to break.

"Of course, how thoughtless of me. You'll want to wash off the night."

Goldie and Big June help her down a hallway ending in two doors, both marked with the same symbol: ♀

"Here we are, ladies' choice," Goldie says. "And…" She produces a neatly folded sweatsuit and a washcloth. "Something clean and dry from the gift shop."

Sam stares at the offering. With every kindness, it's harder to breathe, harder to trust.

"Go on, sweetheart," Big June says. "All for you."

Sam accepts the clothing, slowly, letting her blanket slip from one shoulder, exposing the smiling curve of her pickaxe. Like Big June, Goldie doesn't even blink.

"Hope you hurt him good."

Sam shakes her head. "He said he was a priest. Do you know him?"

"Not him. But we know the breed." Goldie and June exchange dark glances. "Sooner or later, they come for us all."

"We were driving to California," Sam says, "to tour UCLA… But now Claire… She'll never… We'll never…"

"Oh, sweetheart, we hear you, we truly do." Big June squeezes her shoulder. "It feels like these monsters take everything from us."

"But they don't, Sam," Goldie says. "They *don't*." She pushes open a bathroom door, exposing a room of clean white tile. "How about a little privacy?"

Sam nods, already unhooking herself from Big June.

"Go easy on that ankle, sweetheart." Big June lets her go. "That bastard's done enough damage."

Except that's where the old woman is wrong.

The priest didn't crack Sam's ankle. Claire did.

"Anything at all," Goldie says, filling the doorway. "Just holler."

Sam turns to thank them, to get them to leave, but a novelty sticker on Goldie's collar gives her pause: a happy face and the line *BE KIND REWIND*. Above that, a faded purple scar snakes across the waitress's throat.

"Help will be here soon, Sam," she promises, closing the door.

Sam twists the lock, then hobbles to the sink and sets the pickaxe on the counter where it's fast to grab. There's a mirror, but all it reveals are bloodstains and bruises. There's nothing vital underneath, nothing left of her. The congealed remains of her T-shirt and shorts fall away like scabs as she peels herself raw and naked.

She fills the sink, but her hands hesitate and her gaze gets lost in the shimmering white-blue water. The priest gave them water. Their throats were dry and swollen; their skin sunburned from the endless walk for a gas station. He offered them freshly pumped well water in shallow silver bowls, one for each of them.

Even then, Claire's brat pack had snickered. *What a primitive. Dude doesn't even have working faucets.*

They should've been more concerned about the ghost town vibe, the mounds of fresh earth they passed in the churchyard, the muddy-red stains on the vestments he wore. But they were so thirsty, and he promised his new congregation would arrive soon.

Sam doesn't remember who drank first, only that Brie was the first to collapse.

Hell came fast after that. Faces doubling and blurring, bodies slumping to the floorboards. Something in their water.

Nothing holy.

Sam woke to Shawnee and Brie screaming. She tried to stand, but dizzy, sleepy tendrils pulled her back down—that and the shackle securing her ankle to the pew. Claire sat chained to the next row, terror elongating her face, fire rippling in her eyes.

The church flickered, aflame with candles. The first corpse of the weekend sat slumped against the altar. Eyeballs red and bulging, face a purple bruise, a golden cincture knotted brutally around his neck. Jake. The only male member of Claire's brat pack, maybe the only one the priest saw as a threat.

That's when Sam started screaming, too.

Pleased, the priest stepped forward, dressed in ceremonial vestments and a ravenous smile. He appraised his remaining captives, their long, tan legs and pretty faces, and pulled the vestments over his head. No need to disguise himself behind kind gods any longer. There was nothing ordained about this maniac.

But he was their kingdom now.

The sound of her own weeping snaps Sam back to the present, and the bright-white bathroom reclaims her pulsing vision. She reaches for the washcloth—except, it's already in her hand. The water in the sink ripples, dark pink. She blinks at the mirror. She's clean, scrubbed raw and breaking out in gooseflesh. As if time sloshed forward while she was haunting the past. She drops the soggy washcloth into the water and presses a palm against her temple.

Hastily, she dresses in the sweats Goldie gave her. They're a size too big and easy to hide in. Hugging the pickaxe to her chest, she limps out into the hallway. Nobody stands waiting for her, but the air is cruel with warm butter and cinnamon. She holds her breath as she creeps into the dining area.

"There you are, sweetheart." Big June rises from the nearest booth.

Goldie appears at the kitchen door with a plate of waffles.

Sam limps toward Big June, but as she does, the people turn in their seats to watch her, and the café finally pulls into focus.

And Sam sees them. Really sees them.

Goldie's other customers.

Young women with blankets and bloody bandages. Smeared mascara, swollen lips. Girls with bruises and stains, slashes and gashes.

An entire slaughterhouse worth of injuries inside one little café.

They gape silently at Sam, exhausted and broken. Sam gapes back.

"Who are you people?"

"OH MAN, NOW *that's an ending!"* Claire *reaches for the remote and hits* REWIND. *"I always forget what a beast that girl is with a machete. Final girls are so badass."*

"The killer sure didn't see her coming," Sam says, crawling off the couch, feeling a little green. October is awesome but intense. Inside the VCR, gears and wheels hum, spinning the tape back to the start. "What's next?"

Claire considers the array of video boxes on the coffee table and sighs. "I'm really gonna miss this."

Sam's hand freezes over the EJECT button. "Don't say that."

"It's okay to face it, nerd. Our Sundays are numbered."

"Maybe they'll be a little different," Sam hedges, and those world-famous waffles turn to rocks in her stomach. "I mean, there's no way Mom and Dad are gonna let us take their video collection to L.A. But we'll have Wi-Fi in our dorm, we can stream, and we'll bring a waffle iron or—"

"Stop it." Claire nudges her with a bunny slipper, hard. "You know that's not what I mean."

Sam knows. But.

"It's not too late for you to apply," she says. "I can help you. We can take a road trip, tour the campus. Once we see it for real, you won't wanna leave, I know it."

"Snap out of it, Sam." Claire's smile goes flat. "Seriously, stop fooling yourself with this fantasy dorm bullshit. College is never gonna be my jam."

"Then what is? Barhopping with your stupid friends? A different hook-up every night? You wanna be a waitress forever?"

"Wow. Tell me how you really feel."

"I didn't mean it that way."

"Sure you did. And it's fine. Let's face reality."

"You're my big sister, I'm not supposed to leave you behind. If you come with me, we can help each other. Study, party. Like a team."

"And when did that ever work for us?"

Every Sunday morning.

"I can't move to California alone, Claire."

"Sure you can. You got accepted without me, didn't you? I mean, look at you." She chucks an M&M at the UCLA logo stamped across Sam's sweatshirt. "You've been wearing that ugly thing since junior high. It's your dream."

"You were supposed to be there, too."

"You're strong enough without me."

"You're wrong."

"Shut up, nerd, you're gonna be fine. Just remember the number one rule for survival." She slides the next movie across the carpet. "When shit gets real, the boring smart chicks rise up and leave the foxy fun ones in the dust."

THE WOMEN IN the Clover Café regard Sam and her pickaxe with tired empathy, then turn slowly back to their tables.

There are so many of them, ravaged and damaged, hair and darkness in their eyes. One girl sits slumped over an entire pot of coffee, her high-necked nightgown hanging in ribbons. In the next booth, a blonde in a blood-matted wool sweater stares anxiously out the window at the neon parking lot and the rolling fog. Someone in the far corner cackles endlessly and tragically, while at the counter, another tormented soul clutches a blanket to her chest with an arm that ends in a bandaged stump.

"We're all survivors, Sam," Goldie says. "Like you."

"Try not to stare, sweetheart," Big June says.

But Sam can't help herself. There's something achingly familiar about these girls, like phantoms from a past life. "Did the priest do this?"

"They have their own monsters, Sam. You know that." Goldie sets the waffles on Big June's table and steps back. "Sit, please, you need your strength."

"Strength for what?" Her head throbs, her ankle burns. The scenery keeps tilting.

"To make it through this." Big June stands, and together she and Goldie guide Sam into the booth, forever unfazed by her pickaxe. Their kindness weakens her. Her axe-arm slumps to the table. She loosens her fingers but doesn't let go completely.

They sit across from her with gentle eyes.

"What's next for me?" Sam whispers, reluctant. The question spills past the night, past tomorrow, it bleeds into a thousand Sundays.

"It's different for everyone," Goldie says. "Tonight, for you, help is coming. But only you can decide what you do with it."

"I don't understand."

"That's why we start small."

Big June nudges the waffles across the table. "I hear these are world-famous. Cinnamon-fried."

Sam's stomach crawls. Hunger is for people who still have sisters. "These were her favorite."

"Tell us, sweetheart. Tell us about her. Tell us anything you need."

"She was… She…" But there are no words. How do you sum up someone who was *everything*? Sam swallows a sob and shakes her head.

"That's okay. Maybe it'll help if *we* start." Big June sets her trucker hat on the table and pulls back her long silver hair. Her left ear is missing. "There're lots of stories here tonight."

"We're the lucky ones." Goldie lifts her chin, exposing that ropy scar. "I know that doesn't feel true. But there's one thing every woman here can hold on to, one thing that makes us very rare, but very important."

Big June leans in. "We got the bastards that did this to us."

The two women replay their victories for Sam in low voices. Stories of courage, of resilience, of overcoming the darkness against all odds. They tell her about the other survivors, too, filling Sam's head with masked killers and relentless maniacs—and all the impossible, beautiful ways these everyday girls took the bastards' heads or burned them alive or simply kicked their asses back to hell. With every tale, Sam's mind spins faster, whirring round and round until she's certain she's heard this all before. Dread closes around her, icy fingers of déjà vu.

Out in the parking lot, the fog thickens and the first falling lines of raindrops glow green in the light from the neon sign. The storm is catching up with her. Sam's fingers twitch around the pickaxe; the clean steel head catches the light and winks. Her heart starts pounding.

She takes a deep breath. "He kept us in the pews for three days."

"Oh, sweetheart." Big June squeezes her hand.

"The first days were hot, Jake's body started to rot and stink. But on the third day, the rain came..."

Sam can still see him, enormous in the candlelight. He paced in front of Jake's bloating remains, raving about the stench, blaming the girls and their sticky bodies. So vulgar, so weak, so deserving of punishment. At first, the fury of the storm punctuated his words, but eventually the thunderheads outperformed him. The monster stepped down from his altar.

But only to baptize his trembling, sunken-eyed congregation.

He removed their shackles, one savaged girl at a time, and took them into the rain. While he was outside with Brie, Claire sprung to life.

I saw tools in the graveyard before. I'm gonna try and grab one. This is our chance, Sam, do you hear me? You gotta be ready to fight!

When it was Claire's turn for the rain, she locked eyes with Sam. *Be ready.*

But nothing could've prepared Sam for the last five minutes of her sister's life.

Even over the storm, the roar the priest let out shook the bones of the church.

Seconds later, Claire burst inside dripping rainwater and hoisting a pickaxe over one shoulder. She rushed to Sam's side, powerful and radiant.

Shawnee and Brie cried for her help, but it was Sunday, and on Sundays sisters come first. *Show me your ankle, nerd.*

With shaking hands, Claire slid the point of the pickaxe into the shackle, between the cuff and Sam's ankle.

Do you know what you're doing?

Saw it in a movie once.

I love you.

I love you, too. But after I do this, you have to run, okay, nerd? Run like hell and don't look back. I'll be right behind you...

"But she wasn't," Sam sobs. "She stayed to help her friends and he came back and ripped the pickaxe away and he... That fucker, he..."

"It's okay, sweetheart," Big June says, drawing Sam back into the present. "You don't have to say it. Not this part."

"But, please, Sam." Goldie leans forward, a gleam of urgency in her eyes. "Tell us how you ended him."

"He killed the others, and he chased me through the rain, didn't take him long with my ankle. He dragged me back inside."

"What happened next?"

"He slammed my head against the altar. That was it. He thought he killed me. He piled me with their bodies, and I slept for the longest time. I wanted to die. I wanted it to be *over*. Claire was dead. I wanted to be dead, too. If I was stronger—if I was Claire—maybe I could get up and fight. But then what? Claire messed up my ankle when she broke my chain, and I was still lost in the middle of nowhere. Even if I killed him, I was gonna die out there. But then. But then I got up."

"You got up?" Goldie and Big June lean in. The rain beats against the window.

"I took the pickaxe and I—" Sam's mind flashes bright white. The swing of the pickaxe and then... Then she was chasing the brake lights on Big June's 18-wheeler.

Someone screams.

"Out there!" The blonde in the wool sweater backs away from the window.

The café erupts. High-tension girls flock to the windows to get a better look. The blonde raises a machete, another holds a crucifix to the glass.

What's happening?

At first, Sam misses it.

Nothing out there but fog and rain and random cracks of lightning.

Then a hulking shape materializes inside the misty ether, stepping forward, moving with slow and sinister intent toward the café.

"That's the thing about these bastards." Big June slides her hat into place and stands to face the night. "Sometimes they come back."

THE SURVIVORS LINE the windows and watch the spectacle of the shape lurking in the rain.

"What's he doing?" someone cries.

"Who is he? Can you see his weapon?"

"This can't be happening! I won't survive a second fight."

Several girls shout in agreement. Others want to rush out and brawl. Every voice rises up at once. Sam would cover her ears, but a dark certainty freezes her in place. The shape faces the café, waiting, watching, as if scanning a smorgasbord.

"It'll be okay, ladies," Goldie says, but a crack in her voice tells Sam otherwise.

"Does anyone recognize him?" Big June sounds equally tortured, as if she's selecting a maiden for sacrifice. Nobody answers, but Sam's heart thunders.

The shape in the rain produces a shovel. The girls cry out, but he doesn't come forward.

He starts digging.

His shovel should strike sparks on the asphalt. Instead, the rhythmic gritty sound of metal biting through grave-soil fills the café as if blasted from overhead speakers.

"He's mine," Sam hears herself say.

She slides from the booth and starts to swing the pickaxe over her shoulder. But her hand hangs empty. Her weapon is gone. Vanished!

"My pickaxe! Who took it?"

"Did you ever really have it?" Goldie and Big June step backward, and their expressions conceal something terrible.

"Help is coming," they say, but she's beginning to think they're just blowing air.

The shape of the priest and his shovel dissolve into the thickening downpour. Sam only knows he's still out there because his shovel is relentless.

Digging and digging and digging.

The edges of the windows fog over and shards of moving color spread across the panes like a plague of stained glass. Everything coming together and unraveling at once. Axe-hand as empty as her future, head spinning, Sam starts to shout.

"He can't be alive!"

Digging and digging.

"He can't! I killed him, I—"

But the untruth in her voice is as sharp as the sudden jingle of the front door swinging open. The others cry out, and an unexpected visitor steps inside, dripping rain across the floor.

A foxy redhead with blue bunny slippers and a stack of old movies.

"Hey, nerd," Claire says. "Ready to go?"

"HOW DO YOU *think they get home?"*

"How does who get home?" Claire grabs the video from the VCR, makes sure the tape matches the box, then shelves it.

"The boring smart chicks," Sam says. "After they decapitate the monster or whatever, ninety percent of the time they're still stranded in the middle of nowhere. All by themselves."

"I don't know, they hitchhike. Some old lady trucker'll find 'em."

"*And then what? Go to some clueless police station, some cold hospital to be poked and prodded? What happens when the authorities don't believe their stories? Their best friends are gone. Their lives will never be the same. Doesn't get more isolating than that. So, what then? How do they figure out their futures all alone?*"

"*You're overthinking it, nerd.*"

"*Am I?*"

"*We still talking about movies here?*"

"*I don't know. Yes.*" *Sam crosses her arms over her UCLA sweatshirt.*

Her big sister appraises her, seems to be deciding how serious she wants to spin this. The spirit of Sunday mornings wins out. "*If it was up to me, they'd all end up at the same shiny little roadside diner, a meeting place for the sisterhood, every last boring smart chick to ever kick ass and live to tell about it. And the waitress who runs the joint will serve waffles—they won't be as good as mine, of course— but she'll listen to their horror stories forever and ever and…*"

Sam snickers. "*That sounds amazingly awful.*"

"*Right?*" *Claire flashes a goofball grin.* "*Lucky for you, nerd, it's all pretend.*"

CLAIRE STANDS IN the doorway.

Every survivor in the Clover Café holds her breath. Every heart misses a beat.

Then Sam runs to her big sister.

She throws her arms around her and squeezes tight—so, so tight. It's impossible, Claire shouldn't be here, but it doesn't matter. In this moment, every Sunday in history collides. They're a team, everything will be just as Sam always imagined.

Except, Claire isn't hugging her back.

The videotapes waterfall from her hand and her rain-soaked body presses against Sam, cold and stiff. Lightning cracks the sky, flash-illuminating the pickaxe protruding from her neck.

Oh God, Claire…

"Good luck, sweetheart," Big June says. "We truly hope you make it."

"Yes," Goldie says. "Come back soon."

Sam lets go of her sister and steps back, breathing through the scream.

For a heartbeat, Claire remains upright. For a heartbeat, their eyes seem to lock.

You gotta be ready to fight!

Digging and digging and digging.

The neon sign in the parking lot goes dark. All the beautiful, badass survivors nod at Sam, then sink back into their seats as the interior of the Clover Café flickers and dims. Vinyl seats and polished countertops decay and dissolve into the ethereal darkness at the back of Sam's mind. Warm butter and cinnamon become a putrefied reek. This wistful other reality exhales a death rattle, and in a blur Claire and Sam are all that remain. Them, and the scrape of his shovel.

Digging and digging.

Claire topples forward, knocking Sam down with her. They land inches apart. The stiff weight of several corpses presses the air from Sam's chest while Claire goes on staring. Face bloodless and doughy, one cheek scrunched against grimy floorboards. Her marble eyes implore Sam. Then, she too fades into the dark.

Out in the rain, the shovel stops. He's coming.

No pretending this time.

You gotta fight!

Sam opens her eyes.

ACKNOWLEDGMENTS

SOMETIMES, WRITING HORROR can be lonely work. I write in nooks, usually at night, and transport myself to hellscapes full of doubt and shadows and symbolic monsters. But just when it feels like darkness is closing in, I look up from the pages and realize I always have my guiding lights.

Thank you to Kevin McFadden, my forever hero and sometimes mentor, your friendship these many long years has been one of the greatest gifts of my life. The teenage girl who grew braver inside the sanctuary of your books still exists inside me, and she stands in awe of the real-life kindnesses you've shown me. Thank you, thank you, thank you! Every word I write has you as its muse. I will always be your fan from hell.

To Brittany Noelle, my critique partner, fellow movie and TV nerd, and great friend, thank you for the hundreds of hours of genre talk, and for every invaluable insight you bring to my stories. Nobody cheers on my wacky characters quite like you. Your multiverse of creativity is awe-inspiring, and I can't wait for the world to discover every last one of your insanely imaginative stories. It's such an honor to be on this writing (and publishing!) thrill-ride with you.

A heart full of gratitude to my late mother, Sweet Caroline, for introducing me the movie-magic of *E.T.* and the soul-magic of reading, and for showing me how vital it is to be true to myself. And of course, thanks, Mom, for letting me rent all those R-rated movies. I wish you could've read these stories.

Thank you to my big brother T. J. for introducing me to all my favorite old creep shows. You unleashed the monsters that made me the nerd I'm proud to be today. Those VHS gems we watched together mark some of my best childhood memories. *Oh no, a werewolf!*

Thank you to Nick, my heart-drumming soulmate, for brewing endless cups of coffee and supporting me during so many long days and dark nights hunkered down in front of a computer screen. You've been there for every roller coaster and every triumphant scream. (P.S. I forgive you for waiting until *after* the band broke up to inform me your lead singer had played Ricky in *Sleepaway Camp*...)

Thank you to all my friends in the writing community. Huge shout out to David Boop, friend, mentor, author, inspiration—thank you for always cracking the whip. Shucks, you even sent me the prompt for the first short story I ever wrote and sold. Thank you! And thank you to my old YA Avengers, Kristina and Jessi (R.I.P.), I wish our stories could've lasted longer, but I'll always be thankful for the time we had. Thank you to Nova, Micol, Amparo, Beth, and the rest of the Books with Bites girl-tribe who continue to demonstrate the importance and power of strong feminist voices. Thank you to Angela Sylvaine, The Cheerful Goth, for being such a positive and welcoming force in the horror community.

An extra thank-you to authors Brian McAuley, Drew Huff, and Robert E. Harpold for those delightfully killer blurbs.

A big hug and thank-you to Abir for so much behind-the-scenes kindness and for being the muse who whispers in Kevin's ear.

Thank you to all the publishers who took a chance on my short stories, including the fine folks over at Flame Tree Press,

Uncharted, *The Dread Machine*, *Tales to Terrify*, and *Dark Matter Magazine*.

Special thanks to my editor, Rob Carroll, for championing my cinematic visions and giving this collection such an awesome home.

And finally, thank you to all the movies, TV shows, and podcasts that perfectly haunt my soul. Like a fever-dream Oscar speech where the get-the-hell-off-the-stage music is playing, I have the eerie certainty that I'm going to forget some important names, but I'll offer up these titles for sacrifice and consumption:

MOVIES

- *Nosferatu*
- *Frankenstein*
- *Psycho* (and the sequels)
- *The Innocents*
- *What Ever Happened to Baby Jane?*
- *Rosemary's Baby*
- *Night of the Living Dead*
- *Tales from the Crypt* (1972)
- *The Exorcist*
- *Black Christmas*
- *The Texas Chain Saw Massacre* (and the sequels)
- *The Rocky Horror Picture Show*
- *Carrie*
- *Halloween* (and the sequels)
- *Alien* (and the sequels)
- *The Changeling*
- *Friday the 13th* (and the sequels)

- *The Shining*
- *An American Werewolf in London*
- *The Evil Dead* (and the sequels, and the MUSICAL!)
- *Poltergeist*
- *Creepshow* (and the sequel)
- *Twilight Zone: The Movie*
- *Sleepaway Camp*
- *Gremlins*
- *A Nightmare on Elm Street* (and the sequels)
- *Night of the Comet*
- *Ghoulies* (and the sequel)
- *Return of the Living Dead* (and the sequels)
- *Fright Night*
- *Silver Bullet*
- *Transylvania 6-5000*
- *April Fool's Day*
- *Critters*
- *Vamp*
- *Haunted Honeymoon*
- *Night of the Creeps*
- *Dolls*
- *The Gate*
- *The Lost Boys*
- *Hellraiser*
- *Flowers in the Attic*
- *Pumpkinhead*
- *The Blob*
- *Child's Play*

- *Watchers*
- *The 'Burbs*
- *Pet Sematary*
- *Communion*
- *Tremors*
- *Misery*
- *Tales from the Darkside: The Movie*
- *Flatliners*
- *The People Under the Stairs*
- *Buffy the Vampire Slayer*
- *Army of Darkness*
- *Ghostwatch*
- *Fire in the Sky*
- *Bram Stoker's Dracula*
- *Interview with a Vampire*
- *Tales from the Crypt: Demon Knight*
- *From Dusk till Dawn*
- *The Craft*
- *Scream* (and the sequels)
- *Intensity*
- *I Know What You Did Last Summer*
- *Urban Legend* (and the sequel)
- *The Faculty*
- *Idle Hands*
- *The Blair Witch Project*
- *Final Destination* (and the sequels)
- *What Lies Beneath*
- *Jeepers Creepers*

- *The Others*
- *Session 9*
- *Resident Evil* (the games, and the sequels)
- *The Ring*
- *Wrong Turn*
- *Saw*
- *The Grudge*
- *The Descent*
- *The Exorcism of Emily Rose*
- *The Messengers*
- *Paranormal Activity* (and the sequels)
- *Lake Mungo*
- *The House of the Devil*
- *Sinister*
- *The Cabin in the Woods*
- *Mama*
- *The Conjuring* (and the sequels)
- *You're Next*
- *Oculus*
- *What We Do in the Shadows*
- *It Follows*
- *Southbound*
- *The Final Girls*
- *The VVitch*
- *Hush*
- *Ouija: Origin of Evil*
- *The Autopsy of Jane Doe*
- *Get Out*

- *It* (Chapters One and Two)
- *Better Watch Out*
- *Happy Death Day*
- *Hereditary*
- *Anna and the Apocalypse*
- *Us*
- *Midsommar*
- *Ready or Not*
- *The Black Phone*
- *Nope*
- *Barbarian*
- *Pearl*
- *Smile*
- *Terrifier 2*
- *Cobweb*
- *Talk to Me*
- *No One Will Save You*
- *Lisa Frankenstein*

TV SHOWS

- *The Twilight Zone*
- *Tales from the Darkside*
- *The Ray Bradbury Theater*
- *Amazing Stories*
- *Friday the 13th: The Series*
- *Tales from the Crypt*
- *Twin Peaks*

- *It* (the miniseries)
- *Are You Afraid of the Dark?*
- *The Stand* (the miniseries)
- *The Outer Limits*
- *Storm of the Century* (the miniseries)
- *The Walking Dead*
- *American Horror Story*
- *Holliston*
- *What We Do in the Shadows*
- *Scream: The TV Series*
- *Scream Queens*
- *Creepshow*
- *Yellowjackets*
- *Black Mirror*
- *Stranger Things*
- *The Haunting of Hill House*
- *The Haunting of Bly Manor*
- *Midnight Mass*
- *The Midnight Club*

PODCASTS

- *Cast of Wonders*
- *Creepy*
- *The Faculty of Horror*
- *Halloweenies*
- *The Last Podcast on the Left*
- *Psychoanalysis*

- *Tales to Terrify*
- *Teen Creeps*
- *Test Pattern*
- *The Movie Crypt*
- *The No Sleep Podcast*
- *The Other Stories*
- *The PikeCast*
- *The Pod and the Pendulum*
- *Thirteen*

—Amanda Cecelia Lang

ABOUT THE AUTHOR

AMANDA CECELIA LANG is a horror author and aspiring final girl from Colorado. As a die-hard scary movie nerd, her favorite things are meta-slashers, '80s nostalgia, and the rise of a fierce final girl. If she dies after fighting a B-movie monster, she will consider it a good death. Her scary stories currently haunt the dark corners of many popular podcasts, magazines, and anthologies. You can stalk her work at amandacecelialang.com—just don't be surprised if she leaps out at you from the shadows.

ABOUT THE COVER ARTIST

DAN FRIS IS an illustrator and cartoonist. He creates artwork inspired by vintage horror media and Cold War pop culture. He lives in Metro Atlanta with his beautiful wife and their beautiful dog.

CONTENT WARNINGS

"Choose Your Own Destruction": body horror, gore

"Latchkey": child disappearance, divorce, family dysfunction

"The Ash Collector": autopsies, gore, violence, death

"The 31st of October in Locust, Maine": child disappearance

"Salting the Meat": stalkers, implied torture, implied violence

"Medusa with the Heads of Men": sexual assault (off-page), domestic violence, animal experimentation

"Station 99": gore, violence, death

"Tricksters": violence, death

"Ashes Upon Ashes Upon Ashes": forced pregnancy, infant death, family dysfunction

"The Clover Café": PTSD, implied violence, death

A NOTE ABOUT REPRINTS

Please note, the following stories are reprints.

"Choose Your Own Destruction," *Dark Matter Magazine*, September 2023

"Latchkey," *Mixtape: 1986* from *The Dread Machine*, February 2022

"The Ash Collector," *Night Terrors: Volume 13* from Scare Street, April 2021, and *Creepy Podcast*, October 2021

"The 31st of October in Locust, Maine," *Uncharted*, January 2024

"Medusa with the Heads of Men," *Medusa* from Flame Tree Press, October 2024

"Station 99," *Dark Matter Magazine*, October 2023

"Tricksters," *Creepy Podcast*, October 2021, and *Holiday Leftovers* from B Cubed Press, December 2022

"The Clover Café," *Tales to Terrify*, December 2021, and *Open All Night* from Atomic Carnival Books, October 2023

Frost Bite by Angela Sylvaine
ISBN 978-1-958598-03-0

Free Burn by Drew Huff
ISBN 978-1-958598-26-9

The House at the End of Lacelean Street
by Catherine McCarthy
ISBN 978-1-958598-23-8

When the Gods Are Away by Robert E. Harpold
ISBN 978-1-958598-47-4

The Dead Spot: Stories of Lost Girls
by Angela Sylvaine
ISBN 978-1-958598-27-6

Grim Root by Bonnie Jo Stufflebeam
ISBN 978-1-958598-36-8

Voracious by Belicia Rhea
ISBN 978-1-958598-25-2

The Bleed by Stephen S. Schreffler
ISBN 978-1-958598-11-5

Chopping Spree by Angela Sylvaine
ISBN 978-1-958598-31-3

The Off-Season: An Anthology of Coastal New Weird
Edited by Marissa van Uden
ISBN 978-1-958598-24-5

The Threshing Floor by Steph Nelson
ISBN 978-1-958598-49-8

Club Contango by Eliane Boey
ISBN 978-1-958598-57-3

The Divine Flesh by Drew Huff
ISBN 978-1-958598-59-7

Psychopomp by Maria Dong
ISBN 978-1-958598-52-8

Disgraced Return of the Kap's Needle
by Renan Bernardo
ISBN 978-1-958598-74-0

Haunted Reels 2: More Stories from the Minds of Professional Filmmakers Curated by David Lawson
ISBN 978-1-958598-53-5

Dark Circuitry by Kirk Bueckert
ISBN 978-1-958598-48-1

Soul Couriers by Caleb Stephens
ISBN 978-1-958598-76-4

Abducted by Patrick Barb
ISBN 978-1-958598-37-5

Cyanide Constellations and Other Stories
by Sara Tantlinger
ISBN 978-1-958598-81-8

Little Red Flags: Stories of Cults, Cons, and Control
Edited by Noelle W. Ihli & Steph Nelson
ISBN 978-1-958598-54-2

Frost Bite 2 by Angela Sylvaine
ISBN 978-1-958598-55-9

The Starship, from a Distance by Robert E. Harpold
ISBN 978-1-958598-82-5

Dark Matter Presents: Fear City
ISBN 978-1-958598-90-0

Part of the Dark Hart Collection

Rootwork by Tracy Cross
ISBN 978-1-958598-01-6

Mosaic by Catherine McCarthy
ISBN 978-1-958598-06-1

Apparitions by Adam Pottle
ISBN 978-1-958598-18-4

I Can See Your Lies by Izzy Lee
ISBN 978-1-958598-28-3

A Gathering of Weapons by Tracy Cross
ISBN 978-1-958598-38-2

www.ingramcontent.com/pod-product-compliance
Lightning Source LLC
Chambersburg PA
CBHW011133190726
48289CB00012B/3024